BOOKS BY

REYNOLDS PRICE

A GENEROUS MAN   1966

THE NAMES AND FACES OF HEROES   1963

A LONG AND HAPPY LIFE   1962

A GENEROUS
MAN

REYNOLDS
PRICE

A GENEROUS
MAN

NEW YORK

ATHENEUM

1966

FOR

RAPHAEL JONES

Come degnasti d'accedere al monte?
non sapei tu che qui è l'uom felice?

DANTE, *Purgatorio,* XXX

A GENEROUS
MAN

ONE

"**M**ILO. Son?" Emma Mustian spoke from the foot of the steps for the third time that morning, still not raising her voice, trusting her natural power to wake him. But it had not and did not. It was Saturday, no school and Milo was dreaming, and because he so rarely dreamed—waking or sleeping—he clung to it now, her his dream, like money smuggled into his head, chest, hips and abandoned there, sudden and perilous. So Emma gave up and went to the kitchen and told Rosacoke to wake her brother and see him dressed.

Rosacoke said, "How am I going to feed Baby Sister and cook a big breakfast for Papa and Milo and wake up Milo all at once?"

Emma said, "I'll cook—I've cooked thirty years—and if Baby Sister can't feed herself at three years old, she will have to starve."

Rosacoke sighed but quickly went and was glad to go, not having seen Milo since the previous supper. The door to his room was shut—which was new, so new Rosa did not think of knocking but entered, and there was Milo asleep, stretched on top of sheets creased as storm water, naked hair to heel.

The sound of her entry, her happy gasping, finished his dream, opened his eyes. He looked, said "Morning," then clamped down again.

Rosacoke said, "Morning? It's nearly noon." (It

was seven-fifteen.) "Mama says get up, she needs you now." She went to the foot of his walnut bed and waited there.

Milo said "What for?"

"To take us to Warrenton."

"Papa can take you."

"No Papa can't."

"Why?" Milo said.

"Papa's too old," she said. "You have got to go and stick with Rato and explain about Phillip."

"What's wrong with Phillip?"

"If you ever came home when people were awake, you'd know a lot more about all of us. Phillip hasn't moved out of his house since Thursday. Rato has washed him and wormed him good, but he still acts sick so we're taking him in to Dr. Fuller, and you've got to supervise while Mama shops."

"I hadn't got to do nothing but die."

"And you may have to do that shortly," she said, "lying there naked in early October. Where do you think you are?—Africa?"

"I was near enough to Africa late last night." He buried his dark head entirely in pillows (skin dark from sun, hair gold as crowns).

"I knew it when I saw you walking off that porch. I read it on your back as clear as light—Going To The Fair. Well, if the Warren County Fair is your idea of Africa, I pity the natives."

"I'm just talking about that snake."

"What snake?" she said.

Emma called up to her, "Is he wake yet, Rosa?"

Rosa ran to the railing. "Wake and buck-naked.

Slept buck-naked on October eighth."

"Naked? You come straight down here then. You're too old for that."

"I'm not but eleven and he's lying on his stomach."

Emma didn't answer. She said, "Get him dressed" and went back to Baby Sister's oatmeal.

Rosa went back to Milo, fully awake now but playing at sleep. She crept to his feet and tickled the soles so rindy they lasted from summer to summer, not softening. He did not flinch, did not seem to breathe. "Ever try to tickle an elephant?" she said and laid a flat hand hot and sudden on his butt.

That stood him upright among the sheets, rocking with the springs. He lifted his arms and floated them out as though he were soaring—he was only balancing —and looked through the window to the bright morning sky, the road hid by trees. (The leaves would last another six weeks.) Then he said as if to the trees but to Rosa, to tantalize, "If these damned leaves would ever die, I could see through the branches to that ferris wheel."

"If you can see five miles with naked eyes, you got a better night's sleep than I did," she said.

Then he took two sinking steps through the mattress, one long loud step to the floor, then a series of jabs at his underpants. When they were on—they were actually Rato's—he said, "I didn't sleep three good hours."

"Why not?"

"Because I found a friend at the fair."

"Anybody I know?"

"You been to Clearwater, Florida lately?"

"No," she said.

"Then you don't," he said.

"A girl?"

"A *woman*."

"Milo," she said, neither smiling nor frowning.

So he turned in his shirttails, faced her fully, folded his right arm across his waist, his left on his back and gave her the crisp bow boys learn in school.

> *"Milo's my name,*
> *Afton's my hame,*
> *Heaven's my destination."*

Rosa smiled but said, "What heaven? Dog Heaven —you at fifteen sitting up till day with a carnival woman."

"A woman and a five-hundred-dollar boa constrictor. And we weren't sitting."

"What were you doing then?"

He was into his wrinkled trousers, his shoes, so he flung himself upend onto his hands. Pennies rang from his pockets and rolled towards her, and he said from there, "We were taking that snake for a walk through the woods." He stood again, smiling with his eyes flared white. "And we're exercising him again tonight, just her and me."

Rosa laughed and touched him once on the belly, low as she dared, instant and ended as though this were Tag or he were a stove. "Come on and eat or *I'll* snake you. Phillip needs help or Rato will die."

"Let Phillip die. He can blaze my way to Dog Heaven in advance."

"Milo!" She ran.

And he ran behind her, chin held high in the wind Rosa made, arm thrust up as if lifting a desperate flag through war—"On to save Rato, spare him pain, return him to his rightful place in his home!"

Rato waited by the kitchen door—or blocked their charge with Phillip in his arms in an Army blanket, only his neck and head uncovered, the terrier half, white with one black eye. The wrapped half was mystery. (Rato said "Airedale"—he had never seen one —Milo said "Traveling salesman," but whatever, it was Rato's life, had been his companion day and night, waking and sleeping for nearly three years since Milo had found it on the road one Christmas—abandoned by someone too weak to drown it—and brought it in his pocket for Rato's gift.)

Milo stopped and said, "Phillip, smile. Milo's on duty. You're half-cured already" and entered the kitchen and walked to the table where Papa (their own dead father's father) was eating, having finished his morning duties (which was walking to the end of the cleared back yard and staring for a while in those directions—over cotton stalks, tobacco stalks, pine woods beyond as if staring might revive, make grow, harvest). Emma had gone to dress Baby Sister so Milo sat on Papa's right, Rosacoke went to the oven for his plate and Rato laid Phillip by the fired wood stove.

Papa studied Milo, then said to his eyes, "You look like you slept three hours last night."

"I didn't know you slept in your hearing aid."

Papa said, "I don't—wouldn't if I had one—but I heard you. So would everybody else if they weren't doped up." (He meant the children's mother, his daughter-in-law. She took two aspirins at nine every night.)

"Well," Milo said, "since they were all drugged senseless, let's don't tell anything that might just confuse them."

As Rosacoke came to the table with his plate, they could hear their mother two rooms away forcing Baby Sister into something warm so Rosacoke lowered her voice and said "Such as what?" Milo questioned her with dumb open mouth.

She said, "What might confuse the people that didn't hear you come in at four a.m.?"

Papa said "Yeah."

Milo told it above his eating, hoarsely, pretending to whisper to Rosa and his grandfather (Rato hunkered on below beside Phillip, half-listening but not caring). "The main thing would be that I went to the fair."

Papa said "No!"

Milo said, "You know I did—or knew I was planning to."

"Never crossed my mind," Papa said, "never knew you knew plans existed."

"Papa, I got more plans than Douglas Mac-Arthur."

Papa said, "I wish you luck then, General, but I still never dreamed you were planning on the fair."

"Then how come you locked the truck last night for the first time in history? Because some mule was plotting to straight-wire it and drive to the fair and enter himself in the livestock show?"

"Not exactly"—Papa pointed to the trembling dog —"I didn't want Phillip driving in his condition. No telling what he might do."

"Oh I hadn't thought of that. But I wish you had told me—saved me half an hour poking with a rusty wire in that shut lock."

Papa said, "Excuse me. I meant to tell you. Hope I didn't put you out too much."

"I won't say how much but I will just say that Macey Gupton saved five Mustian lives."

Rosacoke said "How?" She had taken a seat on Milo's right. Now they filled three sides of the long dark table, facing or half-facing Rato and Phillip.

"By coming along in his old truck while I was standing down by the road gazing up here and planning axe murders."

Rosa said, "Calm down and tell us the rest."

Milo said, "I'm calm as that frying pan"—holding out one still hand to prove it—"and was last night till oh eleven o'clock."

"What happened then?"

Papa said, "Don't rush him ahead of his story. If I'm going to listen—with all the better stuff I got to do —I mean to understand. So Macey Gupton passed in his Daddy's truck and stopped and you told him you was killing your people and then flagging down a ride to the fair?"

Milo said, "That's it. Except Macey said he'd killed his people—he had the truck and he ain't sixteen —so to let's just save you all till later and make tracks now."

Rosacoke said, "Milo, what sort of talk is that?"

Milo said, "Lies. But from now on it's true—what I can tell of it anyhow." He stopped awhile, chewing, swallowing, then faced Rosacoke and Papa again. "You are looking at me like I went to the moon."

Rosa said "You said Africa."

Milo said, "Hush. It was nothing but the Warren County Fair—from eight o'clock till midnight, that is. We took in the rides and ate a lot of mess that Phillip wouldn't eat—would you, son?" (Phillip slowly looked towards the use of his name)—"and got up with a bunch of girls that are in our grade. They all had tickets in a drawing sponsored by the furniture store so we went indoors for that at nine."

Rosa said, "What were they giving away?"

"A bed about the size of Afton—innerspring mattress and pillows thrown in."

Rosa said "Who got it?"

Milo laughed. "Guess."

Papa said "Puss Ellis."

Rosa said "Papa!"

Milo fell back, struck himself on the forehead. "She *did*. Puss won it!"

"And needed it much as anybody could," Papa said, not smiling.

Rosa said, "Papa, what do you know about her?"

"I know she uses a bed in her work."

Rosa said "Hush."

Milo said "Plug your ears" and Rosacoke did.

Papa said, "Was Puss on hand to claim it?"

"Not only claimed it but stretched out and bounced. You ought to seen people's faces, Papa."

Papa said, "They all ought to been very glad. Giving it to Puss is just the same thing as giving it to the male population. She's slept with them all."

Rosacoke said, "She has not either. Shame on both of you."

Milo said, "Warrenton ain't such a big town, Rosa."

Rosa said, "All right, let's change the subject. What did you do next?"

Milo said, "Same subject. Me and Macey got in the hootchy-kootchy show."

Rosa said, "What happened to the Warrenton girls?"

"We lost them after Puss won her bed. Then after the kootch-show I lost Macey too."

"What happened to him?"

"It happened to his glasses. After they strip down completely, you see, the women come out in the tent where the men are. Me and Macey were sitting about halfway up but on the aisle—Macey was on the aisle, beat me to it, thank God, because this woman (Phyllis the star) came towards us naked as a skinned mole except for a little slave bracelet. The closer she came, the further I moved—I admit it; she was making fools right and left (I got splinters in my tail right now)— but Macey was in a trance. He couldn't take his eyes off of her so after she had ruined some fellow's cigar, she stepped up to Macey and he commenced to shrink and nudge towards me. Too late. She said to him, 'Strip off them glasses, son—you'll melt the frames.' And she reached down and flipped off Macey's glasses and tucked them away."

Rosacoke said, "Where?—if she was naked?"

"She found a place—and told Macey he'd have to come rescue them, her backing up the steps laughing and beckoning him on. He finally went and she stood still while he hunted his glasses and brought them back to me and said, 'What do they look like, Milo?' I told him if they were mine I'd leave them in the sun awhile to purify. Then I said, 'No, Macey, I was joking. They look all right. Just polish them some.' But Macey's night was over. He wouldn't put them on, and he's blind without them. Put them in his pocket and said 'Let's go home.' It was just ten-thirty and I could still see so I told him to drive on without me. I'd catch a ride."

Rosa said, "Drive? You said he was blind."

"Shoot, he could drive laying down. Lot of people can."

Papa said, "Not only can but do. What next?"

Milo said "The snake show."

Papa said "What did that cost?"

"Fifteen cents."

Papa said, "If you'd ever take a work-tool in hand and go back yonder in your family's garden you'd be in snakes knee-deep—no charge."

Milo said "Not boa constrictors."

"Yeah, we got them too."

"Twenty feet long? Three feet around? Weighing two hundred-eighty pounds? I grant you I hadn't been in the garden lately—"

Papa said "Never been."

"—But I overlooked meeting anything that size."

Papa said, "Nothing ain't naturally that size. All

fair shows is fakes—rubber and mirrors."

Milo said, "Well, this fake last night ate a live white rabbit—feet and fur—right before these eyes." He flipped both thumbs toward his blaring eyes. "And the rabbit didn't act like *he* knew it was faked. That's what she says he lives on—live rabbits, white rats, chickens, dogs. Excuse me, Phillip. I forgot you were here."

Rosa said, "Who is *she* and what was that foolishness about you and her taking that snake to walk?"

"You couldn't keep a secret for God Almighty, could you?"

Emma said "What secret?" She and Baby Sister stood in the door, dressed for Warrenton, ready.

Rosacoke stood and began scraping dishes. "Nothing, Mama. I was just teasing Milo."

"What about?" Emma said.

Papa said, "About a new woman he's got him."

Rosacoke standing and Milo sitting—both gazed at the floor, shrunk into their collars, and Emma said, "What is the meaning of that, Milo?"

From the floor, from under Rato's hand Phillip barked—or tried. What came from his throat was nearer to moaning—grated, weak—and Rato said, "What is the meaning of this to Phillip? You set there talking mess while my dog is suffering and dying maybe."

Milo stood and walked to Phillip, bent above him, scratched in the short hot hair of his throat, lifted one side of his upper lip. Over the long teeth his gums were white.

He gave that feeble moan and Rato said, "See what I mean—his whole voice has changed." He touched Phillip's throat—"Can't eat or drink"—showed Phillip's legs, worked one leg gently—"Can't stand or move."

Milo said, "How long has he been this way?"

Rato said, "He ain't been well since Thursday, but since last night he can't do his will."

Emma said, "Thursday, nothing. He hasn't been right since he brought that bat home two weeks ago. I said at the time to get that thing and burn it up—they swarm with lice—but Rato said to let him play, he was having fun. Fun! Gnawing on gristle and leather wings and dirty fur? Well, fun or not, that bat was the start of Phillip's trouble, whatever it is." Phillip moaned again. "See what I tell you? *He* knows the cause."

Rato said, "He knows he's dying, that's all he knows."

Milo said, "He ain't dying, Rato. He's got rheumatism—or something similar. You couldn't kill him."

Rato partly closed his hand on Phillip's throat. "I could kill him in a minute before your eyes. And maybe I should—to keep him from hearing your mess while he hurts. Just because you ain't never hurt, don't mean other things ain't." The tight noose of his fingers slackened.

Milo touched the short hair Rato had pressed. "A lot of things hurt in silence, don't they, Phillip?"

Rato stood to button the collar of his shirt (an old shirt of Milo's), then he leaned to Phillip, took him again in both his arms and walked through the kitchen door down the hall.

Emma said to Baby Sister, "See where he's going."

Baby Sister ran but Rato had heard. He opened the front door, then turned and said towards the kitchen firmly, "Phillip and me are walking to town."

They heard the door shut, heard Baby Sister pound back with the news—as if it were news, had happened at a distance—but before she could start, Milo said to Papa, "Papa, get ready. We can catch him up. He don't know what he's doing today."

Papa stood in obedience, stumped to the mantel, combed his dry white hair in the mirror propped there, and behind him the others twined in preparation—Rosacoke stacking dishes, rinsing her hands, Emma kneeling to inspect Baby Sister again, Milo stabbing his blue shirt into his trousers. Then at once they were ready—lacking only coats which only Baby Sister and Papa needed, it being that warm—and stood for a moment in silence, hands down.

Papa said to Milo "Who's driving?" and Milo's hand went out for the keys.

But Emma said, "Papa. For Rato's sake, let's get there at least."

Milo accepted that and led them out, down the hall, the three porch steps to the smooth tan stones of the yard. They moved out of step towards the truck, passing singly, successively, suddenly through ragged plates of October sun—no longer bleaching but ripening, curing, the color of gold simply though none of them noticed, had ever noticed—Milo, Baby Sister, Emma, Rosa, Papa.

Baby Sister noticed what was noticed, stopped the

line, pointed—"Rato!" It was—farther on his way than they had expected, nearly at the trees that would hide him entirely.

Rosacoke said, "He'll never get there, starting that fast. Phillip must weigh thirty pounds at least."

Milo said, "He'd make it—Phillip ain't yours, Rosa—but we got to help him now if he'll let us. Papa, you drive. Mama, you and Baby Sister sit up front. Me and Rosa will ride in the back. Papa, drive past Rato, then slow down and stop a good ways ahead so he has to pass us. We got to give him time to change his mind."

They looked again and Rato was gone—vanished, blanked by pines—so they moved on urgently, silent, to the truck which Papa managed now as if he were younger—reversing, turning, proceeding quickly, smoothly as the ground allowed, then slowing as Rato showed ahead—his high narrow back, head, shoulders, arms spidered inward on Phillip to warm, shield, hide him. They came to Rato, flanked him silently—Rosacoke waved but he didn't look up—then passed on a little. The dirt of the road was damp and soft so they spared him dust at their stopping, yards ahead. And he and Phillip came on unaltered, refusing to acknowledge by look, gait or course that five people waited in a humming truck to make their amends. When Rato had covered half the gap, Milo stood to his knees and dropped the tail gate. At the clang Phillip looked and continued staring till they were close enough for Milo to use his natural voice.

He said, "Phillip, climb in. It ain't as smooth a trip as you're getting now but it's quicker at least."

Then he beckoned once (a wide slow scoop), and Phillip scrambled, near panic for a moment in Rato's grip till his forelegs were free—surely the most he had moved since Thursday—so Rato took the truck in stride as if it were one more rise in the road. A foot on the bumper, a hand in Milo's, a seat up forward against the cab, shelter. Nobody spoke, nobody signaled Papa to start, but when Rato was with them and Milo had slammed the tail gate, he started—poorly now because they were safe, together, lurching—and soon they were on the concrete for town.

They still went dumbly—the children behind, separately lighted, their rounded features flat in the wind as if stones washed and smoothed by its streaming —and in fifteen minutes when they passed the fairground (Papa slowing), it seemed they would not even speak of that. But Milo and Rosacoke looked to the left past the whitewashed exhibit hall to shapes on the sky of silver wheel, red octopus, swings, brown tented roof of the merry-go-round, all seeming shrunk and squat so early in the day and in natural light so spent, frail, dangerous that Milo quickly thought, "I'm not wasting no money there tonight" and meant it till the truck took a final curve and the back of the fairgrounds spread before them—worse at first than the front, dented old trailers with muffled portholes, rags of black oil smoke lounging from the roofs, but then by one, in a blue bathrobe, chafing her black hair between a towel was a girl maybe sixteen.

Milo waved. The girl saw at once and waved in return with her hand and then the towel as if to flag the truck, quickly, not smiling, as if she were captive and pled for rescue. Her sudden panic thrust Milo scrambling towards the cab to pound and say "Stop," but at the window, seeing Mama's neck, he halted and facing the girl again, merely pointed towards town and said with his lips "Come on, come on." She smiled and nodded, he sat again, and Rosacoke said, "If she's a woman, I'm the mother of a litter of hungry puppies."

Milo said, "She is my age exactly—just a few months older. I know I'm a man and I know she's not, which makes her a woman."

Rosa said, "Well, if you've arranged to meet her, hide her from Mama or we'll all pay for it till after Christmas."

Milo studied the fading fair not his sister, then said, "I got a Ph.D. in hiding things from Mama."

That silenced Rosacoke and seeming the pit of the morning's play, flushed her eyes, seized her throat. She knew already, was learning daily (and mostly from Milo) what she would always have to ignore to live her life, and she huddled lower on the slats of the truck and told it to herself or still hoping, asked it, "When will I learn a way to protect him?"—her face hid from him.

But he felt her trouble, had not yet ceased to know her entirely, and resenting her hold, her try on his life, he left her under the weight she had drawn on herself for almost the final mile. Not until they were in the heart of town—Papa parking the truck by a sidewalk black and laughing with Negroes—did he move to free her. Then he took two steps on his knees toward her, bent to her bowed ear, began the truth. "Rosa, I'm

fooling. She is nothing to me, just a girl named Lois
Provo from Florida. Her aunt runs the snake show back
at the fair and Lois helps her."

Rosacoke looked up, faced him unsmiling but
listening.

And the sight of her face locked the truth within
him. "Last night when Macey had left me alone, I
wandered in the snake show because it was cheap, and
since I was almost the only one there, Mrs. Provo (the
aunt) and Lois started talking (standing in the midst
of dozens of snakes but they were mostly asleep—it was
cool last night). Lois talked that is—Mrs. Provo
watched me from the minute she saw me like something hurtful, a hawk in a henhouse—and I talked back
and watched while they woke up some snakes and put
on their show two or three more times for some colored
boys. Then at midnight when I said I'd be going, Mrs.
Provo finally spoke to me, said, 'Whoever you are, I
need your help.' I said I was Milo and volunteered
gladly to prove my good nature. 'What help?' I said.
'The big snake,' she said. 'Help us put him in his box.'
So we all three did—their helper was drunk—and then
Mrs. Provo gave me one more look and left, left *flat*—
lights on, snakes loose. Lois said, 'Aunt Selma keeps a
lot inside'—in her heart, I guess, but I didn't ask. So
Lois and me shut down for the night and then took a
walk together round the fair—mostly closed by then—
and I hitched home, walked most of the way. That's
all."

It was not. There was, and would be, more. And
what he had told was mainly lies, told to shield her
from his own growing, as if his life, his sudden needs

and powers, were a rising light that could stunt, sear. Meeting his smile, she accepted his shielding, believed his story, suspected no more. But she could not mirror his lasting smile. She knew her day—feared her life— was ruined.

Papa gouged the truck tires into the curb, the engine died, Baby Sister turned and flattened her nose on the glass above them, a Negro girl two yards away said to a boy *"Lead* kindly light!"

Rosacoke stood and said, "Come on, Phillip. It's your turn now." She could smile at him.

Dr. Fuller blocked them in the door of his office, five-foot-four in brown shirt sleeves, straw hat to his ears, round purple face grinning young for his age, stumpy legs set wide in bloused gabardine to brace him on the stream of reek and yelp that washed around him down the steps to the Mustians—all but Emma and the baby who were shopping. They waited in the sun till the doctor moved, told them come or go. He came to them or at least to Phillip, spoke to him not the family—"What's wrong, boy?" knowing his sex though his sex was hid—and taking one hand from the package he held (a thick short cylinder, wrapped and tied), touched Phillip's skull with three fingers suddenly frail, roved for a moment on the waves of bone round the eyes as if the dog were a boy as he said and would show fever there. No one answered—the question was to Phillip—and Phillip withdrew from beneath the hand and strained with his neck to smell the package, moaning in pain and discovery as he moved.

Dr. Fuller smiled to Rato, then pointed to the package
—"He knows what I got"—meaning Rato to ask. Rato
did not so the doctor stepped back, looked round to the
rest, tapped the end of his package and said, "Guess
what I am heading to mail."

Milo said "Something round—a snake?"

"No, a mad dog's head. Belongs to a lady in
Macon—or did till he bit her cook and she sawed off
his head and brought it to me, and I'm shipping it to
Raleigh to see was he mad or was she mistaken."

Rato stepped back, removing Phillip's nose from
touch of the package, and Papa said, "I was bit by a
mad dog—here on the lip, my son's pet hound. She
didn't mean me harm, she didn't know she was mad no
more than I did, just thought the world of me and tried
to show it so one summer evening I come up the porch
steps to eat my supper and bent down a little to scratch
her stomach and she jumped to kiss me and snagged
my lip. Two weeks later she was crazy as a bat, foaming
at the mouth, and I shot her dead on a Wednesday
evening. I say it was Wednesday and I know it because
I waited till then when my boy was at prayer meeting.
Shot her, soaked her with kerosene, set fire to her and
buried the ashes in the hour or so Rato was gone." Rato
at the curb wore horror like a gauze so Papa said, "Rato
my *son*, these children's Daddy, that's dead nearly four
years. Well, early that Saturday they brought me in here
to Dr. Sledge, and he commenced the treatment on me
—fourteen shots in the belly with a needle like a twenty-
penny nail. No sir, you children step back"—he made
shielding wings of his long thin arms. "We don't want
no more treatments to pay for."

Dr. Fuller said, "It ain't half as bad as it used to be. I've had it three times. Gave it to myself. But the health office will do it for nothing, and it's not but seven shots now."

Papa said, "That's seven more than we need. What's wrong with this boy's dog?" He ducked his head to the curb and Rato.

Rato stayed still, not moving closer, but Dr. Fuller asked him, "How's your dog been acting, son?"

Rato said "Sad" and bound Phillip closer inwards to him, offering no more.

Milo stepped up—he had come, been sent for this —"He has been depressed for some time, Doctor, but since last Thursday he won't eat his food, and now this morning he can't seem to walk. Just trembles—don't he, Rato?" Rato swallowed, nodded. "And moans like you heard."

Dr. Fuller said, "Worms. Take him inside and I'll see to him when I've mailed this head. Won't take me long. I'm not insuring it."

He turned right to leave them, and they all entered his door but Milo. Milo meant to wait awhile on the stoop, looking down towards Main Street to see who passed, to see if Lois followed his beckoning hand.

So it was to Milo the doctor spoke after he had gone ten yards, stopped, thought, lifted his straw hat, scratched, turned, walked back halfway—"Who are you, son? I know I know you."

"No sir, you don't. You never seen me. I just let my animals die if they can't find weeds to cure themselves. I'm Milo Mustian from out behind Afton.

That in yonder"—he thumbed towards the screen door
—"is my Granddaddy Mustian and my sister Rosacoke
and Rato my brother. The dog is Rato's."

"What's *his* name?"

"Phillip."

"Phillip. You certainly do have unusual names
around Afton."

Milo said, "I never looked at it like that. We use
the names they give us, that's all. They called me Milo
so that's how I act."

The doctor thought a moment, hitched up his
package. "The only other Milo I ever knew was a
Baptist preacher—Dr. Milo Candler. Fact he used to
ride the circuit out around Afton—oh forty years ago.
You named for him?"

"No sir, I'm fifteen. I'm named for Milo the old
Greek wrestler."

"He one of the fellows wrestles in Raleigh every
Saturday?"

"No sir, he's been dead about three thousand
years. He used to wrestle in the Olympic games and
always won. The first time he won—to celebrate—he
brought in a four-year-old heifer on his shoulders and
carried her clean across the stadium and then on the far
side slaughtered her, cooked her and ate her by himself
in one afternoon. Then when he was old one day
walking through the woods, he came to a tree some
men had halfway split and left, and Milo thought he
would finish the job with just his bare hands. He
almost did but he slipped a little and the tree clamped
on him, and before he could wrench himself loose,
wolves passed and they tore him limb from limb

and ate him. He was old then though—I said that, didn't I?"

"Yes, you said that. About my age, don't you estimate?"

Milo said, "I can't tell you that. I don't know your age."

"Seventy-one."

"That's about what he was, just a little younger maybe."

Dr. Fuller jammed on his straw hat again. "I'll be stepping on. Back in a minute though—won't keep you waiting with a name like that."

"No sir, please don't"—the doctor went a little— "and keep a good lookout for wolves as you go. I saw some last night out at the fair. They smell that mad dog, you're done for, Doctor."

"And so would half of Warrenton be. That fair's a disgrace—brute beasts cooped up in nothing but chicken wire, blood in their eye, death in their heart, waiting for the chance to bolt and kill." He pointed ahead to the sun-lit junction where men and girls— mostly black—seethed slowly. "Let them *all* bolt loose —wolves and vipers. This town needs a drenching, a scourging, I tell you. It's Nineveh now, drinking and lying and hating your neighbor."

Milo thought he was joking and threw back towards him, "Doctor, you be the Jonah."

But the doctor didn't hear, didn't answer at least. He had finally wheeled on his own last word and was at the corner, rounding it rightward when Milo's speech lapped on his back, on the print of the pint bottle riding his hip.

Two people heard—a boy at the corner (white,

about four, rushed by his mother into dwarf man's pants, bow tie, feathered felt hat: he frowned, waved; Milo grinned, waved) and Rosacoke. She had listened inside unseen through the screen till she knew the doctor was safely gone. Then still inside she moved into sight, raking one finger loudly on the wire of the door.

Milo threw up his arms, shied back in mock fright. "It's one of them violent beasts tearing out!"

She said, "Calm down, it's your sister Rosa, and you're no more Milo for some old Greek than I am Rosa for the roses that bloom."

Milo dropped his arms, said, "Sure you are—you're my own rose" and leapt to the screen, bent, kissed the wire at the height of her lips, wore a grid of rust on his mouth when he stood.

She smiled and said, "I am *Rosa* for Mama's mother, *Coke* for Daddy's, and you are Milo for—who was it Papa?"

From deep in the waiting room—"My old blind mule that died the day Emma had the scoundrel."

Milo said, "That's part of my namesake—you're right, I forgot."

Rosa said, "You are named for our human ancestors. I can't remember which one but Mama'll tell me."

"Mama don't know. She named me Milo for her own reasons when I was defenseless. Now I'm a man I choose to be Milo for Milo the great, strong and brave."

"Milo the *great*? Nobody ever heard of him around here."

"Shoot, he's well known. Anybody's been in the

eighth grade knows him. He's in the myth book you study that year."

"I'll recognize him when I get there then. That's something to live for."

Papa said from inside, "What is *my* name?"

Milo said "Mr. Mustian."

Rosacoke turned to where Papa sat, the doctor's Bible open in his lap. "You are *Jasper*, aren't you?"

"Yeah. But *Jasper* for what?"

Milo said, "For your old dead Daddy."

Papa said, "No, for Aaron's breastplate," and he read to them, each word separate, surrounded by waiting—" 'the breastplate of judgment with cunning work . . . and thou shalt set in it settings of stones, even four rows of stones. The first row shall be a sardius, a topaz and a carbuncle—this shall be the first row. And the second row shall be an emerald, a sapphire and a diamond. And the third row a ligure, an agate and an amethyst. And the fourth row a beryl and an onyx and a jasper. They shall be set in gold in their inclosings.' "

Milo said, "The *fourth* row? If I'd have been picking, I'd have picked me one in the first row anyhow —*Topaz* Mustian, how does that strike you? Topaz Mustian up on Aaron's breast."

Rosa said, "Milo, Aaron was a man and Papa was named for his own father."

Papa said, "If Milo can choose his namesake at fifteen, I can sure choose me one at seventy. But maybe you're right—fourth row is pretty poor. Hold on a minute though. Listen to this. I do a lot better in the New Testament." He riffled from Exodus to The

Revelation, slowly sought his place, found it, lined it on the air with a stained forefinger—" 'And he carried me away in the spirit to a great and high mountain and shewed me that great city, the holy Jerusalem, descending out of heaven from God, having the glory of God, and her light was like unto a stone most precious, even like a jasper stone clear as crystal.' "

Milo said, "That's better. I admit that's better. I'd be named for that verse if I was you."

Papa said, "Well, you ain't and there's better yet —'And the foundations of the wall of the city were garnished with all manner of precious stones. The first foundation was jasper.' The *first*—hear that? My name is the cornerstone of New Jerusalem. That beats most wrestlers I ever heard of."

Milo said, "Heaven's hard to beat I grant you that." But Papa barely heard it. It was said not to him nor to Rosacoke but downwards to the corner, meaning Milo was finished discussing names and had moved on to looking, to hunting Lois Provo's face if she came.

Rosacoke heard that in the tone of his voice, and to spare herself watching his hunt, his face, she turned to Rato seated upright on a bench by the wall. He had not looked at a magazine nor studied the dirty framed dogs hung around him but neither had he shut his eyes to rest. She watched a whole minute to see if he blinked, and in the dull room his open eyes seemed to dry as she watched—what shine they had soaking inward till they matched his face (that sallow, that lightless), till they seemed so dry he could never shut them. "Rato!" she said.

He blinked slowly, turned. The deep lower rims of

his eyes held tears.

She had made him show his pain, his fear, his weakness to help the little he valued—the huddle of dog cupped now in his lap—so she said, "*Horatio*. If I was a boy I would want your name, and if I have a son I'll name him for you—you and our Daddy."

His name was Horatio—Rato's name—and though he was second son, he was the Junior. He nodded to her offer, locked his eyes onto blank space again (a hand on Phillip's butt, not moving), and Papa looked up from The Revelation. "He was my only son and I gladly paid for most of his food—even the little he ate at the end—but Horatio's a name ought to stop with this Rato. It hadn't brought none of us no satisfaction—I don't mean you, boy" (but he did half-mean him)—"I mean the drinking I never understood that killed him, drove him wild when he had a good wife, a house, hot food, three growing children and one in Emma. Maybe it was me—I think about that—a judgment on me. Nobody else deserved what he done —walking straight under the wheels of a truck, leaving it all on me, this old. I must have deserved it. He done it to me."

Milo was not beyond them completely. At the end of a moment when nobody answered, assured, denied, Milo threw in the rescue—"Put down the doctor's Bible, Papa. You'll wear it out."

Papa obeyed, set it gently on a table white with dust.

And Rosacoke slowly fled to Milo, relieved by his joking and seeking his help now to soften the knot that had gathered beneath her breastbone since they passed the fair, the standing girl—collecting its mass like a river snag from the sound of their private names, Rato's dumb pain, the inward sight of her dead father, Papa's blame, Milo's adjacent absence. She opened the whining screen and stood to within her arms' length of Milo, silently, trusting her nearness to turn him, return him to his natural friends.

He did not turn, allowed her to stand unacknowledged behind him, laying upon her only the backward edge of his shadow as he balanced upright on the thin iron rail of the stoop. At first the shadow seemed shelter enough, seemed promise of care, but he thrust his loose hands deep in his pockets, hooked his feet on the bars beneath him and hunched far forward, all his body prowed and set for landfall—sight of the girl he had called and expected.

Then his shadow seemed a stain, a small squat bellows as his arms pumped time. Rosacoke stepped back, cleaned herself of its touch and weight and stared at the broad flat base of his neck, scraped bare by Mama the week before of darker twined hair that had gathered since summer. She would stare and wait till she knew his thoughts. For most of her life till lately she had done this—known Milo in sudden right leaps up his spine through his brain to the core of his simple needs, leaps he allowed her, had heretofore (even in anger) not blocked. She stood awhile waiting, then straining to hear—only the sounds of cars and Negroes, desperate exhausted barks from the kennel. So she clamped her jaws to start the ringing that would flood her ears, let her only hear her inward thinking. She heard herself. "He is aimed away from me, hunched like that, but his main aim—the aim of all this sorry morning—is to throw me off, shut me out of his life who had been there eleven years till yesterday evening." Suddenly she knew one way to reclaim him, a way to test if he could be reclaimed. Still behind him, separate, she began to sing—

> *Oh I went down South for to see my Sal,*
> *Singing Polly-wolly-doodle all day.*
> *My Sal she is a spunky gal,*
> *Singing Polly-wolly-doodle all day.*
> *Fare thee well—*

Milo was meant to answer "Fare thee well"—the only three words he would ever sing and had sung without fail since before he could read, in a fake bass croak. But he failed this time, allowed the burden to drop uncaught.

To save the rhythm Rosa caught it herself, took it on to the first stopping place—

> *. . . Fare thee well,*
> *Fare thee well my fairy-fay—*

then stopped and knew he was set to hurt her.

He was not. What she didn't know (mercifully didn't—the truth being harder than any guess) was this, this simply: he had not thought of her (to care or spurn) since facing the corner, since the night before, since this year had rammed him beyond her, for now beyond his own understanding but not beyond his joy in what he was, was becoming daily.

He flagged up a hand in sudden recognition, called "Lois" once, no louder than he ever called anybody, and beckoned inwards to himself, his chest.

Lois heard (people always heard) but waited where she stopped—having followed him this far, quick pride halted her (and fear and shame).

So he rang the railing as his feet unhooked, leapt the four feet down to the pavement and rolled on forward, head half-down, arms bowed again at his hips, hands hid. She had made him a gift (the first such gift he had ever received), and he was still new enough to feel grateful to her, but only grateful—and ready to ask, asking already in his stride, his grin for the gift again, hoping to read guarantee in her eyes. In the little space around her among the Negroes, he stopped, smiled fully, gave her his deep waist bow. "Morning," he said.

"—Which is what it is," she said, looking to the day, the unmarked sky, her waves of black hair chestnut in the light, the white wandering of her nose, chin, neck seeming dusted and dry—for all her quick walk, her helpless search which was ended now (maybe still helpless). Her hands worked rapid pleats in her yellow dress as if by working she could finally lower her eyes to face him.

But she looked on up (at birds now, southward) till Milo said, "I hope you got more sleep than me. I didn't get home till four a.m."

"I slept some," she said and made herself face him. "I can always sleep. Anybody works like me and my aunt could sleep with murder on their soul, I guess."

Milo lurched a step back, walled his eyes in mock concern. "How many murders you got on your soul?"

That eased her. She puffed a little snort through her nose but not in disgust and shook off the hair that lay on her shoulders. Then she smiled a moment.

"How did you get to town so fast?"

She said, "It wasn't so fast. A mile isn't halfway round the earth. On my two poor feet. Thanks for the ride."

Milo said, "I'm sorry. We couldn't stop, you see. We were rushing my brother's sick dog to the vet."

"What's wrong with him?"

"Nothing but worms. The vet's gone to ship off a mad dog's head. He'll be back directly."

"Good thing you didn't stop for me then. If I get the smell of dogs on my hands, the snakes won't touch me for two or three days."

"I don't guess Phillip—Phillip's the dog—would take to you either. Gentle as a baby but show him a snake, he's the Hound of the Baskervilles. I've seen him fight a dead blacksnake the best part of a hot afternoon, wring it to shreds."

"Tell him not to try himself with no pythons though. He wouldn't need a vet—just an undertaker then."

"Not old Phillip. If he don't want you to catch him, God help you—doesn't matter whether you're snake or human. Phillip's *gone* if he wants to be, days at a time, then comes prancing in thin as a slat, tore to ribbons but healing already. He's a expert doctor—eating weeds and grass."

Lois looked to Dr. Fuller's porch. "Who is that girl you were talking to yonder?"

Milo looked. It was Rosacoke still—or until they

had turned on her. Then she vanished inward. "That's just my sister. And we weren't talking. I was waiting for you. She was just waiting."

"Looks like I am too, don't it?"

"What for?"

"You tell me that. You called me in here."

Milo said, "I didn't have nothing big in mind. I just saw you yonder drying your hair, waving at me, and the natural thing was to call you on."

"You waved first."

"I beg your pardon for causing you the trip if you didn't want to see me. I don't have no presents to give you, no big plans—not till tonight. There's nothing to do in town, God knows, and when Dr. Fuller comes I've got to go back in there with him and handle all that. And anyhow I couldn't let my mother see you. It would ruin her day—she thinks I'm a child. So I beg your pardon—I said that before—but there you stood at the back of the fair when we were all worried about Rato's dog, and I said to myself, 'Yonder stands Lois. I'm meeting her tonight,' and then instead of waving and waiting for tonight, I was haling you in. I didn't think it out."

"You ought to," she said.

"—*Milo*," he said.

"Milo. *Milo*, I know it's *Milo*—know it by heart—and I don't mind a morning walk in sun like this, but don't you know I work mornings too? You got your duties, I got mine."

"Such as what?" he said.

"My correspondence school (the Law makes show people study too) and I'm learning palm-reading on my own free time. And forty-odd snakes need a lot of love and care."

"I ought to been a snake then."

Lois laughed, half-whispered "You near about *were*."

Milo blushed scaldingly, the cords of his face locked by rushing blood. Then recalling his age, his powers (but looking at the pavement not her), he said, "Look. I got to go back to my family or they'll be asking a million questions, and I'll be stuck at home tonight. You can go to the fair now and study, can't you? And wait till tonight?" He faced her again.

Lois said, "Sure I *can*. I can tell you to go to Hell too. *Wait till tonight*—what for, I ask you? Forty-five minutes in dirty pine straw with a teen-age farmer that I'll never see after sunup tomorrow? If that's all you're offering, if that's all you're hauling me round town for, you keep it, boy. Keep it on ice for some poor girl that hasn't wandered up the seaboard coast of the U.S.A. since she could remember with four dozen snakes and crooks for friends, no family but an aunt that cannot sit still—wanders and drags me behind her like a load and slides in and out of some speechless grief the way normal people change a suit of clothes."

In fifteen years no one had ever said more to Milo than *Come* or *Go*, *Stop* or *Start*, and to those the answers were *Yes* or *No*. Now faced with pride and hurt and honest need, with all the questions twined and crossed, with new orders rising like *Take* and *Use*, he lacked an answer. He had the age, the abundant power to cause her demands but neither knowledge nor strength to fill or reject them. He said, "Lois, I have

begged your pardon two times this morning. That is all
the angels in Heaven can do." He touched her brown
forearm—"Look."

She looked. Her eyes were dry but coiled, crouched.

He did not even have a sight to show her, except
himself. Having gained her look he had meant to urge
her gently again to leave him now, to wait for night,
but he paused a moment, held (again for the first time
in fifteen years) by an upward flood in his throat which
he did not know was gratitude, unspoken, unspeakable
thanks.

To save him, Dr. Fuller appeared—from town,
behind them. He seized Milo by the shoulder and said,
"Wrestle me, son. If I lose I'll kill you."

Milo said, "You outweigh me, Doctor. How come
you didn't mail your mad dog?" The package was still
pressed into his side, looking hotter, more dangerous.

The doctor looked to it as though it had mani-
fested fresh that moment—a wen, a tumor—in the
crook of his body. "Damned if I didn't forget it," he
said. "But it's just as well. It would just have to sit all
Sunday in some hot post office, baking. I'll put it back
in the ice box till Monday. Who's your friend here? Is
she sick too?"

"No sir. She works out at—" Milo stopped.
Catching at once the doctor's sweet liquor breath and
recalling his rampage against the fair, he said, "She's a
friend of my sister's from out of town."

The doctor studied her. "She sure outgrew your
sister, didn't she? Must have good air where she comes
from—where is it, girl?"

"Clearwater, Florida. But I travel mostly."

Milo frowned to halt her there.

"Travel is broadening," the doctor said, then walked on beyond them towards his office. Milo saw that the bottle he had carried was gone, surely emptied, but before he could turn to Lois and explain, the doctor stopped and called back to them. "Come on, I tell you. Both of you, now. I'll need all the help I can get with that dog."

Where he stood Milo said, "I thought you said it was nothing but worms."

"Maybe I did but I've had time to think, and recalling his face, I don't like his looks. This time of year and the fair going strong, fouling the air—he could be worse-off than anybody knows. So come on and help me." His face was all one downward frown, he seemed in earnest and however wild with drink and age, to wait at the edge of some necessary leap he must make for Phillip—with or without their company or help.

Milo looked to Lois, said, "Stick with me, Lois. God knows what's coming," and they went together behind the doctor, through slotted light (the heat and cold) towards Phillip suddenly the center of the day, their separate lives.

Surrounded at wait on the doctor's table, Phillip seemed to know that—that he bore their fear on his ribbed skull, the color and weight of walnut shell—and at first he spared them by refusing to meet their eyes, even Rato's (Rato still touched him). He watched the empty door where the doctor would come. The doctor had sent them ahead to this room, saying, "Take that poor dog in and stand clear," vanishing himself into some side closet where they heard a drawer open, the sounds of swallowing, the drawer shut quietly, the whisper "Dear God." They listened to that so intently, pressed it so hard for meaning and promise that no one thought to ask Lois's name nor stare at her eyes.

And for all her unease, she stood as what Milo had said she was—his sister's friend—beside Rosacoke on Milo's right in the circle around the bare wood table, and when Dr. Fuller shuffled in towards Phillip (flanked in the door by diplomas on the walls, proving what his gait and smell denied) and Phillip shuddered under Rato's touch, Lois laid a natural unthinking hand on his nose to stroke, to calm them both—Phillip and her, the two in the room who most needed calming.

But sick as he was, Phillip took the old scent sunk in her pores, beneath her scrubbing and the new smell of Milo—the oil of snakes, their leathery threat, his mortal foes. Whatever sickness he bore was light now. He tensed his throat and began a crooning which stood for a growl, not to Lois herself (he saw she was safe) but to what lurked near her, beneath her, behind her. She—understanding—withdrew her hand but Phillip was sure, and he growled on unbroken as Dr. Fuller neared, then seeing the doctor's weaving shape, lifted his lip over ready teeth.

Two feet away, Dr. Fuller halted, stooped from the knees to Phillip's eye level, took his hot cocked gaze, then reached to a bench, took a leather muzzle and held it to Rato—"Muzzle him, son. He's worse than he was."

Rato refused it, shaking his head.

But Papa said, "Do it. You heard the doctor."

So rubbing Phillip's taut neck with one gentle hand (deepening the pitch of the growl as he rubbed), Rato slipped the muzzle on, buckled it down. And Phillip rose or fought through the blanket till his front legs braced and lifted his head which jerked round the circle of faces, growling to each but louder towards Lois, loudest towards the doctor as he finally came and drew back the blanket and started to probe into Phillip's soft thighs, the pits of his chest, his hard hot throat. Phillip yielded his body but none of his mind—his voice continued to rake out defiance and flipped to his back, he staked his legs in the air above him.

The doctor asked him "What you been eating?"

Nobody spoke. Then Rato said "Mostly cold corn bread."

Dr. Fuller said, "I meant the dog. I know your diet."

Rato said, "I meant him too. He eats corn bread after us at night. The rest of his food he gets in the woods."

"He hunts, you mean?"

Rato nodded. He had already said much more than his quota.

"Hunts for himself? What does he catch?"

Milo said, "He's Hell on snakes. But he don't eat them. Squirrels, foxes, muskrats, owls—we got a back-yard full of their bones, clean as whistles. He's a clean dog, Phillip. I'll give him that."

"A bat ain't clean." It had slid out of Papa (helpless to hold it), and everything clenched—everybody's face and Dr. Fuller's hands.

He thrust those stiff hands up over Phillip as in sudden surrender. "Who said *bat* and what did you mean?" He looked first to Lois.

She said, "Not I. I don't know nobody here but him" (touching Milo's arm). "I work at the fair and I work with snakes, but I wouldn't touch a bat—filth, lice, needles for teeth."

"Hold everything," Dr. Fuller said and looked to Milo. "Who are you and whose dog is this, and what is this news about eating bats? You said you were Mustians from Afton, I thought, and now this child comes here from the fair saying she runs a snake show. Who *are* you?"

"I am Milo Mustian like I told you, Doctor, and these are my people—my Granddaddy, sister, my brother Rato. The dog is his. The stranger is a girl named Lois Provo. She works at the fair and come in here to see me today. I vouch for her though. She's all right. The bat Papa mentioned was two weeks ago. Phillip caught him on the wing one evening. I was out back and I saw him do it. The bat divebombed after some bug, I guess, and Phillip shot up and snatched him down—and played with his body for a day or so till nobody knew where it was any more, buried maybe."

"*Buried* nothing—*eaten*, that's what." Papa again.

Dr. Fuller said, "Of course it was eaten. This dog ate it and you haul him in here, teeth bared to kill me."

Papa said, "Doctor, hold it. *You* hold it now. You said it was worms. I heard you say it and that was my thought. Now how come all this noise about teeth? He ain't got worms in his teeth, I know."

"You're right, old brother. Worms are the least of your worries now. You got you a mad dog all to yourself." Dr. Fuller broke off and strode to the door, to flee the danger, turn them out, call the police—he had not thought which.

And they had not thought, only spread back from Phillip one unison step at the sudden news—all but Rato; Rato stayed. Then Papa drew breath and still in retreat said, "*Mad dog?* Look at him—gentle as a lamb, lying there still, dry at the mouth. I seen mad dogs—I told you that. They foam at the mouth and run till they drop."

Dr. Fuller stopped, wheeled where he stood. "They foam and run unless they have got what your dog has got—*dumb* rabies. There's two kinds of mad dogs, and this dog is one kind—the dumb kind that just lies there till he dies, taking you with him if you stand too close. He's paralyzed—*half*-paralyzed, you heard his voice. Now gradually he'll turn to stone, that still, that dumb."

Rato rolled Phillip back to his stomach—Phillip was quiet now—and stroking his neck said, "Nothing dumb about him. Smart as some people that finished school. I ain't saying who."

Milo said "No don't."

And Dr. Fuller said, "For all I know he's a Philadelphia lawyer, but he's also mad and deadly as a dart." He took two more long steps to leave.

But Papa said, "Wait. Don't run from us now. Hell, do something for him." Dr. Fuller stopped again, turned, faced Papa. "Doctor, what can you do?"

"Kill him, that's what." He retracted a step.

Rato said, "Kill him. You try it. Lay one finger on him and you die. Drunk or sober, I don't care which." Again he ringed Phillip's neck with his hand—a finger, a thumb were enough to do it.

Dr. Fuller walked completely back and with his own thumb strummed Phillip's spine. Phillip turned to see him but stayed silent now to listen with the rest. "Oh drunk, I guess." He took out his watch. "Ten-thirteen a.m. by God and more than half-gone. Me, I mean." He looked over Phillip to Lois's face, offered it to her. She nodded receipt. "It's because of—" he stopped; they waited with him. "There's no excuse. It is ten-fourteen. At noon I will lock up here and leave, the best I can, walking home, *home*"—he pointed through plaster and brick as through glass, paused while they looked. "I will eat some rat cheese and soda crackers and stretch out to rest, and if I am lucky I'll sleep a little and *if*"—still to Lois—"if God hears prayer, my heart will seize and I'll never wake." Lois frowned. "I'll wake. Don't worry. I'll wake about ten p.m. in the dark and lie in that empty house, not a sound except what I tell myself—'Get up, Joel (my name is Joel) and take a-*hold*.' I ask myself, 'Take a-hold of what?'—'Your own sorry life, your sorry self.' —'Take hold for who? Who gives a damn?' I spare myself the answer to that. It's one care I take, but I'll tell *you*—not a breathing soul; oh four or five dogs in the dark down here, fouling their cages, waiting for daylight and me to feed them. Well, daylight will come and so will I and any poor bastard that's lasted the night can eat what I give. If one of them's died the others get extra. That's what I take a-hold for every daybreak—three or four dogs that whatever I do, if I was to rise at *three* a.m., will die anyhow, run over, poisoned, shot by neighbors, and nobody grieves more than twenty-four hours. That is my life. Who would have guessed it, who would have thought a man could live it? And you come in here to break my heart with this poor son"—meaning Phillip and still touching Phillip but all said clear-eyed, unblinking, slowly to Lois because he had started with her, could not face the strain of another judge.

For personal reasons she took the burden, said, "Nobody's aiming to break nothing, Doctor. They are just asking you to do what you can."

Milo brushed her flank beneath the table.

Dr. Fuller said "Right" and walked to a cabinet, took an empty syringe, screwed on a needle, held it to the light, withdrew the plunger to fill it with air, then stepped back to Phillip.

Papa said, "Is that some new discovery, Doctor?"

"It's fresh air," he said. "New as air."

Rato understood—but only Rato—and covered Phillip's heart with the flat of his hand.

Milo said, "Phillip, we're pumping you up."

Papa said, "What'll that do for him, Doctor?"

"Put him to sleep."

"For how long, Doctor?"

"Till Judgment Day. That's the best I can do."

"That's *all* you can do?"

"All any human being could do—the shape he's in. I'm sorry to tell you."

Papa said, "We are sorry to hear it, Doctor," and they were, thus: they sensed where they stood among one another, who was left or right ten inches away, kin or strangers—the doctor farthest, opposite, alone, Phillip on the table; Rato at one end and strung out from him down one side together—Papa, Rosacoke, Lois, Milo. They all watched Phillip or chipped quick glances off Dr. Fuller like stones or hooks. They did not, could not face one another nor speak nor touch— and did not know why. Lois knew—she stood in their midst. She had learned that much in sixteen years. So she took a step back, moved left round the table and stopped beyond at the vacant end, on Milo's left. The space she had held shrank as she went; without conscious movement Rosacoke stood now closer to Milo, and Milo said, "Then there's nothing else to do" (which was not a question). "Do you see that, Rato?" Rato nodded. Milo said "Doctor." The doctor extended his left hand to Phillip, Rato bared Phillip's tufted heart, and the doctor aimed the empty syringe, saying "Shut your eyes."

Papa said, "Hold on, Doctor. Excuse me a minute. What do you charge for this fresh air treatment?"

"The consultation is three dollars even; this thing now will be five dollars more—eight dollars total." He was still poised to act.

Papa said, "Just hold it. Doctor, five dollars is more than I've give to *feed* this dog in all his life. Where am I going to find five to kill him?"

Dr. Fuller said, "I can't help you there. I offer a service that would wear and tear the nerves in a rock. I can't do it free."

"I know that. I won't asking that. What I am

thinking is, since Rato's handled him all this week with no trouble yet and since you say he is half-paralyzed and will be completely—well, if we could borrow that little leather mask and take Phillip home, we could handle him there. One of us could. Shoot him, I mean, and Milo could bring you your mask on Monday. He comes in to school on Monday, you see."

None of the family objected to that. It seemed— once mentioned—natural and fitting, and no one had real money to offer. There even rose in them, cool and quick, a sense of reprieve that allowed them to move— scrape feet, scratch arms, face one another. All but Rato whose visible future was silent grief, locked at his end, no longer touching Phillip who had failed, abandoned him.

Even the doctor showed relief though slowly. He continued to feel for Phillip's heart, but he said, "You choose. What I can do is no fun for me, and he might prefer your way after all. Just give me your word—that you'll have this poor son underground by noon today."

Papa said "You got it" and while the doctor dismantled the needle, found in his purse three old dollars to pay for the morning, the news, the duty that lay ahead of him yet, saying, "We thank you, Doctor. Take care of yourself," then "Take up your dog" as he turned to Rato and took the first step to finish the day.

Having their word for Phillip's death, Dr. Fuller let them leave unattended, preceding them only to his dark side closet, entering without a backward look— both saving and depriving them further speech. So they passed single file through the hall, the lobby, then stopped outside in a huddle on the steps in sun again. Papa said, "Now listen. Nobody's telling Emma this news. It would just scare her and start her talking. When we get to the truck, you all shut up and I'll get us home quick as I can." He pointed to Phillip in Rato's arms (seeming smaller now, compressed by his doom)—"Stay way from his mouth but treat him easy. I can't be bringing nobody to Warrenton for fourteen mad dog shots if he strikes. He ain't going to strike. He knows he's licked. All right, let's go."

Lois was gone—three steps before even Milo noticed. He said, "Lois?"—no turn, slowing, goodbye, arrangement to meet—so he said to Papa, "You don't need me. You and Rato do it. I got to catch her." He rattled off three long steps of his own.

Then Papa said, "Hold it. You are needed here and will be, at home. We don't even know that child's last name."

Rosacoke said, "I heard—it's Provo. Milo, stay."

But Papa said "Girl—" and Lois turned. "Are you headed for the fair?"

She nodded. "Yes sir."

"Then we can take you with us in the truck" and he started towards her, Rato following.

Rosacoke hung back knowing she had lost, delaying acceptance, and Milo even said, "Papa, you've ruined it. Wait till Mama sees her."

Papa threw back, "I said to keep shut and leave that to me. I've answered Emma since she caught my son and ruined his life. She's the least of my worries. Now let's go home." He spoke the last four words to

Lois, having faced her again as he walked ahead and, thinking, smiled. She seemed to be waiting for him— the girl—seemed gently nudged from behind by sunlight to meet him, greet him. And smile she did but he gave the greeting. "What you reckon is the trouble with him?—the doctor, I mean?"

Lois said, "Oh drinking and living alone and your sick dog—"

"—Old age," Papa said, looking down on her (the crown of her dark hair coppered by sun) as she took stride beside him, accepting his lead, his final answer— "Just pure old age."

There was little cause to sing and now no right, yet once they had climbed on the truck (Emma waiting), heard Papa say "He's bad sick, Emma," heard her say "Who's the black-haired girl?," then the cranking engine to drown Papa's lie—once they were washed again by wind, Milo (of all the family) was singing though silently. He had no gift nor love for music, never sang in church nor school nor for joy, only if he thought he could make a girl laugh or to echo Rosacoke's "Fare thee well," yet now the spent morning and its opposite parts spun in his mind as music, melody—broadening to bear all he saw and felt, needed or merely wanted for pleasure this Saturday morning his fifteenth October, dawn to the previous night with Lois.

For Lois had caused the song he felt—by giving the gift he had grown to demand (entrance, a hot loud grip on his life), giving it simply because he had asked:

not aloud but by leading her tired at midnight around the fair, then through rusty trailers, dusty cars to the dark edge of trees where just as his heart rose in him to ask, she turned and spoke—not "Take me back" nor "Why are we here?" nor "What are you after?" but only "Far enough," looking out of the dark where they stood towards the fair (her home) that was dying rapidly light by light on the rim of the sky. "*Far enough*," meaning this is the place, the time for us both, which he had agreed to, dropping to his knees, not looking for fear she would change and leave, waiting till she lay to her place beside him, open to the night and presently simply open to him for whatever reason—he wondered that as he huddled above her: why? why me when she barely knows my name or face by day anyhow?—the shelter of pines only ten yards away which she would not use.

She would use it tonight. He would lead her there —into trees—tonight. And to test his will, he looked to where she faced him now in the bed of the truck, seeming darker even by day than night, heavy (among his brother and sister) not so much with memory as promise—of the night ahead, his sudden life he had finally begun in her tight fork and would surely continue (farther from now than he could dream) on handfuls of others of whom Lois Provo was only the first.

But still the first. She knew that and smiled, taking his gaze now through all the wind, confirming his hope, her similar wish. Tonight she would go wherever he led. "Oh will follow wherever I lead," he said—or sang, still silent—and blinded now by his memories and hopes, he tasted in an upward rush from his chest one more feeling he had not yet known. To know it and name it, he rolled back his head to rest on the truck side, accepted the light on his shut eyelids—and found that the taste was gratitude, plain thanks for Lois. So he did not contain his song any longer. Eyes still shut, his mouth burst open on the surge of his joy, the sudden manhood that stood in his groin, that firmed the bones of his face and wrists as the truck bore him on through this clear day among his family, his first known girl, toward his life to come, his life he would make for himself as he wished. What he finally sang—aloud to them all—were the only words and tune he knew.

> *Fare thee well,*
> > (*Fare thee well.*)
> *Fare thee well,*
> > (*Fare thee well.*)
> *Fare thee well, my fairy fay.*

He bore the burden in his own bass voice and nearing the end, he half-expected—from years of habit and because she was near—that Rosacoke would join and help him, that now she would feel and share his fullness. But no answer came and when he had lunged on alone to the end, he peered from eyes that still seemed shut at three people crying—or in silent tears not caused by the wind: Lois, Rato and Rosacoke. Really not knowing their separate reasons nor trying to guess, he sat up to speak, said, "The funeral's not till after dinner. *Smile* till then."

Before anyone could strike back at that, the truck

stopped beneath them. They looked—all but Rato—and saw they had come to the edge of the fair (the town edge; the woods lay beyond towards home). Lois pressed with her hands to rise and leave, meaning to go without a word—to Milo at least who had not spoken except to sing some children's song—but the truck door opened and Papa leaned out and said, "Where must I leave you?"

She stood now. "Oh here will be fine. I thank you, sir."

"That ain't what I mean. I mean where is your tent?" Papa half-stood himself on the running board and waved towards the fair still dead before them so early in the day—ten forty-five, one or two shaggy men with buckets of water, the distant cry of a wrench on metal (someone tightening the ferris wheel in hopes of its lasting another night).

"I'm not headed there," Lois said. "I'm headed home now."

"But we ain't going as far as Florida."

"I meant that trailer." She clutched her black hair with one hand and pointed over tents and rides towards the trees. "The road runs by it but I can walk."

"No'm," Papa said, "Sit tight. I'll take you *home.*" He slammed his door and rolled them forward but she did not sit. She stumbled towards the cab—towards Papa's side—and kneeling on the scraped ribbed-steel floor there, she stared at the fleeing asphalt road which was surely as steady as anything else—any person or place—in her shifting life.

Everyone watched her openly now—Emma and

Baby Sister backwards through the window in blank curiosity (Papa had told them the girl was a nurse that toured with the fair and helped the vet in her mornings off); Rosacoke, opposite, propped by the cab, in understanding hatred; even Rato at the tailgate cupped round Phillip, in hope of finding relief on her person (never having looked to a person for that since he was a child: he was fourteen now)—but nobody spoke, least of all Milo.

Milo watched for signs in her face of what would become of tonight—his plan, her promise, their mutual wish. He could only see half (she turned from him), and though she did not smile, she did not frown, and the recent tears had sunk and dried. How could he, why should he spend his days, his precious life, in straining to know what other people meant—this Lois, his sister, his grieving mother—when they would not speak and ask for their needs?

He would ask his need when the right time came. He looked and the time was almost on him. They were slowing beside the huddle of trailers, and once more Lois was crouching to leave—when Papa turned into the dust and ruts and stopped by instinct at Lois's trailer.

She stood and walked down the truck to Rato. He had gone back to watching Phillip not her, but he roused now, let down the chain for her, drew back his legs so she could pass. She jumped the long step, Rato drew back the tailgate, but she faced him over it—no one but him—and said, "I'm sorry to slow you from getting him home. I have lived with animals all my life —since my parents died. I can guess how he feels if I don't know for sure."

Rato nodded. "You know," he said with that much force.

Lois flagged out a hand to Phillip, then moved along the truck on Milo's side, not towards Milo but towards her duty to the waiting old man who had brought her back and leaned out grinning to take her thanks. How could he know, old as he was, that his kindness had ground her—her expectation, promise, pride—like a slow water wheel every inch of the way (his kindness on the base of his grandson's silence)? She would tell him thank you and leave them for good and, walking, she forced a smile towards his grin.

But Milo laid a hand on the truck side and whispered as she passed, "Ten o'clock, Lois. Like we said—o.k.? I'll be needing to see you and say good-bye."

She stopped and faced him, canceling the smile. "What you'll be needing is a set of feelings and some eyes to notice you are not alone in this world, boy—not after last night—and had better stop grinding on other people that you hardly know, for no better reason than because you *need* to. If anything of yours starts *needing* tonight, you haul it to Phyllis's"—she pointed to the kootch tent—"and if she laughs you out, knot a string around it till your feelings grow to fit it. And as for goodbye, I can say that now—say, Fare thee well. Fare-*thee*-well." She bowed her head, swallowed, looked up smiling—"And you don't learn that in Clearwater, Florida, not at sixteen anyhow." She turned again to Papa, deepened the smile and told him "Thank you."

Papa had not heard—no one had but Milo and

Rosacoke and they were both stunned (for separate reasons) into slack-jawed stares. Papa only saw, when she stepped near enough, the face she had instantly prepared for him. "My pleasure," he said. She moved left homeward. He reached in the air as if to touch her (she was ten feet gone)—"I would pay you to show me your show right now—I don't drive at night—if it won't for the dog."

"I'm sorry for him. Be careful now."

"No'm, he's no harm."

"Well—" she said and stroked the air once, moving on again.

"Clearwater, Florida, didn't you say?"

Lois only nodded, continuing to leave (twelve feet gone, nearer to home than to them now, to the trailer at least).

And Papa threw towards her "Wait," then turned back to Emma rigid beyond Baby Sister—"Won't that the last place I heard from Tommy?"

"Tommy who, Mr. Mustian?" Her fears of the girl, her cocked outrages were tripping one another from speech to speech like a sweep of dominoes.

"Tommy Ryden my boy, my favorite cousin that ran off from home when he was fourteen in nineteen-and-thirty. You ought to know that."

"I've heard, yes sir, but I didn't know he was such a favorite of yours. You hadn't said his name since the middle of the war."

"Hell, Emma, he was *killed*. Killed overseas and buried in a hole three years ago. You want me to march around naming my griefs the rest of my life? I got to forget. I got work to do."

"Well, I have forgot. I never saw him to know who he was, and I don't know if he moved to Florida—or Baltimore. I just know, since you mention work, I ought to be home right now and cooking."

Papa did not answer that but turned to Lois who had waited at command. "Did you know anybody down there named Ryden? Tommy Ryden?—a middle-sized boy." He measured up five-foot-six with his hand. "Rusty-headed, did a lot of laughing?"

She thought a moment, "No sir. Three years ago I was already traveling, been traveling since I was three in fact."

"*I* knew him"—some new woman's voice entered from beyond, firm and deep. "What you want to know?" All the Mustians looked for the voice—Lois knew. It came from a short plain woman, maybe fifty, walking as she spoke, coming from the tents towards the trailer and Lois, to stop like a shield between Lois and the truck. (Milo knew her—it was Lois's aunt—but she had not seen him and he would not speak, being already in trouble with his mother that would take weeks to clear.)

Papa said, "Good morning. I am Jasper Mustian," bowing as best he could from the running board. "I rode this girl from town out here, and when she said she was from Clearwater, I recalled Tommy wrote me his last word from there before he was killed—ten years before so it won't a goodbye and I never knew what he done down there."

"He done plenty. He kept busy. I am this child's aunt, Selma Provo, her mother's elder sister and the child's only kin."

Papa stepped to the ground, bowed again, kept his hat in his hand. "When was the last time you saw Tommy, please ma'm?"

"Nineteen thirty-five."

Papa said, "Oh. I thought you had seen him nearer to his death."

"No sir. I heard of that ten years after I saw him last, read it in the paper. Somebody mailed it to me out on the road. You haven't got any of his money left, have you?—his death insurance?"

Papa frowned. "I never had it to start with, lady. What do you mean?"

"I mean he disappeared owing me money—for room and board, various things."

Papa said, "Listen, lady. I was nothing but his cousin, and I ain't seen him in eighteen years—since he left home with maybe a dime in his pocket. I can't go taking on his debts this late. Not with these to feed." With his hand he directed her eyes to his truck, his waiting family.

She looked in a sweep, landing last on Milo's helpless smile. Then she laughed, kept laughing, came forward saying, "Is this your boy, mister? How come you hid him?" She even looked back to mystified paralyzed appalled Lois—"Lois, did you see who's sitting here grinning?"—but did not care nor wait for Lois's "Yes." She came till she stood three feet from the truck—"*Milo*, aren't you?"

"Yes ma'm. From last night. He is my Granddaddy. That's my mother." He pointed to the small back window of the truck, expecting Mama's face, prepared to take it, braced for the blow that would land on his eyes. But she was not there, only half of the powdered back of her neck. She was waiting now for an explanation—later at home—and the force of her wait shook the truck like voltage, had stunned Baby Sister to sit and shut up, heated the metal beneath Milo's hand. He lifted it again—"That's my sister Rosa and this is Rato my only brother."

Mrs. Provo studied them all for a while, then said to Milo, "Let me get this straight, help me get this straight—every one of you are Tommy Ryden's cousins?"

Milo said, "If Papa says so, it may be so and may not be. Papa thinks everybody is kin to him. Some of his people way back were Hulls so he thinks he is kin to Cordell Hull, just having the name rattling round in the family. He's been waiting for a call to Washington all these years from his cousin Cordell. Hadn't you, Papa?"

Papa smiled but nodded his confidence. "Yes'm there's Rydens that are kin to us. I don't know how close kin though."

Rosa said, "They couldn't be too distant for me."

Mrs. Provo said, "What you got against them?"

Milo said, "Oh she's just talking. There's a Ryden girl in her grade at school that beats her time with the boy she likes."

Mrs. Provo smiled but Rosacoke said, "That's a bluefaced lie. I don't like boys yet. Dora Ryden is nice to me. It's Claiborn her twin that ruins everything. I wouldn't even tell the things he does—to girls mainly, putting things on them. Snakes—slimy!" She shuddered of course.

And eight feet away, Phillip cocked his head at the

sound of snakes. He knew the word as his order to charge—like "Sic" or "Rabbit" to other dogs—but Rato gripped him.

Mrs. Provo said, "They are cleaner than any human being *I* know, shed their whole skin if it gets a little dirty—scale by scale and it's no fun either by the look on their faces. Name me a person that'll go that far."

"Not me," Papa said. He had moved up to join them. "Every seven years is enough for me. But I've seen them do it—grab hold to something with their tail and *strip* and leave it lying there like so much trash."

"Even the worn-out surface of their eyes, peeled off clean," Mrs. Provo said. "I got one in yonder, shedding now"—she thumbed behind her; Milo knew she was aiming at the snake tent—"Come on and see it. All of you, get out. No charge till noon!" She turned back for Lois—"Lois, you and Milo get the snakes out. I already started."

Phillip clenched again and Lois was gone, where she had stood seeming violent, smoky as if she had been snatched away or had vanished in anguish like a speechless ghost.

Mrs. Provo said, "She must have gone in to fix up better. She tore off to town so fast this morning, she barely dressed. I didn't know where she was—or what hit her."

"Milo did," Rosacoke said firmly.

"Did what, honey?"

"Hit your niece. When we drove by here two hours ago, she was drying her hair—standing yonder —and Milo waved and she trailed him in to where we was at the veterinarian's with poor old Phillip. Phillip is the dog."

Mrs. Provo said, "What's wrong with Phillip?" walking towards the tailgate and Rato and Phillip. "You ought to have brought him here to me. I can heal most animals just with my hands." She extended her spread fingers into the light, fanned them twice in preparation.

"No'm," Papa said. "Don't touch him now. He's feeling low and his temper is up."

"These are soothing hands," she said and touched him. And at first it seemed she was right in her claim. Phillip loosened beneath her palms, laid a calmer head back on Rato's arm. "What did you say was the trouble he's having?"

Milo snatched the undrawn breaths of his family, open-mouthed around him. "Worms," he said.

She proceeded to stroke, both strong hands in the pit of Phillip's throat (he had raised to admit her).

Papa neared a little, looked, said to Rato, "What have you done with his harness, son?—that leather thing the doctor lent you?" Rato fished behind him and held out the muzzle which he had removed once the truck was rolling, to let Phillip breathe out his last minutes free. Papa glanced to Milo, then said to Rato more gently than ever in fourteen years, "Strap him up, son, like the doctor told you."

Before Rato could decide to obey, Mrs. Provo said, "Muzzling a dog for nothing but worms? What kind of doctor did you take him to?"

Milo said, "A cracked old drunk but he's all we got."

"Well, any fool knows how to worm a dog, and it doesn't take a muzzle and torture to do it. Bring him on over to Jake Hasty's trailer. Jake runs the dog show. He'll worm him for you and no muzzles needed."

Papa said, "No'm, thank you. We got all the treatment he needs at home." He pointed towards what he thought was west.

Mrs. Provo kept rubbing but said to Milo, "I don't think your Granddaddy trusts me. He thinks I'm after Tommy Ryden's insurance."

"Lady, you are wrong. It ain't I mistrust you. And Tommy didn't have no penny I've seen. His Mama died two years ago—poor as Niggers—so if *she* got a penny she must of buried it."

Milo said, "Old Miss Jack Ryden? Fat as she was, she couldn't of dug a post hole much less buried ten thousand dollars."

"Who said a word about ten thousand dollars?" Mrs. Provo said—but quietly to Phillip.

Milo said, "Nobody. It's just what you get if some of your kin people die in the war. The Bullocks got it when their boy died—and he never left Norfolk, died in port."

They paused as they always did for death—time for one long breath. Then Mrs. Provo looked to Papa. "Excuse me talking so hard about Tommy. I was coming from the tent—from watering the snakes—and Tommy's name struck me like a hand on my teeth. Then I saw Lois facing all you strangers—not seeing Milo grinning over here—and I went cold scared. I didn't know what you might know and tell her, to ruin her life." Her hands on Phillip had stilled when she started, and now they lifted and hung blank before her as part of her asking and offering pardon. "We never told her and I never knew Tommy had living kin till this boy strolled in the tent last night"—Milo gravely accepted her gesture to him—"and my blood froze. It was Tommy *walking*—his face, his voice—like thirteen years had never rolled by so how could I refuse when he took to Lois and she took to him? It was time going backwards like I knew it would, like it always does. Who was I to stop it? But I never knew you were her blood kin too. Well, still, don't tell her. Leave me that much and I'll find a way to ease her the news, later when she can use it."

She had lost them all but in natural courtesy, they tried to hold back the mystery from their faces, the smiles that threatened to replace understanding so they could not look to one another but held their eyes separate, fixed on the lady who was silent now—having opened her life like a vein before them. Her eyes were filled and though her lips parted again and again, her throat was locked.

Papa, being oldest, was now the one to speak. Each silent moment laid the duty harder on him—to comfort or clarify, both if he could. He could not. The mystery craved instant light. "Tell her what, lady?" he said at last.

She had held her open hands suspended this long. They oared once now—"*You* know. Her name, her life, her . . ." They waited as they had not waited before, dreading her tears that were visibly rising to drown the news. She shook her head, blinked, the tears rushed down across a smile broad and sudden as a morning glory—"Let's go see the snakes!" Her healing hands slapped together like cymbals.

And Phillip vaulted the tailgate neatly—from Rato's lap and loose arms to the ground without touching metal, striking all fours a yard from the truck unmuzzled in a small cloud of dust, buckling at the rear knees, then facing Mrs. Provo and rapidly sniffing the air she laid down, the promise of snakes she had trailed from the tent, advancing towards her. The Mustians were frozen in their previous poses, then Milo began a relay of looking—he to Papa, Papa to Rato, Rato to Rosacoke, Rosacoke backward to her mother's neck, all knowing help was needed but helpless, motionless except their eyes.

The first to move was Mrs. Provo. She took a meeting step towards Phillip, leaned to greet him, saying "Looks cured to me," surrendering her fingers to his nose that sucked up, winnowed her scents from palm to elbow. She was squatting now for Phillip's convenience, but she turned to Papa. "See, I told you these hands had healing in them."

Papa broke the family relay of looks by turning to the background, the trailers and tents, in search of help. The only man moving was as old as himself— Jake Hasty the dog man—whom Papa's dimming vision and the twenty yards distance aged and slowed to feebleness. They were on their own. So he spoke to Mrs. Provo in the voice he reserved for corners, blank walls, black-bottomed trouble—"Just hold off your hands if you aim to keep them. Lady."

Mrs. Provo was the one in mystery now. She stood straight with difficulty, backed two steps, then looked to Papa for whatever was needed—a stick, a pistol, relieving laughter—then to Phillip again whose nose had slid to her ankles, her socks, the heels of her shoes, the powdered dust, all in slow motion like a learning child, drunk and lurching but bent on success, a goal in sight and bound to succeed the moment his joints firm and bear him, his nerves obey. "What's his trouble?" she said.

Papa said "He's mad."

"Why mad at me?"

Papa said, "He's mad at the world at large. He's a mad dog, you see. Hold still in your tracks. He used to be gentle. Phillip, lie down, son." He had never said the dog's proper name before, and if Phillip heard it in this strange new voice, it was past too late—he had ceased to fear or love or even care. He was all dog now, with no memories maybe of his life with them. Their last chance was that he recalled his life. Papa said "Rato, catch your dog."

Rato slowly turned from Rosa down to Phillip, free and looking healed as the lady had promised—or visibly healing with each breath he drew, spared of present death. "Phillip?" Rato said.

Phillip looked gradually but accurately to Rato. He partly remembered.

So Rato raised his voice and said, "*Snake*. Snake, boy, snake. Go get it. You are free."

He went of course and everybody stood in respect as he went—those that were seated: Rato, Milo, Rosacoke; Emma and the baby remained sealed off. Mrs. Provo pointed—only pointed to prove she had lived to see this, a mad dog aimed at her livelihood, her twining

snakes, the golden python drowsed in the pit. And
Phillip pursued the line she pointed, the trail she had
laid in the ground as she came, seeming as he went to
be wolfing a strip of irresistible food, now in the dust,
now floating in air at the level of his head cocked and
unappeased. Yet he went so drunk, so slowly at first
that each step he took might have been his last—his
rear legs delayed, hung swaying backwards, either not
receiving or not obeying the fury that sucked his hot
eyes on. Mrs. Provo looked to Papa—"Do something,
man. You know where he's aiming." By then he had
stopped—for good, the Mustians thought; all but Rato.
Rato knew he was on the spot where the lady had
paused when she came from the snakes and announced
her acquaintance with Tommy Ryden, and he circled
the spot in what—to the others—seemed a whirlpool
safely funneled towards death.

Papa said, "Lady, your snakes are safe. He's dumb
mad, you see. He's paralyzed and dying right now."

Phillip stopped in the midst of a whirl facing
them, took Papa's words with stiffening ears, used them
some private way in his brain, wheeled on himself and
plunged on as quickly as in his youth, crooked but
silent between the first tents.

"Paralyzed!" Mrs. Provo said. "He's giving a good
imitation of lightning—Mr. Jake, stop that dog running yonder." She abandoned the Mustians, yelled to
the old man Papa had seen who had a broom now and
was sweeping the ground by his trailer steps, then she
broke into a run more crippled than even the worst of
Phillip's (she suffered rheumatism).

Mr. Jake saw the black O of her mouth, her

flinging arms, but before he could cup a hand to his
ear, the words had streaked past. Still he saw the
Mustians standing in the distant swimming light and
Selma Provo in flight from them so he legged out to
meet her, broom raised as weapon, arms stretched wide
as a safe port for Selma.

But she only saw Phillip—his vanishing trail—and
rammed Mr. Jake full-force head-on. They struck dust
together, scuffed head and heel, he crying from the
cloud, "I'm with you. You're safe;" she crying, "Safe!
We're in awful danger. Turn loose, old fool!" He
turned loose and lay flat, small on the ground,
wounded at heart far worse than in limb, and she
strained to rise—camel-wise, humps and knees—but
when she set weight on her thick right ankle, it buckled
and threw her down useless, frantic. She looked to the
Mustians through settling dust, rage and plea plugged
dumb in her throat.

Papa looked to Rato, "Boy, you have ruined me
—a mad dog streaking towards a wild snake show and
now she'll sue me for a broken leg. Emma! Oh
Emma!" Emma slowly looked through the dirty glass.
"Help that woman. She has broke a leg." Then he
limped off tentward, calling, "Come on, children. We
got to go face him. He used to be ours. We can't wait
here."

But the great snake waited in his canvas pit,
roofless this day as he was dazed mild by the rabbit
slowly dissolving within him—the meager appalled
unworthy offering that had suddenly crouched before

him last night from unknown hands. He had roused to accept it in two airless coils only because of blind hunger, starved pride, and it lay within him humbly, invisibly. Yet though it had not faintly swelled his sides, the rabbit was steadily feeding his pride. He dimly knew that in his warming doze and calmly awaited this mysterious healing, return of the strength he had known in his home—the trees, brown water, white sun of Burma: all stripped from him in his treacherous capture (sated, asleep), his black boxed journey that had ended thus in dry canvas walls, despondent giant among knots of pygmies, the target of a thousand daily laughs or shudders from throats he could crush in one coil. But impervious target, un-scathed, immortal because of his skin which at least they had left him, the scraped but living roots of his former strength, watered by his blood all night, all morning with the rabbit's bright eyes, tense speed, cold fire. He was healing for a purpose, a deed, a foe. He waited to know it and his skin drew towards him the one shaft of sun that pierced the tent. It flowed warm and thick on his still loose coils and flamed his pattern, the outward show of his inner pride: pale brown scales as the ground on which darker shapes were encrusted— unmatched shapes of night, birth, dream, huddled death, darkest at their centers but edged with gold or— now! as he flickered—with amber, bronze, violet, green. Hide and armor for a warrior king. Such a king wore it now, restored and waiting.

So he felt—and was—as Phillip burst on him, no prologue or warning but silent and firm in every joint as he took the top of the pit in stride, landed a foot from the dreaming head and halted amazed, having seen for the first time a foe so grand, so far beyond hope, fear or former strategy that an instant of worship was compelled upon him. Phillip thrust his front legs flat before him, half-crouched behind and laying his head to the cool wood floor, bore that lidless gaze, sleeping? waking?—for such eyes shone as hard in sleep; in death, he knew—as in dangerous life. Which did he face? He waited to know. His awe was now curiosity, *justice*, and he knelt on, losing this vital moment, dazed by the eyes to his own natural aim—restoration of his ruined pride: he tan-haired, torn-eared, welted, called *mad* and thus doomed and desperate but held, fixed. The black eyes soared in their own amazement two feet above him, borne on the flat head that swayed once back over tightening coils, bared a hundred teeth and—awake!— lunged, locking Phillip's heart in one cold coil and humped for the next as Rato's voice came "Phillip, his throat!"

When Milo and Papa reached home at last it was Sunday morning though full night still, and the house was black except the porch light. Papa choked the engine and striking a match, looked exhausted but proud at his pocket watch. "Two in the morning. We left here at eight o'clock Saturday morning—eighteen hours. I ain't been away from home this many hours since Pauline died, since Prohibition maybe." (Pauline was his wife.) "And two in the morning, Great God Almighty! The last time I read a watch this late—well, I hate to tell you what I was doing. I won't telling time, I'll say that much, and neither was she. What the Hell was her name?—married that cross-eyed fellow in Elberon?"

"Old ugly Mrs. Luck, you talking about?"

"You got her, you got her. Ugly, I grant you. Ugly as sin but she let me in every time I knocked. And I knocked regular. She won't *old* though. Fifty-five years ago, who was old?—just my Mama and Papa. I was younger than you."

"You're holding up better than me now, Papa. I died at midnight. Let's go rest. We got tomorrow to get through, remember."

Papa waited and then said "Yes, I forgot," and they walked to the house as softly as possible, slowing at the steps from now useless habit to let Phillip know it was family, safe, that he could sleep on till light woke him naturally.

Inside the house was as silent as dark, but as they tipped past the dim hall lamp, Milo saw a tablet propped against it. In Rosacoke's round open hand was a note—

Dear Milo and Papa and Rato,

Mama fried a chicken which is in the oven. Where in the world have you all been? We are worried but have finally gone to bed, being sick and tired. Please be quiet as we have company in the downstairs bedroom and in my room. Milo, you and me are sleeping together in your room, hear? Papa, you and Rato sleep as usual. If anything bad has happened, wake me up. I know something bad which I'll tell you in the morning. Sleep good.

Rosacoke

There was bad news enough but Rosa woke herself when Milo laid his hand on the doorknob, before he even turned it. She had been in the depths of a dream about him—a sensible story, clear and possible like most of her dreams: he stood in the fork of a tree high above her (his present age and face), then as she looked up he turned loose his hold, high as he was, and spread his arms to jump. She said, "You will die and ruin us, Milo." He said, not looking, "I am almost a man. I must fall to rise." He jumped and he rose and the last she saw—before she woke—was him rising not falling as he had foretold, above limbs and leaves into steady light, a single figure in clear day alone, no thought of when that day might end.

Though torn awake she did not move at first. She lay in total dark, eyes open, hearing him shut the door, walk towards the bed. She knew she was conscious— she always broke sharply with sleep, no confusion—yet as he slid and hunched out of his clothes (his body lined on the unshaded window), he still seemed to lift, his dark body darker than the visible night, to be past retrieving. Nor did she speak. She had not yet hooked from her mind the question that would drain the mild grief she felt and had felt all day so she concentrated on moving silently to leave him a fair share of bed when he came. And when he came—having stripped to Rato's underwear—and lay on his back to face the ceiling, she said what she suddenly needed to say, what rose unsought, "Well, you came back."

"Barely," he said. "More dead than alive," show-ing no surprise that she was awake. (He was someone you could not surprise if you tried. Not that he kept up perpetual guard—just that he always expected what happened, accepted it however sudden or wild.)

"We thought you might be completely dead when Papa at least wasn't here by bedtime. I hope you won't taking him and Rato to Phyllis's right after stopping poor Phillip for good."

"No'm, not tonight. I wish I had. I wish I had stopped poor Phillip too. Papa and me and four show men and the sheriff and deputies been looking for Rato and Phillip and Death. Death is the name of an Indian python, twenty feet long, weighing two hundred pounds. We still hadn't found them, not even their tracks. Now let's shut up and get some rest."

Rosa propped on an elbow, "Rest? *Milo.* You mean to say Rato is not in Papa's room?"

"No, and God don't even know where he is tonight—could be the woods behind the fair, could be he's in Death's jaws or belly."

"Milo."

"I'm kidding. No, Rosa, everything's true but that last. The snake ain't hungry. He ate Friday night. Rato is safe for a week or more."

"Milo, you're lying. After you ran Mr. Hasty got up—he was not hurt—and went to the tent and came back directly saying you had caught the dog and no harm was done but that you all would stay there and shoot him right then and he would drive us to town with Mrs. Provo to fix her leg."

"He was the one that was lying, Rosa. Papa told him to." She was speechless again but she stayed propped up so he knew he must start at the first and explain. "Rato outrun us all to the tent—a lot of men joined us before we got there—and when I tore in ten seconds behind him, he was down in the pit on his knees, wrestling Death. Phillip had jumped in first of course and was already locked in one of Death's coils—"

"Just call it a snake. I'll know who you mean." She had lain to her side, turned to face his black profile.

"Phillip was already strangling (you could hear him), but he had his teeth in the snake somewhere— where does a snake's throat begin and end?—and Rato was struggling with both hands and feet to hold off the snake from casting again. Two coils—you're lost, Mrs. Provo says. The four of us were alone there another ten seconds, and I was waiting for some more men to help me. I figured it was no sense the whole Mustian family getting strangled or rabies, but I want you to know in that twenty seconds of grunting and thrashing, Rato tore Phillip loose from Death and took him in his arms —Phillip, I mean—and jumped the far side of that pit and was gone, and so was the snake like lightning behind them. All of that happened with me standing there not moving a muscle but to open my mouth, and when Papa and the extra men arrived, there was nothing to see but a swinging tent flap and my big mouth and four dozen egg-sucking baby snakes, pop-eyed and crazy—I say *baby*; beside Death, I mean. Well, Papa said, 'Where is the mad dog, son?' and I pointed to the flap and said, 'Gone yonder in Rato's arms and a boa constrictor with them.' The man that is Mrs. Provo's help said, 'That ain't no boa constrictor. That's a python. She just calls it a boa since that sounds worse.' Then all of us scuffled around to the flap and looked out for signs. The snake tent is back on the woods side, you see, and unless they were sucked up in

a tornado, they had hit those woods thirty seconds
before. Some fellow yelled out 'Get your guns, boys'—
they have to travel armed—but Papa said, 'Hold it.
Don't get no guns. My boy's in them woods—my
second grandson—and he ain't a scholar so we got to
be extra careful to save him. Take me to a phone and
I'll call the sheriff. If we got to have guns, have legal
guns.' Just then Mr. Hasty run in and said Mrs. Provo
had broke a bone and was suffering. Papa bowed a
minute and then said to him, 'Go back please sir, and
tell the women we got it in hand but will be delayed,
shooting the dog. Have you got a car?' The man said
Yes. 'Then you drive them all to the doctor, will you?
Emma Mustian is the big woman's name, my daughter-
in-law. She's good in a sickness.' The man took orders
and Papa called the sheriff, and him and two deputies
came right out, and we been scourging those woods
every since. Not a trace of nothing—boy, dog or snake
—once the pine trees start. Pine straw doesn't show
tracks too well, but we all kept looking till around five
o'clock when the fair people had to go back and work
and the sheriff had to leave to round up the drunks. He
left us a deputy—Yancey Breedlove—and him and me
and Papa hunted with flashlights till an hour ago. We
were God knows how deep back in the briars when
Yancey stopped and said, 'Son of a bitch, them
bastards live in *trees*,' meaning pythons. Papa said 'Do
they, Milo?' and I said they did, having thought of that
at sundown. So we gave up and came on out to the
truck and come home."

"Just leaving Rato under the stars?"

"Shoot, it's warm tonight. And listen, Rosa, if

Rato has got through fourteen years on less than half-rations in the brain department, he can sure last till noon in his own home county."

"Why noon?" she said.

"Because the search party is gathering here in the yard at noon soon as church turns out—all the men we can get, white or black, and the sheriff and deputies and two blood hounds. We are going to spread out and comb every step of the woods from here back in to town and the fair. We figure they are aimed this way."

Rosa sat up finally. "I better go wake Mama up right now."

"You lost your mind? It ain't but two-thirty. You'll worry her to death."

"Well, who's going to cook for all those men between sunup and noon? We ought to start now, killing chickens at least."

"Calm down, Rosa. You are eleven years old. You ain't a woman yet, however you act. You got three or four years so lay back and rest. Your time will come. Mama will make out. She'll know how. It ain't your worry. Rest now or hush up and let me rest."

She said "I'll hush" and fell back beside him. "But who's going to rest, knowing their brother is wandering through briars in the dark of night with a mad dog by him—and running from a snake that is going mad too?"

"Where did you get that?—the snake going mad?"

"You said Phillip bit him. So unless snakes are vaccinated, he's going mad."

Milo waited. "I hadn't thought of that. And he's got a hundred teeth, Mrs. Provo says." His neck strained upward, waited, relaxed. "What is to be will be. Close your eyes." He closed his before he finished speaking.

And Rosa closed hers. She lay flat like him, having fallen that way with her hand on her chest, and thought through a quick hard plea for Rato. As it ended her fingers had warmed on her chest and seemed, despite the gauze of her gown, to touch flesh there—the close firm muscle, tanned hide, brown circles where her breasts would be when her time came. She pressed, even kneaded there (careful not to move the bed beneath her), searching for buried but tangible proof—a core, a seed—that her time would come, that what had happened to most human beings would happen in her—fullness, the burden of fertility of which her body bore no certain promise, cleft though it was and had always been, dryly dusted in every pore with faint gold hair. And she found no surer signs tonight. Her hand stopped, she thought in her mother's voice, "Most things are not meant to be understood;" then in her own, "This surely is one—my terrible future. Oh let my time come;" then in Milo's drowsily, "What is to be will be." But they did not calm her. How could she, why should she wait here behind—three years, four —when she knew the shape her future must have and when people she knew (girls in her grade only six months older), people she loved and had understood were passing her, changing before her eyes: Milo beside her breathing slowly but not with the depth or rhythm of sleep? She rolled to her right side, reached and touched him. Whatever had become of in him in these few months, whatever he would be in time to come—

would learn and yield—he was this near now, one hand away, a narrow hand.

He drew a deep breath but did not speak, finding nothing to give her.

So she volunteered what she had meant to avoid. "Don't you want to know who our company is?"

"I guess I know."

"Who do you guess?"

"Mrs. Provo and Lois."

"How did you know?"

"Because their trailer was the only one left when we came through the fairgrounds awhile ago—everything else had broke up and gone, snake show included —and their lights were out and the shades were up so I figured Mrs. Provo was hurt and was here."

"And you didn't ask me?"

"I figured what she broke wouldn't knit before morning."

"She didn't break nothing. She tore some gristle and that's more painful. I'll tell you, hear?" He did not say No. "Well, when you all ran, me and Mama and the baby went to Mrs. Provo. She was still right down in the dust, moaning. Even Mr. Hasty had run off and left her, hot behind you all. Mama didn't know a thing about Phillip—Papa lied to her; she thought he could live—and whenever Mrs. Provo began about Phillip, Mama would look up from rubbing her ankle and tell her not to worry, he wouldn't harm a flea. Finally when she still couldn't get on her feet and the pain was getting worse, Mama said to me 'Go find that nurse'— Papa had told her that girl was a nurse, that girl you know—"

"Her name is Lois."

"I know her name. And I knew she was no more a nurse at her age than I'm a bride, but I ran to that trailer and when nobody answered, I went in and found her crying already, flung down and sobbing like she had second sight and knew what had happened. She didn't though. I told her and she asked where you were so I had to tell her that—about Phillip running. Then she got up and came out and acted like a nurse. She felt her aunt's leg and said, 'No bones broke but the gristle is loose.' Then she asked Mama was there a doctor in town, and Mama said, 'Several—ours is Dr. Sledge. We can take you to him when the men get back.' So I want you to know we squatted in the sun around that woman for a good quarter hour—she couldn't stand up and how could we tote her? She's no bantam hen—till the old dog man Mr. Hasty come back and passed on that stream of lies from Papa: everything was in hand and you all were held up, shooting Phillip. Well, we had to put our shoulders to it and get Mrs. Provo in Mr. Hasty's car. Dog hair! I thought Phillip shed bad enough, but he sheds outdoors—or used to, didn't he? —and he's just one dog. Mr. Hasty has twelve and they ride with him. Anyhow it got us there—the car, I mean —and Dr. Sledge said what Lois had said: torn gristle and was there anybody that could look after her for a day or so till she could walk? Mrs. Provo said she had a white boy working for her that was sober enough to handle the snake show—everyone of Mama's pores stood up; it was the first she had heard of snakes—but all else she had was her one niece and mighty poor cooking equipment in her trailer. What could Mama say? She had seen enough to know we were mainly responsible so she said 'Come to us' and Mrs. Provo accepted. Mr. Hasty drove us back to the fair. You all were still gone and Mama's groceries were spoiling in the heat so he said why didn't he ride us on home? Lois got their clothes and locked the trailer, and here we've been since two p.m., waiting for you. Gradually Mama learned all the facts the rest of us knew, but they didn't seem to scare her half as much as me—because she was busy every minute, I guess: giving Mrs. Provo aspirins and footbaths and frying two chickens. Lois seemed to worry more than anybody else. She sat with her aunt while we ate supper, and she must have been wringing and twisting a lot because we heard Mrs. Provo say, 'Lois, for God's sake, when I was your age I didn't know nerves existed. Get up from here and breathe some fresh air. Take you a walk out in the yard while it's daylight.' Lois didn't answer but she got up and left —and walked beyond the yard and outstayed daylight. When she still wasn't back by seven o'clock, Mama went to Mrs. Provo to ask where was Lois. Mrs. Provo said 'Emma, shut the door'—she used Mama's first name. Mama went in and shut it, and they must have talked an hour in there while I washed dishes—whispering mostly as not a word came through the door to me. Then Mama came out and *she* had been crying. She told me these curious sleeping arrangements—she and the baby would sleep with Mrs. Provo (Mrs. Provo's been in Mama's room from the start). Then Lois came in all dusty from somewhere. Mama and me were standing in the hall. Mama took one look and cried again. Lois said, 'I've just been walking in the road. I knew where I was,' but the tears ran on and that worried me more than all the waiting and wondering about you. When has anybody seen Mama cry? I asked her the trouble. She just said 'Someday you'll understand.' Understand *what?* I want to know. And *when* will my day come? If people just tell me what's going on, I understand more now than they ever guess. What do you reckon she could mean, Milo?" He did not answer nor even seem to breathe. "You are fifteen. Maybe you understand?" Still deeper silence. "This is *your* day, Milo. I'm not that blind. Tell me what you know." His only reply, only move was breath. "Then how come you stay up till four a.m. just to walk some girl as common as dirt round a county fair if you don't learn something for your efforts?" She was not expecting an answer but she could not stop. Rosacoke had tripped within her a hot brown stream that till now had run buried. "It's not but two-thirty yet, Milo. It's not your bedtime. How come you don't go ask your girl what the secret is. She's older even than you, you know, and she's yonder in my room through that wall." She did not point but still the wall seemed to melt between rooms and Lois to be there ten yards away, waiting, awake. Rosacoke tensed where she lay and listened— for any sound, threat or rescue. What came was the pulse of sleep from Milo—half-counterfeit but calming, beckoning—and when she had linked her breath with his and had thought of sinking, she sank and slept.

For how long, how deeply she did not know nor what had seized Milo and shook him, but she woke again cleanly in full possession when he eased back the cover and slid to the floor and stood a long moment

against the dark window holding his arms still shuddering, then picked his way through the floor like a
minefield (safely, silently), took a whole minute to
open the door, left it cracked behind him and started
the five steps to where Lois was. Rosacoke widened her
eyes to the dark. Before this past day, the previous
night, she had understood Milo—him, at least—and
now she forced her mind out to him, not to warn or
halt or even protect him but to share his life as she
shared his mother, dead father, home, bed. She knew
the thing he aimed to do—had learned it from older
girls at school, boys' drawings, the poems they yelled—
and she knew from frequent sight of his body that
whatever he wished, he could now perform. What she
did not know was why?—what force could hold him
awake bone-tired, could seize and rattle his teeth with
need and send him half-naked in Rato's drawers
through the black crowded house past Papa's open
door to one narrow girl on her own iron bed, suspended
above Mama's snoring body? And what would he have
at the end for his trouble, the dangers he dared?—unless
simple calm, the shuddering eased, sleep at last?

He did not know, might well not have cared or
tried to prevent her, but Rosacoke was with him, as
surely with him now as if she were laid against his back
or had entered him ghostly and tapped the currents of
his sight and touch. The stalking paused. Here was the
door. Body drew tall, fists clenched, toes grasped. Then
right hand felt as gently for the knob as for warm bird
eggs, twisted the cool cracked china rightward, pressed
a half-inch—then the lock took hold and shaking swept
again from eyes through shoulders. The lock was a

screen-door hook Rosacoke had screwed there herself
the previous summer to give her the sense at least of
peace for occasional thinking, and here now it threatened to hold off answers she needed far worse than
privacy, peace. Probe finger into crack, lift hook free.
But there is not space for both skin and bone, and the
nearest thin blade is below in the kitchen. O speak!
Surely she waits for word? Say "Lois." It was said in
Milo's whisper. "Lois, it's me." The rustle of cover,
complaint of springs surrounded her waking, her slow
understanding, but once formed, her answer hurled
sudden and final—"No. Leave me alone. You have lost
your mind."

That drove Rosacoke back into herself, instantly,
violently. Her actual eyes stayed open but were blind,
her hands felt only her own dry chest, ears heard only
one rooster crow, then a second, a third—a relay of
pride, for daybreak and light were hours away, might
never dawn.

She almost wished darkness would last on. She was
that exhausted. She strained to stay conscious, to see
Milo back, not that she hung large hopes on him still,
but she wanted to know he was safe, resting, calmed,
that—barefoot, half-naked—he would not take cold.
Both of her brothers were valuable to her for all their
lack of attention and care. She already knew, thought it
four years before when her father was killed—"These
are the two persons I will know when everyone else
here now is gone. They will outlast my mother and
certainly Papa. I must tend to them." And here they
were both wandering lost tonight—one maybe miles
from here and in danger; one, yards away maybe in

worse danger (from inward where deadliest dangers lie).

Yet she slept, suddenly, and did not dream, did not even stir when half an hour later Milo stopped his vigil, came and lay again beside her. He had stood that whole time against Lois's door, looking down towards a window at the end of the hall. Beyond were the tops of trees, invisible. He thought he could stand till light would show through their final leaves and Papa start coughing. He was no longer tired, no longer in hope of any sort of entry but sick with balked want (not need; not yet, whatever he thought) and with shame and bafflement: how could people change like this in a day? —take all you could give one night and leave, promising; then the next night seal you out like a thief, call you crazy through the crack in a door?

Still as he stood from one foot to the next and the last dregs of heat seeped out of the house, his question rested and finally he was calm—a different calm from what he had sought. What pulled him now was his own warm bed, and the moment his head touched pillow he slept and began to forget. He was the agent, had made the try, taken defeat, but he would forget in the rush of his growing, his swelling life. It was his sister, trapped in childhood, who would not forget.

TWO

"**M**ilo." Their mother stood in the open door and spoke towards the bed, firmly, to wake them both with the single name. It was almost eleven and the strong light fell on her worried face and her hands that held the tablet of paper.

Rosa woke first but seeing Mama's forehead, did not dare speak, only rolled to Milo, shook him and said, "Wake up. Mama wants to ask you something."

"*Something!*" Emma said. "I guess I do. I got a list of questions long as my leg" and in proof extended her columnar leg.

Milo said "Shoot" but into his pillow.

Emma said, "Sit up and honor your mother. I have let you sleep past time for church. The least you can do is ease my mind."

He sat up in bed and bowed to his knees. "I'll do what I can but if you're needing ease you better get your aspirins. I'm as full of bad news as a Christmas turkey is of you-know-what—but Papa told you, didn't he?"

"Papa hasn't told me so much as Good Morning. Him and Lois left in the truck about sunup. Didn't wake a soul, didn't eat a mouthful—just took a loaf of lightbread and two hot Pepsis and left me this note." She shook the tablet at him.

His feet hit the floor. "Let me see that."

Emma pressed it to her, "Tell me this first—what is the sheriff doing downstairs now, asking for you, and three men with him milling in the yard, badges shining and hound dogs—they must be—in a rusty wire trailer? What have you done, son? Tell me that first please."

Milo hopped to his clothes, struggled into them, pointed to Rosacoke still in bed—"Rosa knows it all. She can tell you. I'm going," and he tore past her, taking the tablet by force, reading as he went—

Emma,

Me and the girl are leaving early to get a headstart. Milo will tell you on what when he wakes up. But you let him sleep. He needs it bad. Then tell him I said the girl and me will go to the fairgrounds and strike in from there. Him and his men strike in from here and meet us at the old Ryden place at dark.

Emma called after him, "Come back and put your shoes on—it's Sunday," but she knew it was useless, bent for the shoes to take them to him (the laces were knotted) and turning to Rosacoke above the dry shuffle of his feet descending, said "Tell the worst first."

"We got to cook dinner for them" Rosa said and pointed towards the yard. "No, that ain't the worst. Here, sit down, Mama." Emma sat in the warmth where Milo had lain and Rosa began.

But Milo was nearly at the sheriff by then—downstairs, outdoors, across the porch, through the yard

(half-asleep, half-buttoned, barefoot). And being barefoot he had come in silence—no one had noticed—so
he stopped a little short of the various men, gathered
his eyes against broad daylight and searched among the
men till he found the sheriff, studied him—or his back
which was turned: a big man wide but firm in khaki
shirt and pants, stained Panama hat, waddled down on
his hams (holster plowing the dirt) by a little wire
trailer where the two hounds lay.

He was speaking to the hounds as if they were
children, straining to console their obvious grief. "Rest
on, boys. Soon as church lets out, you got to go track us
a snake and a mad dog." They looked towards his voice
but did not even blink.

Then a low dark man (unhitching the trailer)
said, "Take more than livestock to scare *my* dogs. They
seen and caught worse than any Mustians can offer—
rapers, murderers, maniacs, Republicans. You name it,
they've tracked it, treed it and *bayed* and been offered
as proof in eight courts of law in two different states.
Put a man in the Chair last month in Raleigh."

Yancey Breedlove, propped by the big oak,
laughed. (He had hunted for Rato the night before.)
He said, "Buddy, we gas them in North Carolina."

"But not standing *up*, fool," the hound man
said.

"They don't set them down, do they, Sheriff?"
Yancey said.

The sheriff faced round onto Milo not Yancey and
seemed for a moment not to recognize him or to
recognize him as someone else—his narrow mouth
bubbled open on a name (not *Milo* certainly), and his

eyes frowned in pain. Then he knew the boy, his pain passed on, his mouth smiled broadly, and he half-ran to Milo, saying, "Here's the *man*. This man *here* knows." He shook him by the shoulder—"Tell me all you know."

Milo said, "I know things you'd die to know—die in agony, smiling—but I want to know how come he's yelling *Chair* when all my brother done is chase a sick dog?" He bore the sheriff's heavy stare (Milo could stare-down a statue of God) and pointed to the hound man.

The sheriff said, "Son, *he* ain't running this hunt. I am and I won't named Rooster for nothing. Rooster Pomeroy is running this hunt. That fellow's nothing but a Capps from the river that owns these dogs and runs his mouth, but I give the orders because it's my duty—the duty I can *do*, was elected four times to do like F.D.R. So lean on me. Lean on Rooster, son." He reached for Milo's tangled head to make him lean momentarily.

But Milo coiled back, then surrendered, smiled and looked up for the sun. "Ain't you early, Sheriff? I'd of been up and ready, but I thought you said noon."

Rooster said "I did," then dropped his voice. "I did but I tell you, my wife she—" He stopped. "How old are you, son?"

Milo said "Fifteen."

"You know my wife?—Mrs. Kate Pomeroy?"

"No," Milo said.

So Rooster thought back through thirty-nine years till he was fifteen, then changed his mind and raised his voice—"No, I tell you, I just wasn't sleeping last night so I got up early and drove to the river to get these dogs and come here thinking we could stop by your church (since this thing is serious and they all know you) and ask for helpers. Catch them in a body with women present, they'll volunteer like flies to cream." He fished out his watch. It was quarter past eleven. "It's close by, ain't it? If we go right now we can beat the sermon and make our call." He saw Milo's bare feet, ruined clothes. "I'll go in but you ride with me."

Milo said, "Maybe I better stay here—explain to my mother. She's still in the dark."

Rooster said "So am I." He clamped his eyes shut, groped blind for a moment, looked again (not smiling) —"I need you, son" and started for the car.

Milo followed him.

They had covered more than half the distance in silence—Rooster watching the road as if it were a trap; Milo watching the sky, what birds there were—when Rooster laughed and said, "We're going to find your brother, don't worry. The cause for *worry* is your old Granddaddy. What's he up to with that snake girl?" He looked to Milo who had just seen a quail and did not respond. "We are liable to find him dead of a stroke or burned out clean as a cotton gin, ain't we?—" Still no answer. "How old is he? A heap older than me. Well, I tip him my hat." He tipped his straw hat. "I'm fifty-four, my wife is twenty-seven. I married late, you see, and I can't—" He stopped again, again changed tack. "That girl is more your style, ain't she, son? How

come you ain't in there guarding your interest, grab-
bing your share?"

Milo did not turn. He said "I overslept," then
leaned to see the sun. "But the day isn't over—not *my*
day at least. Hadn't hardly begun. I hadn't lost yet."
He smiled but he meant it, believed it entirely.

Rooster grabbed Milo's knee. "The Hell you
hadn't. You've told your secrets to the wrong man, son,
and you're under arrest—corrupting a minor female
child." Then he laughed for a while—Milo not joining
in. "No, I *am* sheriff and sheriffs are paid—not much—
to keep order (if I kept the order I was *paid* to keep,
this county'd be a thicket of gnashing teeth), but this
is Sunday and till those dogs start, I'm on private time
so I'll set you free"—he lifted his hand—"spare you
what you deserve (you'll get it quick enough) but on
one condition: that you listen to this. This is something I know and it won't cost you nothing." He
looked to Milo who would not face him. "Please look,"
he said.

So Milo looked. "You guarantee it's free?"

"Free as day," Rooster said.

"Guarantee it's true?"

"Oh it's *true*," Rooster said. "Anybody can lie. I
ain't paid to *lie*."

"Then I'm listening," Milo said—and he was, eyes
on Rooster as if Rooster were a place he must oc-
cupy.

Rooster said "What's the time?"

"Maybe eleven twenty-five."

"And you think it's morning?"

"For half an hour—sure."

Rooster said "What's your age?"

"I told you—fifteen."

"And you think that's young?"

"Well, I've met one or two older people through the years."

Rooster said it to the road. "It is eleven twenty-five, a clear broad morning that will be noon soon. You are fifteen, a man and the Lord has hung gifts on you like a *hatrack*."

Milo looked down searching, brushed his chest, his thighs but did not speak.

And Rooster went on—"Use what the good Lord give you *now*, and use it every chance the day provides —Hell, day *and* night—till it's wore to a nub and that'll be before you have hardly got started. Son, I *know*. Thirty-nine years ago when I was fifteen, I could of bored through hickory wood with the auger I had and I *wanted* to, but I listened to my Mama and got religion and let shoals of women go streaming by me in *technicolor*—white, black, gray, tan, red, yellow. I could of had me one of each—Hell, I'm *sheriff*—but no, I waited and did my duty by God and my Mama, and then she died ten years ago, and I got married to a girl seventeen, the jail-keeper's daughter. Too late, too late." He took his hand back to his own fat crotch, cupped the fullness there. "This won't stir a warm rice *pudding*, not now, no more. Remember this, son. It won't cost you nothing but it cost Rooster Pomeroy most of the sweetness life can afford—don't wait, don't wait. Don't think it's morning when it's late afternoon."

The car had slowed to a crawl through that, and

Milo had watched Rooster through to the end, but when silence settled he turned to the window, the yellowing trees. "Thank you, Sheriff, but I hadn't been waiting, not since Saturday nohow, around midnight. And I ain't going to wait till dark today so let's get moving. I got to find my brother, a snake and a dog. Then I can pull out my throttle full-steam." Milo pulled an imaginary throttle on the dashboard, pulled with both hands not pausing to his groin and rested them there.

Rooster pulled his own throttle, roared the last quarter-mile and turned rightward into the sandy churchyard, stopped at a distance from the fifteen black cars frosted with dust, baking in the sun, killed the motor and sat still, ear cocked toward the building. A hymn streamed out through open windows—the hymn before collection—so Rooster pointed and said to Milo, "Is that the choir door standing open?"

Milo said "Yes."

"Then I'm going to go and call the preacher out while the singing's still on and ask will he make an announcement for me before the benediction." He looked again at Milo's feet. "You wait. Wait for *me*." Then he struggled to the ground and went three yards, stopped, thought, shook his head and turned back to Milo, face urgently crouched. "And when I get back don't fail to remind me—I *mean* this, son—to tell you one thing I forgot that goes with the rest of my free advice. It's dangerous without it, a loaded gun."

Milo nodded, smiled. "I give you ten minutes."

Rooster said "Thank you" and the flagging congregation launched another stanza (final or not, they would not last another) so Rooster pointed to the gun on his hip, tapped its bright black butt. "A loaded *gun.* How come I forgot?"—meaning it for Milo—and went towards the choir door, turned again on the highest step. "Remind me, hear?" But Milo's head was back, already asleep.

Till the full doxology was finished and he had the money, the preacher (Mr. Favro—tall, stooped, yellow) had had to set Rooster in the high black chair behind the pulpit, pistol at his side, hat between his feet, his small hands creeping about for shelter. Then the preacher shut the Bible and said, "My friends. We all see before us a face we know and trust and depend on, a face that we all sleep better because of. He has just come to us with an urgent need. Danger has struck and still roams among us. Our brotherly help is needed, he says, and I have asked him to come before you now (the Lord won't mind) and say a few words in explanation—Sheriff Rob Pomeroy." Some Guptons clapped. Mr. Favro frowned but stepped back and sat.

Rooster clasped the pulpit like the last floating timber in total shipwreck and began speaking softly, pumping up words with frequent long battings of his round blue eyes. "Reverend, I thank you for those good words. I never thought about my work like that, but now you mention it, if anybody here that has voted for me sleeps better at night knowing I'm on duty—well, God bless their heart, I *am* on duty. Even in my own home and in my bed, I am ready, I am eager, to do whatever I can to serve so sleep tight, friends—Rob Pomeroy's awake. He's awake if he ain't one other thing else, and if you're in need any hour of the night or day, call him—call me, *I'm* him. And I'm ready. For instance, one of your members had some trouble yesterday and called on me with no hesitation, and that's why I'm here—Jasper Mustian, you know him. I got his grandson out in my car—*one* of his grandsons. Wouldn't let him come in. He forgot his shoes. But anyhow all the Mustians rode in to Warrenton yesterday morning, and on the way home as they passed the fairgrounds about eleven-thirty—" He paused, drew his watch out. "Twenty-four hours ago exactly." He turned to Mr. Favro behind him. "It's *your* fault, Doctor. You dragged me in here and now I've took over. Looks like I'm preaching the sermon, don't it? Give me your text."

Rooster had only meant it in fun, but Mr. Favro's face drained potato-white, and his purple lips recited from memory, still seated—"And when Jehu was come to Jezreel, Jezebel heard of it, and she painted her face and tired her head and looked out at a window. And as Jehu entered in at the gate, she said, 'Had Zimri peace, who slew his master?' And he lifted up his face to the window and said, 'Who is on my side? who?' And there looked out to him two or three eunuchs. And he said 'Throw her down.' So they threw her down and some of her blood was sprinkled on the wall and on the horses, and he trod her under foot. And when he was come in, he did eat and drink and said, 'Go, see now this cursed woman and bury her, for she is a king's daughter.' And they went to bury her, but they found no more of her than the skull and the feet and the palms of her hands. Wherefore they came again and told him. And he said, 'This is the word of the Lord which he spake by his servant Elijah the Tishbite, saying, "In the portion of Jezreel shall dogs eat the flesh of Jezebel. And the carcase of Jezebel shall be as dung upon the face of the field in the portion of Jezreel so that they shall not say 'This is Jezebel.' "

Rooster said, "*Uhhh!* You bound to know. Somebody *told* you!" Mr. Favro shook his head in denial. "Then the Lord laid it on you. That's *my* text too— 'the skull and the feet and the palms of her hands.' Raving dogs." He faced the congregation. "The Mustians' dog got loose at the fair and run through the snake show and on in the woods. Well, the dog is mad and he's loose right now with the *other* Mustian boy and—I'm sorry to tell you—one of the snakes. Twenty foot long. Can swallow a calf. Break every bone in a grown man's body."

Everyone shrunk about six inches inwards, and for maybe ten seconds nobody looked at anyone else nor moved more than hand to open mouth. Then Arnold Gupton stood to leave while he could—not to help but to run; he had no mind—but Macey his brother wrestled him down. "Arnold, it ain't coming in no *church*."

Rooster leaned to them across the Bible, "In the words of Jehu from this great book, 'Who is on my side? Oh *who?*' I come here to ask your help today. I got two blood hounds and two armed deputies setting in the Mustians' yard right now, waiting for reinforcements to hunt. Mr. Jasper has been in the woods since sunup—him and the girl that owns the snake." (Macey fought down a laugh that rose stronger than Arnold.) "I'm calling on every strong man and boy—just so he's fifteen—to join me soon as your preacher is finished. Don't bring no guns. I got four guns and they'll more than kill what might need killing." He bowed to Mr. Favro and motioned him forward, "Preacher, I thank you. It's all yours again."

But Mr. Favro was looking ahead and could see. His face resembled all leaders abandoned—say Moses' face as he came from direct sight of God, the Law in hand, and found his men on their face in the dust, bowed to a gold calf flashing above them.

The men were rising and shuffling toward the aisles. The first to rise had been Buck Russell. His wife had said, "Sit down, Buck. This is Sunday." But his coattail carried her detaining hand with him— "That snake don't know it's Sunday. Come on. I'm riding you home and getting the pistol." He did not turn to hear her say "I'll walk," and though they had tried to whisper their quarrel, the whole church had heard, and the men were pulled silently up and out.

It had not been his purpose to end the service, but Rooster did not try to turn the flow. He had not raised his voice till now and would not—that was the duty of an ordained preacher. He only watched them go and when there were four men left in the church (Mr. Favro, himself, Arnold and Macey Gupton), he said, "Reverend, I never meant to ruin your day, but I know you have heard of the ox in the ditch—Jesus Himself rescued it on Sunday—and anyhow most of your ladies have stayed." He surveyed the remnant—seventeen

women, some scared knots of children, Macey and
Arnold. He did not know Arnold's mental history, but
seeing his size he said to him gently "Ain't you
coming?" Arnold shook his head. "You're a big strapping boy. You could handle that snake right by
yourself. He'd never swallow *them* shoulders, one sure
thing." Arnold's shoulders shook and he pointed to the
choir and the women there but did not speak.

Macey said, "Sheriff, his pleasure is music. Louise
Rodwell was going to sing a solo. He's living for that."

Rooster smiled to Arnold, "Live on, son," then
turned to the choir. "Miss Louise, I don't know which
one is you, but excuse me please for taking your crowd.
I hope you'll give this boy his song." He bowed again
in an arc to all and aimed for the door he had entered
by.

Before he was out the piano began. Miss Louise
was giving—or starting to give.

Every volunteer had gone home first (for whatever
reasons—mainly for guns) so when Milo and Rooster
and Macey Gupton (invited by Milo to ride with
them) stopped in the Mustian yard again, there were
just the two deputies and Mr. Capps, and they were all
standing at the porch steps together, drinking cold
Pepsis, eating cold biscuits and looking up to where
Selma Provo sat at the edge of the steps in a rocking
chair, Emma beside her standing with a plate and
Milo's shoes.

Selma was dressed though her hair still hung in
one long plait, but her face was pale as a ghost in need

and seeing Milo rolling towards her through leaf-broken light, she paled even further and whispered to his mother, "You say you never saw him. I don't understand. Not knowing Tommy, how could you make his picture?" She pointed to Milo.

Yards away he accepted her notice and said to her loudly, "You lasted the night. Now maybe you'll live."

Selma's mouth opened towards him but no sound came, and her gray lips wrenched in memory and grief though Milo chalked it up to pain. Then she said, "Your mother has told me the news and helped me out here to see these men."

Rooster tipped his hat, said, "Sheriff Pomeroy, lady. Hope you ain't hurting or worrying no more. Help's on the way. I have just broke up a whole Baptist service, and all the men are coming on here. Your snake's good as dead—and your boy's good as caught." The last was to Emma.

But Selma said, "Dead! You kill that snake and you owe me five hundred dollars cash. What do you think he is?—an eel? He's an Indian python from the jungles of Burma. I've nursed him through more than twelve long years—from a scrawny baby to a strapping beauty—and I won't have him shot by a hot-headed gang just because a mad dog scared him into running and him full of rabbit, drowsy and slow. Excuse me, Emma, but if I hadn't fed him Saturday night, he could save himself, could wrap any one of you in lightning hoops of steel, but full as he is, he's asleep yonder somewhere gentle as a lamb." She made a wide sweep toward the visible woods.

"I'd hate to be a lamb and cross his path." Mr. Capps said that, having nothing to lose—or so he thought.

But Selma pointed towards his trailer in the yard, his valuable hounds. "Laugh all you want but he loves a nice dog. I feed him puppies from city dog-pounds when he gets homesick or is shedding his hide."

Milo said, "Macey here smells like a dog. We can use him as bait and save the bloodhounds." Macey butted him flat and they rolled down the yard twenty feet towards the road till Macey had won and rode Milo's chest, knees in his armpits, both of them laughing to strangulation.

Emma said, "Shame! Shame on both of you. Get up—it's Sunday—and here come the helpers." The boys struggled up, covered with white dust. "I can't smell from here but no dog would get as filthy as you two."

They did not even brush at the dirt with their hands nor acknowledge Emma but ran towards the help —two trucks and a car turning into the yard, loaded with faces, not one of them smiling.

Rooster said "Lady" gently to Selma. "Please do me a favor. When my men are all here, just talk to them *calm*. They are doing this free and despite my warning, they have all got guns hid on them somewhere so be nice please, but make a little speech about how you are grateful and how much you trust them with your private property, and then tell us some of that snake's likes and dislikes."

Emma said, "Selma, listen to the sheriff. That's just good sense. You told me last night you had ruined your life through hot-blooded words—"

"—*Acts*," Selma said but nodded agreement, and Emma went in to the kitchen and Rosa, leaving Milo's shoes (Rosa was working on refreshments there, and the baby was with her).

Meanwhile Milo was bringing up his men—Macey and seven that had good sense. They had all but Macey changed to hunting clothes—the oldest dirtiest stuff they owned—so they all matched Macey, and with Milo half-dressed, they resembled a set of old cyclones coming, tan and gray, torn and creased, spent. Rooster said, "General Lee has finally surrendered. Praise God, here come our boys *home!* Welcome home, boys." They heard him but the oldest was in his sixties so they still did not smile as they reached the porch, and to make amends Rooster quickly said, "Thank you, gentlemen. You know me I guess—I am Rooster Pomeroy, the Apple King."

"Apple *what?*" Milo said.

Rooster said, "Apple *King*. That's what Pomeroy means."

"Means in *what?*" Milo said.

"In the language of love—what else? Now you know. But if I don't know everyone of you boys—well, all that means is I ain't arrested you for bootlegging, tom-catting or beating your women, ain't caught you anyhow! I'll have to get all your names in a minute, but this sick lady—she's tore her ankle—is Mrs. Provo from Clearwater, Florida. She runs the snake show that travels with the fair, and the snake we are hunting belongs to her. She raised him from a baby and knows his mind, and she's agreed to tell us all she knows." He gestured to Selma.

Selma said "Nothing."

"*Nothing?*"

"Nothing. I have had that python for thirteen years, and if he knows me from Adam's housecat, *I* don't know it. He lets me touch him and eats the rats and rabbits I give him—when the spirit moves him. One time he fasted from Christmas day till my next birthday, September tenth, nine long months. Laid there and let rats crawl all across him. Then he struck one day, ate a two-pound rat and has eaten regularly ever since—two or three times a week in hot weather."

Macey said "You call today hot?"

Selma tilted her chin to test the day. "Yes sir, I do."

"I figured you did." He slapped the crown of his head and dust flew.

"I'm calling him *him,*" she said, "but I don't know that even. The boy that gave him to me way back when, he said you could tell by him having big feet. Pythons got feet out beside their behinds, and the male's feet are bigger—so this boy said—since they hide their nature, their thing, in there. One in each foot, drawn in and covered. That's what he said—the boy he belonged to, that gave him to me. I never have seen it but I call him *him.* And that's all I know— nothing, like I said. I've raised him thirteen years from a baby—three foot long to eighteen foot. I say he's twenty foot when I show him on the road, just to round it off. Maybe he is. You ever try to measure a live python? Anyhow he's been with me all these years, never tried to escape and know me or not, he means something to me. He has been one thing that stayed, and he didn't leave now of his own free will. So when you find him, he'll be asleep. Two or three of you just move on him gentle—he hasn't got ears but he feels you in the ground—and take him by his neck and middle and tail. He won't struggle much. I bet he'll be glad. You won't *know* that though. He won't show feelings. It took me five years of standing in snakes ankle-deep day and night to figure out the terrible thing about them—they haven't got faces, just eyes and a mouth. Dogs, cats, horses, even pigs smile or frown but a snake just stares."

Milo said, "Sounds like your Mama, don't it, Macey?" Then to Mrs. Provo—"Macey's Mama has lost all her teeth and won't crack her mouth, even cats in private." Macey sucked in his lips, crossed eyes to show his mother's predicament, and then another truck pulled into the yard. Milo looked and said, "Hide your money. It's Hawkins Ryden. Who told him?" and a high lean man maybe forty years old started towards them.

"Ryden?" Selma whispered urgently to Milo. "Any kin to Tommy?"

"Who's Tommy?" Milo said.

Selma searched him as disbelievingly as though he had asked, "Who is God? Who am *I*?" Then she gradually found herself and said, "Your Granddaddy's favorite cousin that's dead, your *own* cousin—killed."

Emma stepped out of the door with more biscuits. She had heard that last and catching Selma's eye, gave a deep shaking frown.

Milo said, "I can't tell you that but don't ask

Hawkins. He'd charge you for an answer."

Macey nodded. "Listen at him squeak—tightest man in America."

Hawkins came on and Rooster said "Morning, Mr. Ryden."

Hawkins nodded. "Sheriff. I didn't know you knew me."

"I know everybody that's voted for me."

"I never voted."

"Costs too much"—it was Macey whispering, clear as a bell.

"My wife come home from church and said you was wanting some men to help you hunt."

"Need all I can get."

"What are you hunting?"

"A boy, a mad dog and a twenty-foot snake."

"That's what my wife said. I never believed her."

"She's right today. Welcome to the crowd."

"Hold on a minute here. How much you paying?"

"Mr. Ryden, I'm paying out the best thing there is, that will outlast money by a hundred years—a satisfied heart, knowing you have helped a friend."

Hawkins thought a moment. "Who are you speaking of?"

"Mrs. Mustian here and this poor lady that owns the snake."

Hawkins thought again.

Milo said, "Hell-fire, Hawkins. You are blood-kin to us. What else do you want?"

"I don't know," he said, "but I wasn't looking forward to donating time on my day of rest."

"Isn't your name Ryden?" Selma said. "I'm Selma Provo that owns the snake."

"Yes'm, it is."

"Are you any kin to a Tommy Ryden?"

"I was. He's dead."

"I know that," she said. "How well I know."

"Selma—" Emma said.

Selma paddled a silencing hand. "What kin were you when Tommy was breathing?"

Hawkins thought, then worked it out on his fingers. "Tommy's Daddy was my Uncle Gid, my Daddy's brother. His Mama won't a bit of kin to me, but I had her to feed after Tommy left—and she lived till nearly two years ago, back in them woods." He pointed them all to the woods they knew, behind and around. "What do you know about Tommy, lady? None of us saw him after 1930—cleared out of here and never sent his Daddy or Mama a penny. But I knew he wouldn't. I grew up with him. He wouldn't of give a aspirin to a dying woman."

"He give me the snake that's lost today."

Hawkins laughed. "Might of known but I bet it was just part-payment—won't it?—on some big debt. He was famous for paying on things piecemeal even as a boy. Never paid for all of nothing in his life."

Rooster said "Amen" but no one seemed to hear.

Emma said, "He paid for *freedom* with his life. What was that please if not total payment?"

"Shirking," Hawkins said. "Just one more way to shirk his duty and throw his old folks on his relatives to keep. Broke his Mama's heart, I can tell you that.

Starved her to death on pure cold grief."

Selma said, "I know what you mean."

Milo said, "*I* don't—old Miss Jack Ryden? Starved to death? I saw her the Sunday before she died. I was squirrel hunting back yonder in the woods, and late in the day I come on her place. Well, I had to do my business and there was her johnny-house standing empty, nobody in sight, so I went in and took a seat, and directly buck-shot was blasting the walls. Talk about business! I never knew you had to buy a ticket. Anyhow once I got hold of myself, I looked through a knothole and saw this woman on the porch of the house, old as a turtle, holding a shotgun and looking like she weighed three hundred pounds stripped—except she looked like she hadn't stripped in years. It was Miss Jack Ryden and don't tell me she was starving. She won't. *I* was thin though and I saw a loose board at the back of the johnny—just a six-inch scantling—but I squeezed through like a ounce of butter, gun and all, and when I got to the edge of the trees and out of her range, I hollered, 'Miss Jack, it's Milo Mustian. I won't doing nothing but borrowing your johnny. Ain't that what it's for?' 'Hell no,' she said. 'The woods is for that.' She flung out her arm at all them pines. 'There's woods enough here to hold all you can do, you and every other thieving scoundrel. That johnny is mine!' So I been using the woods ever since, and don't tell me Miss Jack Ryden starved. She died of meanness."

Selma said, "There's more than one way to starve."

"Amen," Hawkins said. "She was full of fatback and bread till she died and I bought every slice."

Rooster said, "I'm glad she could die on a full stomach. Now Mr. Ryden, are you with me or not? We got to get moving."

Hawkins said, "How long is that snake again, Sheriff?"

"He *was* twenty foot but he'll be a heap longer if we don't get moving. This day is hot and everything's *growing*."

Macey said to Milo, hand cupped for secrecy, "Milo's growing—from the hip outwards, ain't you?"

Milo frowned but seeing his mother had not heard, nodded and grinned and measured off his forward growth with both hands as if it were a fat catfish he had caught.

Hawkins said, "Listen, if I catch that snake, can I have his skin? That's what I'll ask. I'm the best snake hunter in the U.S.A., and I call that a bargain."

Milo said, "If he catches you, can I have yours?"

"Hold it," Selma said and wept. Everyone waited, watching the ground, till she swallowed her grief—its sudden plug at least. "I've said it strongly and I'll say it again—don't kill the snake." She thrust her bandaged ankle at the men's eye level. "If this fool foot would bear my fat, I'd be with you now, be leading the pack and I'd get him whole. But I've been struck down by the hand of God so I'm pleading to you." She paused and stared every man in the eye, separate in turn, then coming last to Milo she rested on him, said the rest to him. "I can see you thinking, 'She is cracked as deep as the Liberty Bell, raving on a snake like it was human.' And maybe I am. But I've told you he's worth over five hundred dollars, and I've told you the thirteen years

I've struggled, bringing him to his full color and power. Still to tell you the truth, he's fully insured, and I've also told you he don't know me—I don't know he does—and I know you are worried with him running free. *I* know he's gentle, has been mostly gentle with me and Lois, but if he took a mind he could do real harm—kill a grown man and I've got a book that says a python swallowed a boy in Sumatra, head and heels. So why am I pleading round a knot like a fist in my foolish throat?" The knot constricted, then eased, gave her breath. "Because like I said, he was *given* to me—by someone more harmful than any live snake, any cobra that spits. Snakes don't strike unless they're cornered or hungry but *that* boy—" She stopped. The boy had been hungry. She saw that now, after so much time. "It was his first cousin"—she pointed to Hawkins—"and some kin of yours"—she pointed to Milo. "And Tommy said to me, 'I'll leave you my snake'—he called it Death even then as a baby—'and if I leave he will be my spirit and carry my messages to you from the grave.' I laughed but took it and have kept it and waited. Not a sound, not a sign."

Emma touched Selma's shoulder. "Take a ham biscuit, Selma. They were hot awhile ago." Selma took one and ate it like the last shard of food on Judgment Day.

Then the plate passed round to every man, and over his loud chewing Hawkins said, "You got any papers to prove he's yours?"

Selma said "Why do you ask?"

"Because if you ain't and Tommy died owning him, rightly he may be mine not yours. I'm Tommy's nearest living kin and five hundred dollars—if I caught him and sold him—would be partial payment on the food I poured down his hungry Mama when he broke her heart and left her penniless."

The biscuit plate had returned to Emma in the course of that, empty again. Her wish was to sling it into Hawkins' teeth, but looking, she saw it was Rosacoke's, a gift from her drunk dead father (Emma's husband)—thick blue, Captain John Smith bearded, *Jamestown Exposition* 1907. Where had he got it?— the year he was born? She had never thought to ask him, too late, too late. She said, "Hawkins Ryden, this ain't my house and it ain't my land. I come here a bride twenty-one years ago, and I've scoured and scrubbed every inch of it since till my hands are raw." She extended her right hand—it nearly was, flamed with labor. "But it still ain't mine, not a splinter of it. I tell you this though—it'll be my children's when their Granddaddy dies, and in their name I am telling you to leave. Nobody needs your kind around here. Mean people grow on trees, Hawkins Ryden. Start making tracks." He walked three steps and Emma turned to Rooster. "There's one big thing all of you have forgot and that *is* mine—Rato my boy. Carrying on all this time about a snake when a human being is in dreadful trouble every second you waste here fanning your gums. Selma, I know what the snake means to you but you didn't *bear* it. It was just a gift to you. Rato is something I worked on, believe me. And if you say he's a mighty poor job, that he hadn't got the sense of a snake or a dog and sure-God wouldn't bring five hundred dollars nowhere on earth—well, I'll say you're right, but he's *my* job, *my* failure, mine and his sorry dead Daddy's, Sheriff. So please get moving or next election I'll stand in the street like a prophet of God and shame folks into not voting for you."

Rosacoke broke the following silence by coming through the door with a stack of lunches, wax-paper parcels of fresh ham biscuits, and Baby Sister tagging behind. Rooster's eyes seized her like port in a storm. "Little lady, did you make these?" She smiled and nodded.

But Milo said, "No, Rosacoke's religious. She just blessed the crumbs from last night's supper and lo and behold!"

Rosa gave him the snaking length of her tongue, and Rooster said to Emma, "I need Hawkins Ryden. He's well known for hunting and anyhow I ain't got enough without him."

Emma nodded. Then she said towards Hawkins who was leaving, "Hawkins, I'm sorry. I'm out of my mind. Come back and help them find my boy. All I can pay you is a ham-biscuit dinner, but he is kin to you. Help your people."

Hawkins took another step, stopped in his tracks, his back to Emma. His shoulders hunched. Then he turned and came towards her, eyes down, carefully reusing his previous tracks in the crusty ground, a secret economy. He stopped a little way from the others, and nobody faced him but Emma. She thanked him.

"All right," Rooster said, "let's call the roll. I got to get everybody's name and age. In case that snake should swallow one of us, I got to know who to notify!" He took out an old envelope and a pencil and licking the lead, said, "File by me and I'll write you down. You might get a medal from the governor, who knows?" They came as he wished in Indian file.

"Milo Mustian, going on sixteen."

"Macey Gupton, ditto but smarter."

"Staley Goins, and I'm going strong. Sixty-three last May thirteenth."

"Buck Russell, forty-two."

"Felton Driver, twenty-nine."

"Ballard Stegall, twenty-one."

"Ernest Umphlett, thirty-six."

"Malvin Thrower, a hundred and one." (His voice cracked saying it. He was nineteen.)

"Hawkins Ryden, forty."

Rooster looked up. "That's all but the paid employees then." He began to list them, "Me and Mr. Capps, sixteen plus. Deputy Lonnie Wilson—how old are you, Lonnie?"

"Thirty-five, Sheriff."

"And Yancey Breedlove?" He looked to Yancey— "Pushing fifty, ain't you?"

Yancey said "Twenty-one last Tuesday."

Rooster said, "That's right. You're just *looking* old lately—wore out, Yancey. Ease up, boy." He grinned towards Selma. "Yancey got married two weeks ago. If the snake swallows you, boy—and well he might, you looking so pale—we'll feed him your wife too. She'd die anyhow, grieve her heart out, the Widow Breedlove. See, it hurts me to say it." Rooster drew a dark line at the end of his list and began to count it backwards.

"Speaking of Breedlove," Macey said, "ain't you going to list Mr. Mustian and his girl? They are in the

worst sort of danger, *I* think. Especially that girl."
Macey looked to Milo and fought not to smile.

Milo said, "She can handle herself all right, let me
tell you. Anyhow I'll be meeting her soon. I'll give her
a hand."

Rooster had counted—"Thirteen exactly."

Selma gasped. "One of you drop out or Fate's sure
to strike."

Milo said, "Shoot, that's the number of Jesus and
His men. And all the apostles could handle snakes
harmless as fishing worms. That's well known. Macey,
you be the Jesus—Macey's beard has started and he
walks on water."

Macey raised both hands in grave benediction—
"Who is my Judas?" and waited for an answer.

Nobody looked at anybody else, not at any adult.
They looked to the children, the baby and Rosacoke,
for rescue, relief.

But Rosacoke said, her voice like a blade, "Let Milo
be Judas."

Rooster lurched to Milo, grabbed him under the
chin. "Cough up them thirty shekels of silver! Yancey,
find him a rope to hang hisself with. Sorry scoundrel,
I've got him at last!" Milo submitted and Yancey
actually started for the rope.

But Emma said, "Sheriff, I meant what I said,"
and Milo was free, blood-red round his neck.

Rooster said, "Lady, I heard and believe. Your lost
boy is good as back in your arms. The reason I've
carried on about that snake was—we don't get too
many calls for pythons, but boys get lost several times a
day. And we generally find them, white or black,

Methodist or Baptist. Boys is easy. I think like a boy and I know where to look. It's snakes and dogs that worry my *mind*—they just ain't human. But the closest thing to my *heart* is your boy. He'll be home for supper. Start frying right now." Then he faced his men and solemn heavy authority seemed laid upon him by the falling light. "Now here is the plan. We are hunting separate in two even groups—one with the dogs, one with me. Since Mr. Mustian and his girl are hunting westward (if they are still *hunting*), we'll hunt east and north and since you mentioned it, meet at old Miss Jack Ryden's place. Hawkins, who lives there?"

"Lizards and owls. Some Niggers did after Aunt Jack died, but they claimed it was hexed and left in the night, owing two months' rent."

So Rooster knelt and taking a stick, gouged a map in the ground.

Then he stood. "That's your orders, boys. Don't take no chances. If the dogs strike a trail, Mr. Capps'll fire once. If they find what we're hunting—any one of the three—fire three if you can, if you've got the time. We'll come hauling. And we'll use the same signs if *we* strike first. Remember we are dealing in precious property—a human being and a snake that's as much God's doing as

you are. The dog?—poor fellow, shoot the dog on sight."
He let that register, then stared at each man. "Anybody
that's got other business at home, go now." No one
moved. "Right. Anybody that can't take orders from me
or Mr. Capps, go too." No one moved. "Then we'll split
this way." he consulted his list. "Mr. Capps and the
dogs and Deputy Wilson take Ryden, Goins, Thrower,
Umphlett and Driver. Me and Deputy Breedlove'll take
Mustian, Gupton—they'll be our dogs; they'll smell so
good the snake will come to *us*—Stegall and Russell."
He removed his hat. "I ain't said much this morning,
have I? Let me just say this much before we go. In all
my years as elected sheriff, I have *done* some deeds.
I have captured several pondsful of moonshine liquor. I have took razors out of crazy Niggers' hands,
blood on the blade and a gal cut to ribbons laid dead in
the ditch. Just last week I arrested a man that had bit
off and swallowed another man's thumb—his wife's
boy-friend. So I've had a full life—I'm honored to have
it—but this job today is the *height* of my life. And I've
got a strong feeling—come on me in the night when I
couldn't sleep—that all of us here, every man and boy
with a part in this day will end bigger men in the eyes
of their loved ones and enemies if they *play* that part
the Lord has give them. Also a man from the *Warren
Record* will meet us at four p.m. for pictures. So I want
us to pause here one last minute and leave with a
prayer. It's the least I can do, breaking up a church
service. I'm going to call on the one that's got most to
gain or lose—Milo, give us a prayer." He reached to
touch Milo but Milo stood farther away than he knew
—and frowned at first, for a relay of reasons: disbelief,

embarrassment, scorn, final ignorance of what to ask. "Don't worry, son. The Lord will provide."

Milo's lips were suddenly separate from his face, red and long and as clearly, firmly lined on his skin as if worked with a blade and intended for silence. But they moved, opened, and this was provided—"Today we are hunting three valuable things that have give some pleasure to several people. My brother Rato is valuable to us. His mad dog Phillip is valuable to him. And Death is valuable to the Provo ladies. Help us to always remember that, all day today. Help us be worthy of what we are hunting. Help us to live with whatever we find."

Rooster said "Amen" and looked to Mr. Capps but thought to himself, "Let this be the day I prove to Kate the man I can be if she lies still and lets me be what I'm meant to be, what the Lord intended—a help to others, to keep their peace." His mouth hung open but no speech followed.

So Mr. Capps said to Emma Mustian, "Lady, I'll need a scent for my dogs. Give me a piece of your lost boy's clothes that ain't been washed."

Emma nodded, turned but thought before going, "What will I do if you don't save Rato? You did not save his sorry father. Save one helpless thing, for me." She pointed Milo to his shoes beside her (the laces unknotted), then vanished inward.

Selma Provo sought Milo's face (which he freely gave), took its ghostly shock. "Leave me," she thought, "what little You've left. At the end of this day bring me Lois and Death, the things he left me."

Rosacoke sought her brother's look. He had not

faced her, by light, all day. He did not now. And Rosacoke thought, "Bring Rato back safe. Bring Milo *back* in his old right mind."

Milo looked to the waiting woods. "Let me find Rato, let me find Death, then let me take my ease on some girl."

Macey looked to the sun and its light sucked from him a long high laugh and this, aloud—"Keep it burning, Lord. I'll need it today in them black pines." The light found an unleaved hole in the trees and struck Macey broadside, laughing again. "A-*men*. Thank you, Lord. Prayer is heard. Now save Macey Gupton from the jaws of Death!" He ran to the car and the men could only follow.

Rooster was tired by three o'clock and lonely, having walked alone for more than two hours through empty woods—apparently empty though how could he know what had slid through their net, so loose and feebly cast? Every step now seemed a step away from what this day was meant to be—a gift to Kate in hopes of holding her—a step into tiredness, helpless age, abandonment, the long wait for rest. He suddenly knew an important thing, the thing he had meant to tell Milo this morning after the church service—the shield, safety, to the otherwise deadly advice he had flung out, unasked, unwanted but plainly taken. He called for Milo—one word, the name, not loudly to his right. If his orders were obeyed, Milo was there fifty yards away, and Macey was fifty yards to his left (and the others at equal spaces beyond). But no answer came. Then he broke into a small natural clearing, a pine-needled bowl, shaded but light, and he paused to listen for Milo and Macey. No help came, not so much as the sound of a human foot behind or beyond. They had surely passed him or left and gone home or disobeyed and arranged themselves into better ranks that could work without him, leaving him here with only the rest of his life to face. Then above his head unseen in a tree the nasal click of a squirrel began, certain warning. He braced to listen—warning of what? Up from the earth, from somewhere near came the gentle unhurried displacement of leaves by something that shouldered its way towards him, low and long. He reached for his pistol to summon help—if help was near—but whirling and seeing no visible threat by the roots of trees, he found a rusty whistle in his pocket and blew three times. The sliding silenced and he heard distant Milo passing the call to his righthand neighbor and him to his—sweet fading music to Rooster Pomeroy, the ring of his unquestioned authority spreading through woods like the hump that will rise through a length of rope from a flickering hand. He was not alone, there was day still ahead.

Yet it took Milo a minute to burst through the trees, crouched to struggle—"Which is it, Sheriff?"

Rooster pointed up. "I heard a squirrel talking, then some sliding on the ground but I don't see nothing. Just another false alarm. Let's all rest a minute. But before they get here, listen to this and don't forget it long as you live. You recollect what I told you this morning?—not to wait but to use every kind of strength you got while you're young and don't *care?*"

"Yes sir and I said I wasn't waiting, remember?"

"That's what worries me, you saying that. You ain't got a Daddy and the one you had never knew this, never acted like he did, so listen to this. This keeps you from harm—" Yancey Breedlove broke in from the left, rifle ready, and then in loud succession from the right, Ballard and Buck—Buck with the pistol he had so far hid. So Rooster said to Milo "Wait" and calmed them.

They laughed and loosened, began to squat and light cigarettes, but Milo stayed up and said "Whereabouts is Macey?"

Yancey said, "Where is he supposed to be?"

"Well, here before you. He was fifty yards closer to the sheriff when we started."

Yancey said, "God Almighty, Sheriff. It's Yancey's day off. I'm a newly wed. Now damned if we ain't lost another moron."

Rooster said, "Son, you don't own that badge. I can rip that off so fast you'll see stars, and what'll you feed that gal on then?—a diet of hot loving?"

Yancey looked at his badge that his wife had shined this very morning and saw his own face. It was smiling at him, black-haired fool. He smiled back and not looking up said "Yes sir."

Rooster said "God," then cupped his mouth and called Macey to the left, then another long "Macey" in a left semi-circle. Ringing silence, then the clicking squirrel now clearly from the west. Rooster stabbed a hand in the general direction, and sliding began in the dead dry leaves, slow as before, on their west flank, northward.

"There's your snake," Buck said.

Ballard Stegall said "That ain't no snake," living in hope.

They listened, it continued. Yancey raised his rifle. "What is it then?—U.S. Highway Number One creeping north to Niagara Falls for a honeymoon?"

Rooster whispered "Wait," walked to the lip of the bowl they were in, drew his own pistol, then beckoned to Yancey and Buck to follow. The three of them spread abreast, guns cocked, Milo and Ballard six feet behind. Ballard plugged his ears. Then a low cedar moved, swayed rhythmically, and above the natural brush of its limbs came a soft steady "Wooooo"—moan or threat?

"Can they talk?" Yancey said.

Buck said, "Damned if I know. That woman didn't say."

Rooster said, "Sure they can talk. They talk in the Bible like college professors. Speak to it, Yancey. You finished high school."

Yancey said, "All I studied was Spanish. This bastard's Burmese." He cuddled his rifle in the notch of his shoulder, sighted it dead at the heart of the tree, then said, "Come out if you're aiming to live!"

The "Woooo"-ing continued, then dipped into words, "I'm dead already"—both pistols ached—"but I bring you word from the Great Beyond. Woooo."

Rooster said "Shoot" and Yancey fired. The woods took the sound as if they were brass—rang on and on—but nothing moved. In his nerves Yancey merely had topped the tree. "Not you, fool," Rooster said. "I'm speaking to *it*. Shoot your message, I mean. We're listening, ghost."

A long pause, then "Woooo—the snake you are hunting is with you now."

Rooster said "Didn't I tell you?" to Yancey. "Where is he at?"

"Woooo. Above you, beneath you, beside you, behind you."

The row of guns whirled round looking. Milo and Ballard stared into three barrels. Yancey said "Well, it's invisible then."

"Woooo. You're right. It's a *holy* snake from the Great Beyond, a messenger. Prepare to meet it now. Fall on your knees and it will appear with generous blessings for all who kneel."

Ballard's knees dug two deep sockets in the ground. Milo said, "Hell, Ballard, you *want* it to appear?" Ballard half-rose, half-knelt, not sure.

But Rooster knelt and whispered firmly, "Kneel down, boys. The golden rule in this line of work is to not take chances with peculiar cases. Do what your victim tells you to do—within reason, of course." They obeyed, knelt, lowered their guns, and Rooster said, "Right. We're down in the dirt like a bunch of Catholics. Now where's the snake at?"

The cedar shook hard as a woman in labor, then gave a kind of birth of its own—a figure in man's clothes, five-foot-six, its arms stretched towards them, legs hacking wide stiff steps in the ground (clods of dirt coughing back from its heels) and whatever head it bore, hid from them by thin white cloth that hugged

its neck (the vague print of features lurking behind).
Everybody, kneeling, fixed on the head, but Milo down
in the second rank heard the gentle threading through
leaves again—not made by those feet, nearer than they.
He studied the foreground, then said, "Hold it, Ghost.
Excuse me asking but you hadn't noticed that copperhead, have you? Put on your glasses."

Macey fumbled in his pocket, unveiled his face,
put on his glasses, studied the ground, bent like
lightning to a spot beyond his feet and stood with a
copperhead two feet long, salmon pink and brown,
lashing his arm. He smiled and came towards them.

Rooster said, "I hope that's a ghost you're *holding.*"

"This or this?" Macey said and extended his left
hand first—his face cloth had been a pair of ladies'
bloomers—then his right with the snake which he
waved within a foot of Yancey's nose (they were all,
but Milo, still kneeling in shock). Yancey fell back and
spat and his rifle struck ground.

Rooster said "That" to the twining snake which
rung Macey's arm like an Eastern disease.

"No sir, that's a real snake. Copperhead, Milo?—
didn't you say? Just a little old egg-sucking copperhead.
Friend to man, eat rats by the pack."

Milo nodded and Rooster said, "Yes but—hold his
neck tight—he'll kill you *dead* as any ghost if he takes a
mind to bite."

Milo said, "A copperhead isn't no king snake,
Macey. I told you that last summer, remember?"

Macey turned his wrist to face his snake. Its
snouted head was locked by his clamping fingers, but it

fended his gaze with a forked black tongue slick and fast as the girls in Phyllis's tent. Then he looked to Milo. "I forgot," he said. It was offered as both apology and plea.

Yancey stood and pointed to a bare spot beyond. "Fling him down yonder and I'll blast his damn legs off."

Milo stood. "You got a lot of blasting ahead of you then. He hadn't got legs. Mrs. Provo said just pythons did. Didn't you hear her?"

Yancey said, "No, I didn't—she was raving on so —but that explains a lot. That bastard we're hunting is probably way on past Richmond by now, legging it home."

"Burma ain't that way," Rooster said. He pointed east. "And nobody's shooting no more till I say to. That'd be a signal and we ain't caught *squat*—"

Macey said, "Well, *I've* caught something and it's waiting to kill me. *Do* something please."

Rooster thought and said, "Listen, just let him go. There's no other way. Walk yonder ten yards—where we already been—and fling him as far as you can to the south. This is my day to spare things anyhow."

Macey went, drew back and flung the snake. It traveled as stiff as a shut umbrella end over end till it struck a pine and fell and streamed for cover. Then Macey stepped into his bloomers and twisted towards them. He swayed up to Yancey, said, "Hey, big boy. Give me a quarter and I'll strike your *match.*"

Yancey nudged him in his rayon crotch with the rifle. "I'll strike *your* match. Where in the Hell you get them things?"

"Off a Nigger girl."

"That's a lie," Yancey said.

"How come?" Macey said.

"No Nigger gal that thin wears pants."

Milo said, "You know, don't you, Yancey?"

"Damn right I know. I'm the county expert on women's underwear, black, white or red."

Macey said, "Son, you're wrong today. These were give to me ten minutes ago by a gal as black as Moses' butt." He slapped his own butt, slung it out towards Yancey. "She left them anyhow when she heard that whistle. I was way ahead of you all, minding my business, stomping through briars chin-deep when I heard some laughing. I eased up and crept on nearer to the noise till I found me a hole in the briars to peep through. I'm scratched up terrible." He showed his welted arms.

Yancey said "What was it?"

Macey said "What you mean?"

"What you saw through the briars, fool."

"Another hole, fool. Ain't you never been hunting in here before? You have to step high or break your ankle, falling in some gal, Nigger or not." That was meant for Yancey but said to Milo—"Ain't it so, Milo?"

They all looked to Milo and he began a nod, but it drowned in the hot blood rushing to his face. Milo's blushes were as rare as his songs, and this one was doubly scalding for him—he did not understand its secret cause: that he no longer stood with Macey here (in knowledge, experience) but with Yancey, Buck Russell, the worn-out Rooster. Macey seemed shrunk, blotched with stinking dirt, mouth streaming igno-rance. "Shut your mouth, Macey," Milo said, look-ing down. "You don't know what you're talking about."

Macey wavered, swallowed hard—the gristle beak grated up, down in his tightening throat. Abandon-ment rushed like warm wings against him.

But Yancey said, "Come on. What did you see?"

The story he had made to amuse Milo—the kernel of truth, the cushion of lies—crumbled in his head. Even the words to tell it betrayed him, seemed clearly childish guesses, but Yancey's face waited so he flew blindly on as if through flames, hoping to survive—"A Nigger girl laid out flat in the dirt with her bloomers beside her and this Nigger boy that was giving her—"

"What?" Yancey bored like a drill.

"You know," Macey said.

"No I don't," Yancey said.

Rooster said, "I do—a free driving lesson. Ain't that so, Macey?"

Macey laughed. "That's it. I predict she'll get her license soon. He's a A-1 teacher—I saw that myself." He laughed again tightly, then found he could smile.

Rooster said, "Yes sir, Yancey, you take heed. There's a college education lying free in these woods for a fellow with eyes. You ought to come strolling out here more often."

Yancey said, "Shoot, I'm enrolled in night school in my own house on a Beautyrest mattress, no flies on me and my gal's white."

"Don't knock black," Buck Russell said. "It's a

good-wearing color—black don't show marks. 'Learn on
black and pay at the hole'—that was my motto when I
was still loose. It worked like a charm and all it ever
cost me was fifty cents a throw, sometimes a quarter if
the gal was dumb or had one eye, but you don't see the
mantel when you're poking up the grate. Only trouble
I had was the year I got married. I stopped running
round oh a month before the wedding—to purify my
blood. The Nigger I was punching hadn't never seen a
washrag. And luck was with me. I passed my blood test
to get the license, and the wedding come off and the
honeymoon. We went to Washington—took all I had,
October '29 and the stockmarket crashed before we got
home. I didn't have no stock of course but poor is *poor*,
and for six or seven years we kept from having children
—I won't tell you how but it won't much fun. The
Lord was just with me—He's mostly been—but I'm
getting ahead of my story here. Two or three months
after I was married and settling down, I was at the
store, standing there talking, and my Nigger gal come
walking towards the door, her baby sister with her. I
saw right off she was toting a load, was far-gone
pregnant but I didn't worry. I never told myself I was
her only business, never wanted to be. Well, I went on
talking and she come in looking dead ahead and stared
at the showcase. You know how they do—ain't got but
a nickel and hope if they stare at the glass long enough,
it'll melt away and the candy come streaming so all
they got to do is just reach out and take it. Then she
asked how much were the Mary Janes—do they still
make those? pull your teeth right out—and Gip Ro-
land said 'A penny a piece.' (I well knew that—I paid

for many a piece with Mary Janes.) She untied her rag
—took another five minutes—and there was a penny. I
ain't Santy Claus—a seventeen year old gal can live
without candy—but there stood her baby sister all eyes
and teeth so I said 'Come here, girl'—I was talking to
the baby—but Della came over. Now you know who it
is—"

Milo said "Della Brame."

Buck Russell nodded. "So I gave her a nickel and
she didn't say a word. She bought her sack of candy
and went out the door and stood on the steps with her
back turned to me. She was already hunch-shouldered,
toting her load—used to stand straight as wild poke-
weed—and all she was moving was her jaws on that
candy. She gummed down the first one and took out the
second and tore off the paper and threw it towards the
road and then turned around and walked to the door.
The door was closed—it was late December—but she
knocked on the glass and we all looked up. None of
them knew I had ever touched her. I won't a big talker
then—you always can tell; the ones that are talking
ain't doing much else. But she pointed at me and said
'Mr. Buck' loud enough to hear. I went to her, walked
with her far as the road, then she said, 'Buck, how
much you paying me for this?' —'This *what*?' —'This
youngun,' she said. I said, 'Della, I paid at the hole
every time in money or goods and you give a receipt.'
She didn't give no receipts but I said it, and she
recollected and knew I was right. She just nodded and
called her sister's name that was scratching in the dirt,
and they walked on home eating Mary Janes. So like I
said, black don't show marks. Don't knock black."

Milo said, "Did she have a baby?"

"I guess she did. She took up with Boot sometime that winter, and they've had all that yardful of children."

"But you were Jack's Daddy?—the one that's in prison for killing Ella Grant?"

"Well, he don't look like me, black as Egypt. She could have snagged him from half the men in Afton, white or black. Boys used to come here by *car* to see her when cars were scarce as camels. No, I don't know. I never did ask."

Milo said, "How come?—since you remember everything so clear?"

Buck said, "Because I had changed my ways. Because it won't none of my business to ask."

"And it ain't none of yours, son," Rooster said.

Milo looked down. He had made little parallel ridges of pine straw like furrows as he listened, like a well-tended field. He made his hand a spade or a single claw and canceled that, slow and deliberate.

"Speaking of black," Yancey said, "look yonder."

They turned west to where a Negro girl was flanking them, twenty yards away, looking dead ahead, a small load hid in her far right breast. Macey whispered "That's her," still squatting in her bloomers.

Yancey hollered "Come here."

Macey whispered, "Leave her alone. I want these bloomers for my Mama's birthday!"

She walked on south, no faster, not looking. "You girl, come here."

She stopped in deep shade, half-turned to Yancey.

"You hollering at me?"

"I don't see your *sister*. Yeah, come over here."

She faced south again, pointed that way. "My Mama is sick. I'm heading home."

"Well, I'm sick too and I'm a deputy sheriff. You coming or not?" Yancey stood, his rifle downwards, and took a step towards her.

Rooster said, "Yancey, let her go. We got business."

Yancey said, "Maybe I got business with her." Anyhow she turned and was pumping towards him as if she would not stop but pass through Yancey, a new way home.

But she stopped on the lip of the bowl they were in—her right leg thrust on as if not obeying, her bare dusty foot, and the blade of her black shin flashed in the light, violet, gold. ("She has greased her legs," Milo thought, "for some boy. She ain't studying *Mama*.") She drew back the leg and stood to her height which was tall for a girl and which leveled her thin eyes with Yancey's where she stared, not flicking once to his rifle, his badge, the sheriff or Macey in bloomers. No one knew her so no one could use her name to break her gaze which Yancey returned. (Milo thought, "This girl isn't waiting, on Yancey or God. She's doing her own will.") Then Yancey laughed and swept her with his eyes—from her high narrow head, the short hair brown and preened back stiff as wires, held from her skull like wings that, strutting, lifted the corners of her brows, her eyes (so black their whites were diluted brown), her vaulted cheeks, lifted all but her mouth, purple, oval, slit straight as a razor, laid in her face a sideways copy of what Milo could almost see in her fork, downwards, slung from her canted hips.

Because he stood farthest and lowest of all, Milo could see what Yancey could not—that she stood at the edge of a pool of sun flung from behind which seeped through her yellow dress, lighting this private sight for Milo (he looked to the others, no one had seen it, they all stood wrong): her legs were spread and the sun set a perfect hourglass between them, the shape of the seal on a Black Widow spider. The bottom bell rested on earth and rose, bound by her shins, rusty knees, hid thighs to shut in her crotch. Then it swelled again there to the upward half—black bell, black bulb— hid by a single thickness of cloth, by nothing else but as surely there as her tan fingernails, her wiry head. A cloud broke the light. She was solid again but Milo knew, and only Milo. He said to himself, "Let Yancey talk. I got information. Whatever Macey saw, this girl is naked as peeled sweetgum."

Yancey stepped up and asked her "Cat got your tongue?"

Her face was no more than two feet from Yancey's though lower now since he had risen. Her lips split open, her tongue thrust out like Macey's copperhead's and wiggled at Yancey, pink and wet. Yancey drew back a hand.

Rooster said "Yancey."

Yancey said to the girl, "Don't you know who I am?"

She looked down his length—badge, rifle. She touched the badge, left her fingerprint on it. "I see that badge. You say you the sheriff."

"I said I'm a deputy but the sheriff's right yonder." He pointed, not looking.

She lowered the load she had held at her breast, slid it half-behind her—a quart Mason fruit jar full of clear liquid. Her eyes had still not moved off Yancey. "What you call me for?"

"Well, *two* things now." He pointed to her jar. "I was just going to ask you had you lost anything." He pointed to Macey, the milkwhite bloomers.

She would not look. "I ain't lost nothing. What I got to lose?"

"You got a point there—lost it long ago, eh? But you ain't lost no clothes today?"

"I'm dressed, ain't I?"

"Far as I can see. Course I can't see through cloth."

"You telling me to strip off?"

Rooster said "No" and stepped closer to her, pressing Yancey back with one firm hand. He pointed to her jar—"What you carrying there?"

"Some water for my Mama."

Rooster said, "Ain't you got a well? You tote it by the *jar?*"

"My Mama is sick and this is the spring water helps her misery."

"Where's the spring at?"

She looked north. "In yonder."

"And where's your house?" She lifted her chin, hooked it south. "Do I know your Mama?"

"You know Dump Wilson?"

"Yes."

"That's her."

"*Old* Dump Wilson? I thought she was dead."

"She going to be if you don't let me go."

"You sure that's nothing but water?" She nodded. Rooster thought, then reached his hand for the jar. She gave it to him and he gripped the lid to unscrew it, then stopped.

Yancey said, "If that's water I'm Margaret Truman" and he sang three notes. "Let me taste it, Sheriff. I'm thirsty now you mention it." He volunteered a hand.

Rooster said, "I ain't mentioned nothing to *you*." He turned to Milo, smiled. "Come here, son." Milo came. "Taste this and tell me is it water or not."

Milo slowly unscrewed the lid, sniffed at the rim— (Macey said, "Look out, your eyebrows are scorching")—then tilted his head and sucked a good inch out, ramming it down with his Adam's apple like an iron pile driver. He rose and his eyes shut, lids clamped as if planning hibernation. Then he looked to the girl, to nobody else. "Water," Milo said. "Nice cool spring water—make old Dump think she's gone to Heaven and hadn't even had to die to get there." He screwed down the lid and handed the jar directly to the girl. "That's a spring and a half."

She said "Thank you, sir" and looked to Rooster.

Rooster said, "Tell Dump I said to get well soon but to go easy on them water treatments. At her age and mine, your bladder gives out, and then where are you?—leaking all night."

She said "Yes sir" and turned to go.

And had gone five steps when Yancey said, "She sure made a damn fool of every man here." He looked

at them all. No one agreed or disagreed. They were
watching her go, the shock of her wide steps calmed in
the shivering halves of her butt. He looked to Milo and
by force of will tore his eyes off the girl—"Water, my
ass." Milo smiled, turned back to the girl whom he
already saw through waves like heat, rising from the
pure corn liquor on his belly. Yancey said, "Sheriff, you
just going to let her go? Get nothing out of her?—not
even where that still is at?" Rooster nodded (he knew
where it was, had known for years) so Yancey said to
Macey, "Give me them bloomers, fool, and quick!"
Macey hopped about rushing out of the bloomers, and
Yancey snatched them and followed the girl.

By the time he reached her she was far enough
away from him to speak and the others not hear. He
touched her elbow. She stopped, not turning, and he
stepped round to her face and said, "*I* know you're
lying and if I was sheriff you'd be in trouble up to your
bare ass. Here, put these on. Keep the ticks out of it."
He stuck out the bloomers—which she accepted, not
looking at him (she remembered his looks), not
speaking a sound. "Now where's that still?" She was
folding the bloomers to a neat handful. She did not
speak. "You and your Mama want a friend or a enemy
in the sheriff's office?" She met his eyes and pointed
north. "Far?" he said. She shook her head. "Niggers?"
he said. She nodded. "Your kin?" She nodded. He dug
in his pocket, found fifty cents, laid it between her
unresisting thumb and the cheap white bloomers. "Buy
you some candy." Then he looked to where the others
waited—the young ones at least. Rooster and Buck
were down again, resting, and Ballard was squatting,

but Milo and Macey stood guard towards him, Macey two steps ahead of Milo. Yancey found a dollar bill in his pocket, showed it to the girl, said, "Want to make some money for your poor sick Mama?"

"Doing what?" she said.

"Nothing new to you," he said. "You know what I mean?" She did not answer but did not move so he beckoned to the young boys. Macey looked back to Milo and they came on together though Milo stopped again two steps behind. Yancey said to Macey, "How old are you boys?"

"Fifteen—both of us but I'm the oldest."

"Have you ever played the game of ten toes up and ten toes down? If you ain't it's time."

Macey thought, understood, looked back to Milo. "I ain't," he said. "I'm speaking for myself."

Yancey waited for Milo but he would not answer. "Bashful, huh? Well, everybody's got to dive in sometime, and you know what Mr. Russell just said." He said to the girl "How old are *you?*"

"Eighteen," she said.

"Old enough to be drafted," Yancey said. He looked to her bare feet dug in pine straw. "Your toes just turn up naturally, don't they?" She stared at her toes—the big toe did ride high on its neighbor. Yancey handed the dollar bill to Milo, pointed south to where briars and low cedars set up a shield, said, "Take her down yonder. It's all on me and in years to come think of Yancey Breedlove."

Milo studied the dollar, rubbing with his thumbs as if to test it. He looked up to Macey (looked down in fact, Macey being shorter).

Macey smiled. "I'm game if you are, Milo. Always a first time. Nice cool day. Spring water to drink."

"Perfect conditions," Yancey said. "Just don't lie down on your copperhead."

Macey laughed, searched for Milo's answering eyes. They were down on the dollar which he still was rubbing. Then he raised his thumbs. They were faintly green (from veins beneath, from the light off leaves). Smiling, he held out the bill to Yancey—"Yancey, even Niggers can't pass fake money. Your ink is fading. Come on, Macey." He slowly turned and, Macey following, went towards Rooster, and before he was there said, "Sheriff, what was it you been trying to tell me?"

Rooster looked up from his seat on the ground, saw the boy, thought, said, "Oh nothing new. Nothing you hadn't learned."

Milo shrugged and said, "I'm a terrible learner, terrible memory. Ain't it time to hunt?"

They had walked ten minutes when Rooster said "Yancey's pouting" and stopped. The others stopped too and they all looked back to where Yancey stumbled and kicked his loud way, twenty yards behind. Rooster said, "Yancey, come on and walk with us. We ain't contagious—just smell like we are." Yancey stopped where he was and would not look. They waited awhile. Then Rooster led on, whispering to Milo, "Leave him alone. Maybe he'll recover."

"I hadn't done a thing to Yancey, Sheriff."

"I know you hadn't and I ain't neither—I'm his

second Daddy. It's that new wife. Never known it to fail—take a boy like Yancey, a good faithful boy that'll follow you around like a puppydog and work round the clock a week at a time (just so you let him blow steam on Sunday), then hitch him to a girl (nine girls out of ten; hitch him permanent, I mean) and in two weeks' time you can look at his face and you'll barely know him. His eyes will be tired, his neck will look broke. What's happened? I'll tell you. I've thought about it a whole lot lately—his pride is ruined. He's caught what he thought he always wanted, was always hunting, what he thought he was working and saving for, training his hair for, washing and shaving for. And what has he got?—if he's lucky, about a hundred and twenty pounds of curly-headed trouble that won't being hunted but was hunting *him,* a free footwarmer for cold winter evenings and a scuttle to haul his ashes in every Saturday night as the years toll by. He'll strut around for a year or so, acting up, showing off, doing every fool thing that comes his way just to claim back a little of what he's lost, what hurts so bad—the notion that somebody *cherished* him but was running from him for fear, and for fun. He don't of course—get none of it back, won't ever, won't *meant* to. And after a while he'll understand or give up trying. Some never do though—"

Macey said, "Are you talking about Yancey?"

Rooster thought. "I may be. I meant to be."

Milo said "My Daddy too."

Rooster said, "Your Daddy. You remember him? Seems like he died fifty years ago."

"Three years," Milo said, "nearly four. Yes sir, I

remember. My memory's in my eyes. Anything I ever *see*, I remember."

Buck Russell said, "That's an awful affliction—good eyes, I mean. Near-sighted, night-blind—only way to live."

"That's me," Macey said.

But Rooster said, "Buck, you have said a mouthful. And it's nearly my motto, has to be the motto of every law man otherwise jails would outnumber churches—then where would we be? Hell on earth. No, I tell you boys, my rule is this—if a razor don't flash or a loaded gun, if the fellow can crawl home somehow or other and not get hisself run over or drowned, then leave him alone. Oh scare him a little—let him think he's bound for the electric chair—but remember he's *some* kind of human being and maybe that beating was what his wife needed, maybe that gal just needed that humping to calm her nerves, maybe that moonshine soothes more pain than all the doctors in Warren County." He looked to the sky, flung an open hand to the visible blue—"Roll on, world!" and waited a moment as if for obedience.

Macey said, "I noticed it was waiting for your permission" and Rooster walked on.

Buck said, "And that's how come we've changed course?"

Rooster said, "Yes, I figured you knew, figured everybody knew but poor old Yancey."

"Knew what?" Macey said.

"Hush, fool," Milo said.

Rooster said, "Knew that liquor still was right in the path we was taking before. Been there long as I've

known about liquor—twenty, thirty years—and I pure
forgot it. I'd have led you all smack into the boiler if
Yancey hadn't dragged that gal over to us and she
hadn't said Dump Wilson was her Mama, her
Grandma maybe. We used to live near Dump when I
was little in a house just two cuts better than hers.
Main difference was we had a tin roof—and we had the
well. Dump came to us for drinking water, and when
my Daddy died my poor Mama worked beside Dump
in cotton many a year, right down on her knees like a
Nigger in the dirt—I did too and will tomorrow if
crime should cease—and some of Dump's kin were
running this still even then, her brothers or sons or
some of her husbands. I've always spared them since
I've been powerful so why lead Yancey—hobnailed—to
their business after all these years? That's how come I
said hunt together and led us off here. To the best of
my knowledge we are passing it now. It's just about
there behind them trees." He pointed east and nobody
spoke, but nobody stopped—even Yancey behind, baffled, in pain.

They tramped on silently, watching the ground,
the upper trees, and soon their minds had separated
and they went together but secret and alone with
whatever private need they were hunting besides the
python, the dog, Rato. They of course found nothing
they needed or could use, but every few yards a foot
would scuff out something worthless and beautiful—a
turtle crazily gouging a hole in a spot of sun to lay
more eggs (and first frost due within the month)
whom Macey flipped to her back and stranded, stacks
of brittle mica that Rooster gathered for Kate's mantel-

piece, bleached oyster shells from God-knew-where (the sea two hundred miles away) and the wolfish skull of a murdered weasel which Milo paused and lifted to study.

Its globed brain case was cleanly drilled by a perfect hole—bullet or tooth?—and though every uneaten muscle and nerve had been leeched away by months of rain, it was still so fierce in its rigid symmetry of fissures, foramina, nerve-paths, arches that it seemed to burn, to radiate, and Milo held it at full arm's length to ease its threat, to focus and calm his blurring eyes (the liquor had struck). Then Macey laughed so he brought it to his nose. The stench of its secret clinging life scalded his nostrils, and he said to himself in his new man's voice but silently, "I am drunk like my Daddy the night he was killed, like most of the nights I remember my Daddy—and God will punish me surer than sunrise. Rato will die some awful death out here alone or Death will strike down on us from above or Lois will tell Papa what I done and what I have started, what I'm aiming at tonight, what I need so bad"—(he saw it, felt it in his groin, his mouth)— "Will slam in my drunk face. Serves me right!" Tears rushed upward in him and he dared not swallow nor blink his brimmed eyes. He drew back the skull and flung it so hard that, striking a tree, it exploded and sent down a flying squirrel like its sudden ghost, web-legged and red, that glided beyond them to earth and vanished.

Macey pretended to chase it though, needing to run after their long rest, and he ran out of sight beyond the others. Still they could hear him—his heavy feet and occasional grunts, his high-pitched calling for "Rato, Rato. Hot-damn, Rato, where are you *at?* Give me a clue, give me something to go on."

They heard a second voice, lower, answer Macey— "How many? Cash money"—and they heard Maccy halt.

Without breaking step Rooster whispered, "Damned if he ain't stumbled on it after all. All my fault, leading you wrong. Been so long I lost my way. Bear left, boys," and they bore left but too late—Rooster looked back at Yancey.

Yancey had heard and understood. He was aimed like an arrow for the hidden voice that came again— "Cash. How many you want?"

So Rooster took hold and did what he must. He headed too for the voice—whoever—and the puzzled others fell in behind.

The voice was a child and the child was black, a boy maybe seven or eight years old, dressed for Sunday in ragged white, stood in the midst of another small clearing, buried to the calf in Mason jars, Macey before him slack-jawed and staring. Rooster said, "All right, Macey. What you found?"

Macey said, "A parrot—can't say nothing but 'Cash' and 'How many?' "

Yanccy had come up even and said, "It's a bootlegger, that's what. The youngest bootlegger south of Washington. I knew he was in here—spring water, Hell!" He turned to Milo—Milo was swaying—then back to the boy. "I reckon that's pure spring water you're selling? Well, take along a jar when you go to jail. It'll taste good there."

The boy said "How many?" to Yancey's badge which the sun was on.

Rooster noticed that, unpinned his own badge and dropped it in a pocket, said "Step back, Yancey" in a firmer voice than the previous time. Then he asked the boy, "Who's your Daddy, boy?" The boy looked down at his dozen jars. "I know you didn't make this by yourself or tote it all here. Is Wilson his name?" No look, no answer. "Are you some kin to old Dump Wilson?"

The boy looked up to the sheriff's pocket—the two pin holes where the badge had been, the bulge where it was—and he made the starting grunt of a speech but halted.

Yancey said, "Maybe you some kin to that gal we saw just a little ways back with one of your jars of healing water?" He turned to Macey—"Or maybe he's the scoundrel that was humping that gal when you caught them, Macey?"

Macey narrowed his eyes to examine the boy. "Could be," he said. "Could very well be"—which the boy sustained in patient mystery.

Yancey said, "Then he's under arrest—statutory rape, carnal knowledge of a female minor. Handcuff him, Sheriff—looks dangerous to me."

The boy's black wrists had been in his pockets. He withdrew them now to take what came though he did not extend them, and Rooster reached down and rung one wrist with thumb and finger, tight as steel for a moment. Then he eased his grip but still held the boy and said, "Who are you, boy? What's your name?" The boy shook his head but took pains to leave his wrist with the sheriff.

Yancey said, "Search him. His pockets are full. Probably got pictures of his whole sorry family—his Mama and his Daddy, his sisters and brothers and that hot bitch Macey saw him hunching. All we need—put them *all* in jail. Ought to been there thirty years ago."

Rooster pointed to the Mason jars. "What you selling? You a snake-oil doctor?"

The boy said "How many?" and pointed also.

Rooster said "Two."

The boy said "Cash money?" Rooster nodded so the boy took two jars and gave them to him, then kept out a hand. "Three dollars cash."

Rooster said "Wait," handed one jar to Yancey, then opened his own, filled the lid full of liquor and finding a match, lit the liquid into flame that even by daylight was clear hard blue. "It's pure," he said. "No lead in this. You and your Daddy run a clean still, don't you?"

The boy said "Cash."

Rooster said "Wait," drank off an inch of his private jar and nodded to Yancey. Yancey opened his, turned up and drank, then passed it to Buck and from Buck to Macey, even to Ballard who wet his lips, and then to Milo.

Milo again drank an inch without pausing, and at once it affected his mind and eyes—his eyes, barely open, seemed heavy magnets toward which each sight —person or tree within his clear half-circle of day—flew helpless and raw to wait for his gradual merciless judgment. So he looked on and waited. Time seemed his to bestow like pardon. He bestowed it, silently, saying to himself Rooster's words to the sky—"Roll on."

Rooster rolled on, shut his jar, asked the boy, "I said was you any kin to Dump Wilson?"

The boy said, "You said 'Cash money' too but I don't see none."

Rooster set his jar between his feet, found his black snap-purse and laid three dollars in the boy's ready hand.

The boy neatly folded the money to a wad the size of a peanut shell, stuffed it in his already bulging pocket and then seemed free, seemed twenty pounds lighter, raked every face with a smile as wide as a piano keyboard, rested on the sheriff. "You the Law, ain't you?" Rooster nodded. "I thought you was. That's how come I didn't say nothing but what Daddy told me. But now you bought it, you guilty as me."

Yancey said, "We ain't bought nothing, boy. We loaning you that to pay the electric bill when we electrocute your sorry Daddy."

Macey said, "Shoot, you behind the times, Yancey. We gas them now. That's cheaper still. You'll have about a dollar left over, boy. Buy your naked gal a new set of bloomers."

Yancey said, "No, we still fry Niggers. Can't gas a Nigger. Niggers don't breathe."

The boy's smile had survived—towards the sheriff, not moving off him. Then Rooster said, "Is that right, boy? Niggers don't breathe?"

The boy broke his smile to gasp twice deeply. "Ain't that what you call breathing?" he said.

Rooster nodded.

Yancey said, "Then we can gas you and save juice. Just fry your Daddy. What else can you do besides breathe?"

"Sing," the boy said. "I can sing and dance. You want to watch me?"

Rooster said, "Wait. Where is your Daddy?"

"Gone to church."

Rooster said "What's his name?"

"I just call him Daddy."

"Where's your still at?"

The boy jerked left and almost pointed to the hidden still, then thought and said "You don't know?"

"I got a good guess."

"That's all I got then. I don't know myself. Get lost every time I come back in these old woods." He stamped both bare feet and went to digging fiercely at his thighs—"Snakes and chiggers, they *live* on Niggers" and as he scratched his feet began a shuffle.

Yancey said, "He asked you where the still's at, boy."

Feet still shuffling, the boy looked steadily left to the woods, balanced on the rim of certain betrayal and —for all he knew—maybe jail or death. Then he looked in order at the ones nearest him in height and age—Macey was looking at the older men, hoping to take his expression from them; Milo's eyes were mostly inward since his second drink but still were drawing the day to them, planning no help only waiting to judge. No help, no hope so he looked to his own feet, and slowly the shuffle became his dance, so powerful it shook him, body and arms, and forced from his mouth his notion of music, a quiet low wail broken by smiles and by odd understandable words ("My *Papa*, my *brother*") which flashed like rags of signal through his song—to decoy, deceive, beguile, claim real distress.

They all watched awhile but as minutes passed and the boy continued to imagine and act his unrepeated patterns of chaos, fresh and desperate, Yancey lost patience and said above the singing, "I'm going to break me up a still" and raised his rifle and feinted east, walking towards the trees where the boy's eyes stayed. Macey followed. Yet the dance went on, faster and louder—Buck Russell even clapped time like gunshots —and as Yancey and Macey reached the edge of trees, Rooster told the boy, "All right, you can stop," but the boy still shook, so louder Rooster said "What's your name?"

The wailing died, the boy drew air to surrender at last, but Milo lurched forward and stopped the boy's mouth with his own flat hand, yelling to the boy's eyes, "Don't tell them nothing. They get your name, that's all they want. You and your Daddy and all your brothers and your naked-assed sister will be *under* the jail or building roads the rest of your life."

Yancey and Macey stopped where they were. Yancey retracted some steps and said, "Goddamn. Don't you recognize a joke?"

With both sudden hands Milo shut the boy's ears. "Don't hear no more. *I've* listened last night and all day today, and every damned word they *say* is lies. You think they are out here hunting your still? You're sadly mistaken and so am I. I thought they were helping me hunt my brother and his mad dog and a twenty-foot maneating python snake. They ain't, they *ain't*. They

are running their filthy mouths, that's all—running away
from their moron wives just so they can roam out here
and *lie*—telling me about their sorry lives, the mess
they have made on other people, asking me to think
the world's like this, that they've come this far—sheriff
and deputies, badges and guns, blackjacks and jailkeys
—on the sense you could stuff in a crab-louse's heel,
asking me to think that God Almighty would leave
them living, mean as they are, if He anyway cared.
Look at them, would you?" He pointed to each—"A
sheriff that can't even serve his wife, limber as beeswax
soon's he hits the bed; Buck Russell yonder with a half-
Nigger son in Raleigh in prison; Yancey Breedlove;
Macey Gupton that I've known all my life—" He tried
to spit, nothing came. "They have broke my heart.
They've done that much. My brother is dying, a snake
worth five hundred dollars is loose with a foaming mad
dog, and you know where I'm supposed to be?—riding
on top of a girl named Lois—and what are we doing?
I'm the only one knows—we are looking, hunting for
valuable things. Come *on*." He spoke to the boy and
tears poured down his cheeks, "Come hunt with me. I
don't know your name and I ain't going to ask." He
staggered two steps towards the north, the trees. The
boy took a step to obey, follow, but Milo bolted to a
low briar thicket and spreading his legs and buckling
deep, he wretched at the partial cause of his fury as if it
were barbed and hooked to his heart.

Rooster said "Wait" to the boy and the others, set
down his jar and walked to Milo who was turned from
them. He stood back till Milo's rasping stopped, then
leaned and said (from behind, not facing him), "Son, I

had you figured for a sport. I take it all back. But I can't blame you. I brought it on myself and the Lord let it fall—telling you this morning in sight of a church to do your will anytime it rose. What I left out, what I ought to told you when you asked me was this—when you start prancing, don't step too high. Keep your feet to the ground else you'll be flinging dirt on your own pretty belly not to mention people's eyes or kicking by mistake. You know what I mean?" He moved up and touched Milo's still-bent neck.

Milo said "Leave me alone" and jerked his head, then was shaken by another harsh rising from his belly.

Rooster said, "Son, you have cut me deep but you don't know what you are saying. I forgive you. Soon as you feel up to walking on, we'll find your brother. He can't be far."

Milo hunkered to the ground above his own mess, shook his head to clear it, then said from the ground, "If you're cut so deep, you ain't up to hunting no more than to humping. Go back to bed, I'll hunt my own brother and when evening comes and I lay a-hold of Lois, I'll have up a hard you'd give your little badge for."

Rooster kicked him and he sat in his mess.

Milo looked up slowly and around and faced him—"Am I under arrest?"

"No, but you will be if you keep on many days like today."

"That leaves me tonight then." Milo stood with difficulty, brushed at the seat and sides of his pants and started north again, not looking back. Rooster let him go—they all let him go—and he went ten yards. Then his right leg sank into a rabbit hole, and he fell completely, not fighting the fall, not sparing his face which dug into dirt.

Macey ran towards him but when he passed Rooster, Rooster said "Wait, I'm handling this."

Macey stopped but said, "*Handle* it then. He's nothing but a boy—him and me both."

So Rooster went to Milo and knelt by his head. His eyes were shut but his breath was steady. "Son, are you hurt?"

"I'm dying," Milo said. "Least I feel like I am, wish I was."

Rooster said, "You'll live but listen to me—you better let me send you home in the car and we'll hunt on."

Milo said, "*Home?*—and me drunk as my Daddy ever got? Rooster, you're sick. You're crazy, friend. I'll lie right here till the Lord forgives me."

"We can't wait for *Him.*" Rooster thought a moment. "Listen, here's my plan—first thing I'll do is beg your pardon (I don't know for what but I'm on my knees, begging), then I'll call Yancey here and give him the keys and you and him walk back out to the car and drive to Warrenton and leave that liquor at my house, hear? We'll be hunting and you'll be sobering, and when you get back we'll meet you and Yancey at the old Ryden place." Milo opened one eye but was silent. "You hear what I say?" Milo nodded (his chin plowed dirt). "Do you take my advice?" No nod, no word. Rooster laid a hand on Milo's back—drunk as he was, sick and filthy, emptied for now of his hurt and meanness, it was still the back of a prime dray-horse, as lean of fat as a walnut table. Rooster bent towards his ear and whispered, "You be the chaperone of Yancey—hear?—when he sees my wife. At heart she's younger than him if that's possible. You ready now?" Milo thought, smiled and Rooster turned— "Yancey, come here."

Though they walked out a straighter way than they came (in total silence) and drove in silence at eighty miles an hour, it was still as late as four o'clock when Yancey stopped on the far edge of town by a squat Dutch oven of a house, weathered gray, not a leaf of shade, dead morning glories roasting by the door on a stringwork trellis. Milo looked to test his eyes. They saw clearer now despite the pounding so he turned to Yancey to offer amends, thumbing to the house—"Is that all the house old Rooster can afford? Shoot, that ain't a cage for a sick killdee much less the hot wife I hear he's got."

Yancey killed the motor but left in the keys. Then he unpinned his badge, laid it on the seat and slid out the door. He slammed it and leaned through the window towards Milo. "It ain't Rooster's house. It's Yancey Breedlove's and you're mighty right—it's every damned cent poor Yancey can afford and his hot new wife is in yonder now, lying on her belly on the dirty daybed reading funny papers and frying in the heat. Well, I'm heading in to turn her over and fry her some on the other side—which'll take me the rest of the afternoon. She's a slow damn cooker but the walls is asbestos so don't you worry, and you tell Rooster that I ain't coming back not today nohow, that here's my badge and my rifle's in the trunk and I wish him luck, and if he wants me back on the force Monday morning, to come around here after eleven a.m.—I'll wake up then—and beg my pardon and offer me at least a five-dollar raise." He drew back, rounded the front of the car, aimed for his house and had reached the porch before Milo could speak.

"What about me and the sheriff's liquor?"

Yancey smiled from the top of the steps. "You such a big man—deliver it yourself. You can drive, can't you?"

"Sure but I hadn't got a driver's license."

"Well, I'm still the Law and I give you permission. Drive on in peace." Yancey waved a hand.

"Yeah, but where am I headed? Where's the sheriff's wife *at?*"

Yancey sniffed at the air, then pointed upwards. "Smell that?" he said. Milo sniffed—some distant burning, rank and stinging. "That's her," Yancey said. "Just a bitch in heat. So follow your nose but don't fall in." He turned and vanished through a rusty screen door.

Milo called "Yancey!" but did not repeat it. The house already seemed derelict and falling. He sat a minute to confirm his solitude, then slid to the wheel, cranked the engine and smiling, sniffed the air a second time before he rolled. He would ask directions from the first passing Negro.

The sheriff's house was no bigger than Yancey's, but it stood on a mild rise of ground, was white and had had some grass till the August drought. Beside it was an open lot deep in weeds, and staked out there near the side of the house was a fat tan cow and a gallon handcrank ice-cream freezer that the cow was licking. Not a flower in sight except goldenrod, not a clothesline, outside washing machine, freezerlocker nor any other sign that a woman lived here and waited inside, but when Milo had sat a good three minutes and no face had shown at window or door, he reached to the foot for his Mason jars. As he rose he caught his face in the mirror—streaked with tears—but he said to himself, "I can call it sweat if anybody asks" and did not notice his other dirt. He stepped to the ground and started the climb to porch and door.

He knocked four times and stood back to wait. Nobody came and no sound came through the open windows. He would knock once more but first he tensed his feet in his shoes, alerted his toes to sense vibrations in the soft wood floor. Rock, or so it seemed, bed-rock—floor, house, cow, still air. He turned and heavily walked to the steps and faced the opposite lower houses, equally still. He thought of something he had read in the paper—that a human body is nearest to death the instant before it is forced to yawn. Milo yawned and thought he would shout to the street "Yawn!" but a car scraped round the corner below him, the street caught breath and a black Chevrolet-load of boys tore forwards. He saw at once it was no one he knew nor had seen at school, but seeing him the car slowed and stopped and a squirrel-faced boy maybe eighteen leaned out—"How much you charging, sport?" Milo frowned, not understanding. "For your white lightning, buddy? I can't use *you*."

Milo stared at his jars. "This is nothing but pure
spring water," he said, trying to whisper and still make
it carry, "and this is the sheriff's house, I warn you." He
pointed behind him, then raised that finger to his lips
for silence.

"It's also the sheriff's *wife's* house, Ham-hock.
When he ain't home she charges two dollars and
sometimes—if the wind's blowing right—she'll take it
out in trade, don't you know?" The boy wet his index
finger loudly and shoved it up Indian-style to the wind.
"Just right," he said. "But you got water, huh? Hang on
to it then. It puts out fires—and you're smoking already,
just standing on her porch." Another boy, hidden,
sailed out a high laugh that even struck the cow—she
threw up her head, upset her freezer—and the car
whined away.

Milo saw himself, in no glass except his own clear
mind, jerked sober by a laugh—a grown boy old
enough to be a father (could have had a baby more
than two years old) yet offering himself to public view
on a peaceful Sunday in green army pants, a blue
workshirt (both stained and stinking with spew),
face filthy, hair matted, waiting in borrowed underwear for a woman he had never laid eyes on before to
hand her two jars of bootleg liquor made in the woods
by high-hat Negroes—and his brother roaming desperate not five miles away maybe wounded, dead. He
walked like a hunting cat to the door, set the jars there
in Mrs. Pomeroy's path and was standing to leave when
he saw a thing he had previously missed, the day being
bright—to his right, hip-level, was a dim orange light

the size of a dime. He bent to see it and saw it was a plastic button, lit behind, and beneath it on the wood were these words in pencil—

> *In case of emergency day or night*
> *Press this light*
> *Direct hookup to sheriff's bedroom*
> *Be right with you*
> *Thank you for your corporation*
> > Rob Pomeroy

Milo stood and as clearly as he had just seen his own shameful self, saw Rooster Pomeroy rise in a vision from that bell light as if from a jug upward like fume, shedding hat, pistol, badge, all clothes as he formed and rose to float buck-naked on the Sunday air, pink-skinned, blue-veined, sparsely tufted with limp white hair, a firm low belly deeply dimpled where it shelved above his groin—a shed to guard his prized possessions, a mother brooding on his nest of squabs doomed not to rise, to wither unfledged—and on his round face a helpless smile directly at Milo. Milo smiled back, even pointed to the jars, said to Rooster (but silently), "Two quarts of liquor isn't no emergency. I've set them down and am heading back to help you," but Rooster's smile went frantic and opened—"No, *press* that bell. Son, help me *here*. Son, rescue the Rooster!" Milo laughed aloud, said aloud "Saved by the bell!" licked his broad thumb and jammed the button till the back of the house hummed like a hive and the soles of his feet took the coming steps.

The door swung open before he was ready—he

stood too close (six inches from the screen), his actual laugh hung on unfinished at the rims of his mouth—and there stood a woman, more nearly a girl, in a pink bathrobe, huge black eyes eye-level to him for the instant it took her to see Milo pressed close, half laughing. Then her lips pursed and gasped like a fish for air, then smiled, said "Oh!" One hand opened, reached towards him in greeting. Then she folded to the floor like a well-oiled hinge.

Milo leapt back and said, "Lady, I'm your husband—*from* your husband, I mean. Whatever I am, get up—I'm harmless." He had whispered it fiercely, but if he had shouted she still would have lain in her compact heap—he stepped to the screen and saw she was out, fainted or dead. He turned for help to the empty street, the opposite houses, but the same black car had also turned and was bound down on him, slowly now, intending to stop. So he reached for the china knob of the screen. It opened, he rushed in, straddled the body, took her by the wrists and dragged her back three feet, then slammed the wood door and fell against it. He could hear two things—his pulse in his ears and the same boy's voice from the car outside, "Go easy, sport. She'll grind you to dust," then the same high laugh as the car drove on.

Milo said to himself, "She's ground her last. Now what must I do?"—and in fact no visible atom moved; even her wild black curls were still—"Drive back and hunt up the sheriff and say, 'Sheriff, your wife fell dead at my feet before I could even give her my name. You never told me she had a weak heart'?" Macey's favorite joke clattered through his ears—girl says to boy "Oh, honey, my *heart;*" boy says to girl, "Never mind your heart, hang on to your *hat!*" He said "Lord forgive me," then went to her head and knelt in hope of faint signs of life.

Since he had dragged her she lay nearly straight—only her legs were folded to the right beneath her robe, her face was profiled and her arms were hooped above her head—but she still volunteered no visible breath. If life was there, burning inward—banked—he must hunt it out, hunt pulse or heart. He rocked to his buttocks to brace himself—just a week before in health class at school they had felt their own pulses; it had taken Milo a good while to find his and when suddenly it humped out as if from ambush, he yelled in the room, then laughed with the others but secretly tasted terror for an hour (and since, in memory). Her left wrist was nearer. Still reared back, he took it and turned it till the cords of gristle, the sunk purple veins struck his eyes like a shout. He knelt on though, bent closer, stared and daring a finger, lightly traced the path of a scar, still pink, ruthlessly straight for two full inches through all that tangle like an ideal route, the shortest way. Then his finger probed for the pumping blood. If it was there it shrank from him. Yet her flesh was warm and her joints were free, showed no threat of stiffening. He would strike for the source, seek her heart. He gently laid her wrist on the floor, more gently laid his own straight fingers above her heart on the cloth of her robe and gently pressed.

She whispered "Tom" and her whole trunk shuddered, shoulders buckled inward, rolled left, relaxed—leaving two of Milo's fingers stranded on the slope of her left breast exactly half-bared where her robe had gapped to beyond its crest that was stained the color of one blackberry crushed in milk. Milo shut his eyes. He had seen something new—in person, at least; by touch, at least. Oh of course he had seen magazine photographs—the *National Geographic* at school—and a book Macey bought when their class went to Raleigh for the legislature (women like gourd vines) and then hot Phyllis and her girls at the fair (hot as fruit Jello and about as thrilled) but not a bare *woman* whose name he knew and beneath his own hand the first time out (by the time he had been old enough to remember his mother bathing, the breasts he had nursed had been dug at by Rato and Rosacoke till they hung like bladders at hogkilling, full; and even Lois on Friday night had kept on her shirtwaist, he aiming elsewhere in the time they had). His eyes stayed shut but his fingers stayed still though the bones shivered. She had spoken and moved but was she awake and were her eyes open? That was the next ordeal to meet. He met it, looked. She was still sealed against him, but leaning to see, he shifted balance and laid new weight on his three touching fingers. She murmured again, "Tom, look. I have waited; I have met you at last" and shuddered, rolling back rightward, gown closing slightly.

It had closed over Milo's hand still there and hid it to the wrist in its new resting place, for it did rest now—he had clamped his teeth, tensed his neck but surrendered his whole hand, heel and palm, to the shielding service she seemed to demand, sought in her sleep. He guarded her heart or told himself so, but it beat so far beneath his cupping that he could not filter its thuds from his own. Still the woman was alive and warm, and he—content. He knew that slowly, felt calm rise from his hidden hand to numb all fear but also desire. He was tired (he had slept very little lately, had only just struggled from his first shameful drunk), and this seemed rest—to sit above a sleeping woman, her black hair crowding about his knees, who trusted him enough to sleep, to take his guarding. Thinking of sleep, he fought to stay awake but only half-succeeded. He began to rock above her mildly like a well-anchored boat, and in another minute his mind was blank so that when his thumb of its own accord began to flick across the hump of her breast, it stirred him no more than rubbing a child or the clustered grapes at the head of his bed, walnut and smooth (which even now he would reach back to rub when he could not sleep), and it did not notice her various risings, her nipple's quick budding, the slower strengthening of her heart.

But he rubbed her awake. Her brown eyes clicked open, upward, backward. He did not think to remove his hand nor to stop his thumb. He smiled broadly at her (knowing she saw him upside down and would not notice a gentler greeting), leaned to within eight inches of her face, said, "Lady, my name isn't Tom. Wish it was but it isn't and I am sorry. Believe me, I'm sorry from the bottom of my heart."

She said "Oh!" again and though she was prone, sank deeper even than at the door.

"Well, damn," he said and sat back from her, noticing then what his hand had done, holding it out for thorough inspection, then quickly raising and dropping his brows, pouting his wide amazed lips as he gave it a grin of pride and envy. Then he said, still aloud, "If I'm this ugly, knocking ladies out, I better get me an operation, trade in my face on an easier model. I've certainly sunk this helpless soul—two times now; three times, you're drowned." He thought of remedies—spirits of ammonia—but thought he had done enough already, could hardly afford to ransack the house hunting ammonia. He thought of the jars that waited on the porch. If it cured Dump Wilson's private misery (and drove himself crazy, just two clear inches), then surely if he barely wet her lips, she would come to and welcome him normally, hear his name and simple business?

He went to the door, opened it carefully, checked the street for cars or walkers, then took up the jars and was safe inside. But seeing from there the poor sprawled woman, he thought, "She'll drown if I dose her there. I got to prop her up. Where? Against the wall?" A wall was the only prop in the hall as bare as a blighted chestnut. The bedroom would be that door at the back (the bell had rung there), but her robe still gapped too freely to risk it—Rooster *was* sheriff even if he couldn't stir tapioca with the tools he had). Milo looked directly right—a sitting room, a brown couch and pillows. So he went there and set the jars on a table by a thick white mug, empty of coffee but the spoon still in it, and piled three pillows on an arm of the couch. Then he tipped to the woman, knelt again, lifted her so easily he shivered in surprise, never having lifted a woman before, and took her to the couch and laid her there, arranging her robe in case of visitors. Then he unscrewed Rooster's jar—the fuller one—and licking dried coffee off the spoon from the mug and tilting the jar, dipped out a level portion of liquor. He crowded her gently back with his butt, sat by her waist, raised her head with the crook of his arm and prying her lips with his thumb, poured it through her teeth (her teeth were short, nearly square like a baby's but were white and dry and bit as perfect as the jaws of a trap), then followed it at once with a second spoonful.

She frowned and groaned but her throat slowly swallowed, and her eyes were seared open—again on him where he sat beside her, cradling her head. She stared till the liquor had struck her stomach, then she said, "How come you have dyed your hair?"

He set down the spoon and roughed his hair. "I hadn't," he said. "It was born this color. Maybe the sun has bleached me a little but—"

She shook her head. "It was red as a penny. And you look so *young*."

"Lady, I *am* young but I'm eating and growing. Now let me tell you this but don't be scared—for God's sake don't pass out again (I ain't a doctor)—my name isn't what you think it is."

She raised a quick hand and stopped his mouth, nodding as she said, "I understand. I won't ask questions." Then she sat upright and turned to face him, touched his shoulders with the ends of her fingers, ran down the length of her arms to his hands—they were open. She stopped there. "What are you running from this time, Tom?" Tears large as peas fell on their joined hands.

Milo met her eyes, which was no easy meeting, but he did not answer. He thought, "Two things—she is

crazy or drunk. Whichever one, I can see she's in
misery deep over her head. You don't get eyes like that
from laughing. I owe *somebody* one decent thing to pay
for all my mess since Friday. Let it be her. Let me be
what she needs." He pressed her hands. "I'm standing
still now—and I brought you this." He nodded towards
the liquor. She would not take her eyes off him, seemed
to be feeding or drinking off him like a famished mare
that will not raise her head from water, once found, for
any cause other than thunder or lightning. He was
neither one so he looked away, inspected the room.
"Nice place you got."

That broke her stare. She saw the room she had
seen for ten years and wondered again how she had
lasted it (Rooster was how—his red heart's blood)—
nine feet by fifteen, beaverboard walls the color of liver,
low ceiling, one card table with an old radio in the
shape of a church window, one green easy chair by the
open window as swollen as if it were dying of dropsy
(the window curtainless), one ladderback chair with
sideposts like spears, a coffee table with lions feet, the
couch they were on and on an endtable beside the
couch her two wedding presents—from Rooster an
electric clock dead accurate that marked time as if it
were grinding grist, quiet but endless; and the lamp
from her parents. She pointed to that. *"That's* nice,"
she said. "That's all I like." The base of the lamp was
blue mirror glass cut and laid in a winding upward
stairs around the pole; the shade was darker blue and
was spangled with dozens of gold foil stars, some of
them already peeling at the prongs. "Stairway to the
stars—get it?" she said.

"Yes," Milo said.

"All the balance could burn down tonight. I wouldn't shed a tear."

Yet more tears fell onto Milo's hands (his hands rode hers now). "You wish that on poor Rooster, do you? Death by fire?—little sleep as he gets?"

"No, I don't," she said. "He has saved my life one time already and may have to again any day. My precious life. That's more than you done."

"You're right," he said. "Still I nursed you when you fainted just now, brought you in here, got you comfortable. I swear I never knew I was such a shock. I'm taking plastic surgery early next week."

She smiled but said, "You still ain't told me what you're running from *now*."

He knew he must decide—to stand, beg her pardon, say his name and leave or to follow her further, one lie on another, towards whatever gift she would finally ask. But maybe she would ask for something he could give—something painless, harmless, free—so he said, "*You* know, my same old trouble—prancing too high, kicking up mess in somebody's face, then clearing out till the dust can settle."

She said, "I won't ask that somebody's name, but looks like most of the mess hit you." She meant his clothes. She had noticed them.

"Generally does," he said. "That's life."

"Oh it's life," she said, "but it ain't *living*. Take off your clothes. I got to go wash them. You can't go nowhere looking like that. They'll know you right off."

"I hadn't got time—" He paused for her name but

it would not come. Rooster had said it once but he had
forgot.

"*Make* time," she said. "It won't take long. I can
dry them in the oven."

"And I just sit around naked while you do? What
if some company walked in and saw me?"

"*Company?*" she said. "Listen, if somebody walks
through that door, it'll be Rob or the undertaker to get
my body or a ghost out of Hell. That poor door hadn't
been knocked in ten years and Rob's poor bell—when
it rung just now, I thought it was Judgment. That's
why I fainted—that and seeing your face so close,
laughing like thirteen years hadn't passed, hadn't
pressed you no more than a feather quilt."

"They *hadn't*," he said and stood before her,
leaving her hands. "Thirteen years ago I was nothing
but a child. But I have learned things. Thirteen years
ago I was lonesome as the moon, but people come to
me now." He extended both arms like wings beside him,
flapped once silently, rose (on his toes but as if on air),
and still drew her eyes though his own looked upward
—"People need me now since I'm a man."

His arms stayed up, trembling with the strain, so
she stood and began to unbutton his shirt (the two top
buttons), then stopped and said, "They always did.
You just notice it now but it's nothing you've learned.
Don't fool yourself. It's a gift from God." He made a
ring of his thumbs and forefingers and lowered it over
his head like a halo, rapidly blinking worshipful eyes.
She rolled out a laugh like a spool of thread, thin and
cutting, which reeled itself in and thickened to a moan.
"You got to understand that, believe that," she said.

"Believe me, Tom, I have told you before. I know what I say—you have got powers. You could heal the sick, ease troubled minds, draw poison from sores. How come you don't?" She reached to his head where his hands rested now, took one by the wrist and laid it on her own head, bowed, eyes shut.

He waited a moment, allowing what power there might be to flow, then whispered, "Honey, you are welcome to it—all five fingers—but I ought to warn you, it ain't going to work. It won't even cure a fever blister, not to speak of troubled minds."

Yet she stood on beneath its mild weight another minute, eyes still clamped, teeth clenched but rattling. Then he took back his hand, and she opened her eyes, raised her head and said, "My mind is eased. I told you. I told you. I been waiting for this thirteen years, Tom." She held out her own left wrist between them (the wrist where he had hunted her pulse). "Ease this," she said and he did what he had done in her sleep—traced a finger down the route of her scar, down, back. She grasped his hand. "Ease *this*," she said and thrust it to the lapping V of her robe, left it there flat in the trough of her chest. Her eyes shut again, her head rocked back, rolled limp on her shoulders.

He said "Peace."

She said "*Peace*. Tom, give me peace. You owe me that."

Was that her demand, the final gift he was called to give? Final or not, it seemed in his power—in the moment he wondered, it became his desire. His fingers moved of their own accord, honest not stealthy, spread the neck of her robe, took their previous seat above her heart which was also her breast that drooped slightly now because she stood. His hand moved on to lift that droop, then pressed, then rested, waiting for his previous calm to rise. The calm did not.

She said again "Thank you," stood straight and smiled, then stepping sideways, slid from his hand as if from a spear—it hung on an instant—and walked to the door. "Now give me your clothes—keep your underwear—and go take a bath. The bathroom is yonder through our bedroom." She pointed, not looking, towards the back of the hall.

He saw himself again, thought of explaining the mess to his mother and started undoing the rest of his shirt buttons. He carried it to her. She took it, looked away. He untied his shoes, unbuttoned his pants and stood in Rato's underwear, staring out the window at a child in the road—a girl at least ten, maybe eleven, long straw hair, long bones, blue dress, writing with her finger on Rooster's dusty car. Writing what, thinking what, seeing what now as she turned and stared directly at the window he stood behind? He did not retreat but he lowered a hand to cup his groin, harmless as it now seemed, lazed in the heat of the low small room, the afternoon. The woman came, took his pants from the floor and left him alone.

He had never bathed in a tub before, never covered all his body with warm water (never with cold except when he and Macey had swum in creeks or on church picnics at Mason's lake or at his baptizing) so the bath he had drawn had been deep and scalding,

and he had lain sunk maybe fifteen minutes, floating
his arms, his heavy head, eyes shut (feeling his hair
snake clean behind him, feeling through drowned ears
the poor woman's steps in the opposite kitchen). He
had lain and thought, "I must think about her," but
eyes still shut and the water not cooling, he had only
managed one thought of her—"Maybe this isn't the
sheriff's house" (forgetting the bell); "Poor Rooster, if
it isn't"—when he pictured Lois Provo instead. Fully
dressed—he had not seen her otherwise. And when he
had mildly strained to strip her picture, he had left
himself with only her head—he had not seen the rest
(having touched what he had touched in darkness),
and what he had not seen he could not imagine. So he
had opened his eyes, raised his hot neck to study what
he could see—his own sunk body. Even to him it
seemed carved and pressed from two kinds of lean
wood—hands, arms, neck and face (which were bare to
the sun all summer in the field) of walnut or cherry
and shoulders, chest, belly, legs (which were always
covered) of white pine, unstained but haired with tight
coils of gold. He had plowed one finger from throat to
groin and freed a line of small milky bubbles and
looking closer had seen that he wore a whole skin of
bubbles, clung to his true skin, to every hair like a
loving armor and had thought again, "Things come to
me," then he swayed himself shoulder to hip to shed
them. The bubbles had clung. Only his limber handle
had danced—left, right—at the pit of his belly. Hands
still floating, he had stared at that, had smiled and said
aloud, "Calm down, son. It's still afternoon. I got to
find Rato, Phillip and Death before I can think about

feeding you—but oats it'll be when nighttime comes!
That's a promise, son." Its swaying had already stilled
by then—it had lain left and rested, floating in no need
of calm or soothing speeches. Drowsed as he was with
heat not liquor, he had noticed that, had smiled and
spoke again, "This *is* Rooster's house and looks like
Rooster's trouble is catching." He had seized it in his
fist, gritted his teeth, exhorted it as if it were a coward
in battle, "Cephas, arise! We got puddings to stir,
wounds to heal, hearts to ease. You got *powers*, son.
You can ease the world and the world is waiting—
listen!" He had listened and heard two things, out of
reach—the chink of the cow's chain among the weeds,
the poor woman washing for him in the kitchen.
"Cephas, you have only begun to fight!" He had
stretched it up to twice its length, then released it
suddenly to stand alone as his present and future banner
of triumph. It had settled lazily into hot water, floated
like the butt of a soft old log half-sunk for years. Then
he had felt that his heart barely beat—only twitched in
his breast like a frail metal thread stretched thinner,
thinner—and had realized with what mind was left
that the heat had struck, had secretly drained his once-
proud standard, his clear hard mind and was reaching
for his heart to silence that.

So he had stood with difficulty, stepped from the
high tub and clinging weakly to walls, doors had
staggered dripping into the bedroom. He had stopped
in the middle and extended his arms, no longer as
wings but as boneless props against walls and floor that
buckled and heaved, as rudders to right him. But the
whirl had begun. Blood had instantly chilled and

funneled to his feet, head had roared vacantly, ears had filled with tissue paper above whose crackling he still had heard two solid things but rapidly fleeing—the cow, the woman—and had opened his mouth to ask their help but knowing he was naked, had shielded again his shrinking handle and surrendered alone to what seemed death, a rocking, a leaning, a final fall. But had landed sprawled on the unmade bed which was Rooster Pomeroy's cross to bear and had thought as his last thoughts on entering night, "I am costing Rooster his precious badge, dying here, and my own mother will perish with shame—when I never intended to harm a soul. How come I'm punished, so young and harmless?"

So that when she had laid his clean clothes in the oven, washed her face at the sink and in a hand mirror, arranged her hair, bit color to her lips, she came to the bedroom door and listened, and hearing no noise of water or drying, she pushed the door which was only half-shut, and he struck her across twelve feet of space —the shape of thirteen years' hope and need, waiting simply. She stood on that far, one hand on the door, thinking he would hear or feel her presence and rise, shamed or ready. He did not hear (he was whirling on down), but blinded and weak, he did feel her gaze, accept her hopes and turn them in his mind to a momentary dream—Lois at last, clear in perfect nakedness, waiting on a porch as he moved towards her, answered her smile, extended his open hands to hers and heard her say, "I have been afraid, waiting in the dark. I have kept my promise. Why have you failed? You said you would come to me long before night." He

answered, "Night? It is still clear day" but looking up
saw it was really night, that the light was from her, her
readiness, so he said, "I am sorry. I was tending to
duties but now I am here and look, I am ready."

She walked towards the bed, stooping for his flung-
off underclothes, and stood by the edge folding them
neatly as his dream became his visible force, as his
heart restored new blood to his limbs and his sleeping
senses crouched to wake so that when he woke he saw
two things as clear as his dream but solid and in reach
—above him, the woman washed and younger (and
though healed, wilder), loosening now the cord of her
robe; and on himself cresting up his belly at last like an
emblem earned by his youth, his joy, given (by whom?
by the clear day itself) for his generous use of healing
powers, in this room rare as the unicorn—a ready horn,
his one-eyed son, prodigal returned.

He spoke to it first, "Welcome home, old son. I
thought you were *gone*. Kill the fatted calf!" Then he
looked to her, moving only his eyes, not rising from the
sheets—"You be the calf," he said and blushed to the
breast bone. "I thought we was both gone, him *and*
me. Lady, your tub is a killer but look, I lasted, *we*
lasted." He looked down again. They had more than
lasted, had come from the bath another size grander,
another new man. Then back to her, "I'm too young to
die, too pretty and harmless. I must have been spared
for a wonderful purpose. Maybe I've got them powers
you mentioned—reckon I have?" She nodded but did
not smile nor move forward, did not touch the long
bared stripe of her body—from crown to sole ten inches
wide a map in relief of unknown countries (well, once-

known; by night), colored like no other map he had seen: black, white, milky berry, white again, oh black again. Marking whose possessions?—was all that Rooster's, every hill, valley, bottomless gorge? His if he fed and guarded them daily. He could not see all from where he lay but he lay on, prone. "I've almost eased your troubles," he said.

"How do you know I ain't all healed?"

"Eagle eyes," he said—he flickered his eyes, then left them shut—"and various pieces of signal equipment." He raised his arms above his chest, oared them as if taking delicate signals—all of him oared, till he slowly rose from the waist still blind and oared before him till he brushed her arm, slid down to her hand. Then he looked.

"Who are you?" she said.

"I'm a boy," he said.

"I figured that," she said, still not smiling. "No, who are you?"

Now he held both her hands and knelt before her, his knees on the mattress. "Tell me somebody's name you expected."

"You know," she said.

"Well, I'm him," he said. "Just Tom," he said. He gave the mildest pull to her hands, and she gave in smiling, like the side of a dry hill after first rain, that slowly, entirely, having waited thirteen years, accepting the name he had finally offered, a name which seemed no lie to him but the gift he had meant (and now wanted) to give, which any Tom alive—young enough, brave enough—would freely have given.

*   *   *

He did Tom's spadework for half an hour, never dismounting, hardly pausing, and took Tom's pay (Tom and Rooster's)—thirteen years of back pay with interest paid down sweetly in five installments but silently. (Her last words had been "You know," then eyes and mouth sealed and she only breathed.) Then he did pause in saddle, not from exhaustion—his body had thirstily obeyed each order, having waited nearly as long as she, and still stood and waited; his belly and groin still cradled a lake, tapped but bottomless. He paused for the heat and lay perfectly still, her as his mat, face in her hair that was wild again, hoping to cool but feeling only—in the ebb of joy—an acid bond of sweat between them. He stiffened his arms, raised his head to see a clock in the room. There was no clock so he guessed the time by the weight of the air—past five o'clock, the desperate minutes before the sun loses, as it threatens not to. Past five o'clock, his prime hunting hours all but gone, and what did he have to show for his day?—a woman beneath him firm as a horse and as ready to run but crazy maybe and without the manners to say even "Thank you" or ask his true name and look to watch his broad back, working. He rose a little higher and looked down his chest, his belly to their joint, thought to himself, "I am firm as a fiddle and lady, I've played you some lovely tunes but I ain't no Tom. I've done Tom's work—and was glad to get it —but I'm somebody else and I want you to know it before I leave to save my brother." Then he saw her face—flushed and wet and so calm that he could not consider blurting his name and claiming his rightful recognition. But her face was so closed—"She is locked in behind them eyes with Tom. This has all been a homecoming party for Tom and I'm not aiming to break up her party so I'll *be* Tom but who the Hell's Tom? I got to find out and I'll dig to find it."

He dug awhile, deeper and slower than before. She bent with the spade and soon her breath was thinning, quickening so he dug on still deeper (she was years and years deep), one stroke faster than her shallow panting till she drew a long breath and spilled over into a string of little moans by slowing and slightly shortening his dig, and when he had her on the verge of blooming, he said in her screened ear, "Tell me if you're happy."

"Mmmm," she said.

"No, say a word. You can whisper, I'll hear you."

"Yes," she said.

"Is it me makes you happy?"

"Yes," she said.

He spaded on but slower. "Me and who else?"

"Just you," she said.

"Just me," he thought and he threw her such a promise from the hip that she hiccuped. "Not sixteen yet and no driver's license but can't I drive?—I'm the driver of the century, pilot and jockey thrown in to boot. Wrong-way Mustian but I've found the way!" He had thought that not said it, and he eased a moment to taste the honey banked in his thighs but soon realized that joy was not knowledge—he was still in the dark— so he started again so slowly so sweetly and whispered, "Just *me?* I ain't that conceited now. Me and who else?"

"Just you," she said.

"Who am I?" he said.

"Silly—you know."

"I don't," he said. "I have hunted for you so long and hard—halfway round the world and back, I have lost my memory."

"That's all you've lost."

"Thank you," he said, "but who am I?"

"Tom," she said.

"And who are you?"

"Kate Pemberton—I was anyhow when I first knew you."

"Where was that?"

"In jail," she said. "Remember now?"

"I'd forgot that too." He was moving still. She was answering in the gap between breaths. "What had you done?" he said.

"It was you," she said. "That child you stole."

He had not intended to lose control, but he was fifteen and all he had was strength not skill so in the silence that followed her words, he dug on in rhythm and before he could open his mouth to laugh, his spade had forced her into bloom, slow but huge, and much to his own surprise, he followed with a sturdy sprout of his own that branched and leaved upward within her into warm white life—to fade and fall with gradual speed, leaving him the sense of loss for a while, the witness of death where delight had stood.

They both were still, his eyes were open, his cheek in her hair, but what he saw was his brother plainly— eight years before, Rato's first day of school, his own second year. He was drawing a ship awhile before lunch when the class door opened on Rato, escaped and in silent tears, searching twenty faces for his brother. The teacher said, "Can I help you, son?" Rato shook his head and went on searching, and he himself laid his head on the desk, praying no one would yell that Rato was his. But hid as he was, he saw Rato and knew from his fumbling hands his distress—stiff new overalls he could not unhook. Milo knew his own duty clearly as now (to stand, claim Rato, lead him to pee), but he left him to stand till the stain began and spread down his leg to his bare foot and watched him turn and leave. And at six years old though he couldn't do buttons, Rato could walk five miles and find home— which he would not leave again for weeks nor speak his brother's name till Christmas—Christmas morning he mumbled "Thank you" for a celluloid statue of Popeye and Milo himself said, "Rato, thank *who*?" —"Thank you, *Milo*" (the *Milo* was whispered).

He was shrunk now and separate so he rolled off and lay ten inches from her, facing the ceiling. His right hand searched the floor by the bed, found her robe and his underwear (Rato's underwear). He wadded it, left his hand on the floor and facing the woman, took her eyes once more and spoke in the voice he thought was harmless. "My name is Milo and, Lady, I'm not but fifteen yet so I'm grateful to you, but this ain't why I'm here at all. The sheriff sent me in with some liquor he found while we were hunting my brother in the woods. Now I got to go back. But I thank you again and I beg your pardon. I lied—but didn't you want me to?" She nodded, smiled. "You knew all along?"

"I knew you *thought* you were lying," she said. "I ain't sure you were. I believe in ghosts. You could still be him—years ago, before I saw him."

"Maybe I am. Hell, I'm several dozen people a day. So people tell me—my sister, my mother. Always telling me, 'Milo, behave. Act natural. Act your age. You're still a child. Don't act so big—you ain't a baby. Calm down. Cheer up. Be yourself. Try to change. You're acting more like your Daddy every day.' Who was he? Tell me."

"Your Daddy or Tom?"

"Well, either one. No, Tom, I mean."

"That's too long a story."

"How long?" he said.

"I don't even know the beginning or end, but my part alone takes thirteen years."

He paused to feel the time again—the heat focused on them by the black tin roof—and felt slight relief, nothing like a breeze but at least the news that the day was broken, twenty past five. "Tell me the first ten minutes," he said. "Then I got to hunt."

"You been hunting," she said, "for the last half-hour. More ways than one to hunt in this world."

"My brother, I mean."

"You'll find him," she said. She smiled, looked down. "You got a built-in compass—look."

He looked and he did, of its own accord. "You don't know much about compasses then—he's pointing due-south. A compass points north."

"He's pointing to you."

He said, "Do you blame him? Wouldn't you point at me if *you* had me?"

She rolled to her right side, facing him, nearer. "Yes," she said.

"Then *point*," he said to her side-drooping breasts,

her leaning belly, and threw his dropped hand which laid her flat and pulled him in one unbroken move to his left side, his knees, then high astride her—his knees in her arm pits, his tight butt settled in her wiry fork. Her arms reached out to draw him down. He seized her wrists, pinned them behind her head to the pillow. "Tell me ten minutes of your story, please ma'm. Then I'll give you your final treatment and leave." He freed her arms, rocked back to listen.

She began to tell it to the shaded window. "Thirteen years ago when I was your age—or one year younger—I was pretty and as forward in my growth as you. I had eyes, I knew it, and boys at school passed me all sorts of notes—poems, drawings. They understood what was happening in me and acted like dogs round a bitch in heat—as best they could at fourteen or fifteen. But I flung them off like summer flies. I was aiming to find my equal in the world, and also I had a job after school so I had no friends and lived to myself. My job was helping my mother and father. They were jailers—my Daddy still is, here, now—and my mother did the cooking and cleaning for the jail, which was also our home. We lived downstairs, the prisoners overhead—what few there were, old drunks asleep or rarely a maniac waiting for a vacancy at the asylum and locked up with us, having no other home or bed to wait in—and what Mother cooked, I delivered on trays— good country vegetables, corn bread, gravy. My Daddy went with me to chaperone or if Daddy's back was bad, a deputy—and though we ran the nicest jail in South Carolina (number-10 cans of red geraniums in every cell window), I hated my life like a snake wrapped round me, choking me, shaming me—young as I was, unseen, untried. So I planned all sorts of ways to escape, but every way involved a man. (All my life I have leaned on men.) I needed a man to claim me, see me. I knew if the right man could ever *see* me, he would rescue me in fifteen minutes—and when I wasn't crying for him, I was praying, telling the Lord I would give Him a year to repay me for His awful mistake or I would take measures. Well, He repaid and in less than a year. One Sunday morning Mother woke me up when breakfast was ready and I woke in tears— straight from peaceful sleep into tears, just seeing my room and thinking of Sunday. Sunday is of course the big day in jails, coming on the heels of Saturday night. Mother said, 'Kate, stop crying. We're lucky.' 'How come?' I said. She said, 'Guess how many men are upstairs.' I said 'Black or white?' 'White,' she said. 'Three,' I said. 'One,' she said, 'but guess what he done.' 'Rape,' I said. She said 'Not that bad.' 'Arson?' I said. 'Kidnaping,' she said, 'and we got the fellow to feed this morning. Happened in your sleep about two a.m. Nice young fellow, neat as a pin. Come on let's go.' All our previous real criminals were black so I was curious but no more than that. Just put on the nearest dress at hand and went—and it wasn't nothing special, at first sight nohow. A young fellow, red-headed, maybe nineteen. But the image of you—that's how come I fainted, today not then. Though even then I thought I had seen him. He looked at you that way, open and grinning like you were the one he was thinking about just the minute before, aching to see, and now here you were—and him with crime on his hands and heart. But as I say I wasn't struck at first, just nodded to him as he said 'Good morning' and studied his hands while Mother talked to him. I'm a student of hands—whole hands not palms. I can tell a person's whole life from his hands, if I can watch them doing several things— handling bread or buttoning their pants or the way they touch theirself, feel their own face."

Not thinking, Milo took his own hands (they had been on her waist, as if to resuscitate) and hid them behind him.

She smiled. "Too late. I've studied them good."

"Tell me what you know."

"I know you don't hate yourself," she said. "That's half the battle."

He looked down and grinned at his standing pride. "Hate that?" he said. "The Lord made that and it's Sunday—praise Him! Tell me what else you know?"

"I was *telling* you the quick of my life. Do you want that or not?"

"You think I need it?"

She looked at all of him. "Yes," she said so he nodded for her to continue and listened. "Mother was asking him his religion. 'Baptist,' he said, 'till I heard about Hell and decided it sounded like more fun than Heaven.' Mother said, 'Hush, you *need* faith now.' He said, 'Lady, I left home at age fourteen and your friend the Lord stayed home when I left—He don't like to travel, that's o.k. with me, but don't ask me to go calling on Him at this late date. I got faith but in just two things—the U.S. dollar (silver if possible) and my two hands.' His hands again."

"What had you learned about him by then?"

"That he didn't care whether he lived or died. Not that he hated himself like some that claw at theirselves for a simple scratch or gouge their red eyes or hawk at their gullet like a bone was stuck. No, he just never touched himself at all, kept his hands at rest some inches from him or if he was standing, just slightly hanging like them and his body were total strangers. But he smiled a lot as I already said, and when Mother said she would bring him a Bible, he said, 'Wooo, no! I don't read dirty stories, lady.' She laughed and said, 'Well, how about Kate here reading *to* you? I can send her up when the dishes are washed.' He looked me over —mess that I was—and agreed to that. So I went to him after a while with the Bible, having washed and dressed, and sat on a stool beyond his cell just out of reach. (He had short arms.) I asked him did he have any special requests, meaning Bible verses, but he stared at me and said 'How old are you?' I said 'Fourteen.' He said, 'Old enough. I request you, Kate.' I didn't pay no attention to that—working round a jail you learn to be deaf—but went on and read my favorite part about Jephthah's daughter. You know that, don't you?"

Milo said, "No, I'm going to Hell too."

"Jephthah was a general that promised the Lord if he won a certain battle, he would sacrifice the first thing that came out to meet him when he got home. So the Lord accepted and he won hands down and rode to his house and who came out?—his only child, a girl about my age (my age then), dancing and beating tambourines. Jephthah tore his clothes and gnashed his teeth and said, 'Alas, my daughter, thou has brought me very low, and thou art one of them that trouble me, for I have opened my mouth unto the Lord and I cannot go back.' You see, I know it by heart since then, but that morning I read it and didn't look up till I got to the end where he gives her two months to roam the hills and mourn her virginity and then cuts her throat and burns her for the Lord, keeping his promise, young as she was—'She knew no man.' But at the end I looked and he was crying—not sobbing out loud, just great tears dropping which he did not lift a finger to wipe. I didn't speak but looked back down and commenced to hunt for a happier passage. They are pretty scarce—in *my* Bible at least—but just as I stumbled on Jacob and Rachel, he said, 'Hold on. What was her name?—the dead girl's name.' I didn't know and turned to see. She didn't have a name so I said, 'Poor girl. She's just been Jephthah's daughter countless ages. Let's you and me name her.' I said it for fun—to ease his pain not to be sacrilegious—and started to reeling off modern girls' names. 'Alice, Carol, Phyllis, Mavis.' He hollered, 'Shut up—woke up the two drunks—and the tears rolled again and this time sobs. I stood up and said I was joking with him, that I didn't know he took the Bible so serious and I turned to go. He looked up—his face all ruined like a child's but he still wouldn't touch it—and begged my pardon and said 'Don't you *know*?' 'Know what?' I said. 'The reason I'm here?' I said, 'I know you've kidnaped something—that's all,' and he broke down again so I really left and left the Bible where he could reach. I have always believed that is how to give, to lay what you're giving in the other one's reach, let him take it or not."

She halted, flickered her moist thighs in Milo's clasp to rouse her blood that had drowsed with his weight. Milo misread her last words, her moving; reached down and upward to accept again, give again their mutual gift. But Kate turned serious eyes back to him, slowly shook her head. "I am offering something different now. Stay still and listen." He nodded, looked down a little embarrassed to show he was hearing but left his one reaching hand in place, a claim postponed, unurged for now.

"So I went to Daddy and asked him the crime. 'Whose?' he said and I didn't know—the boy's name, I mean. Neither did Daddy. The boy wouldn't tell them, and when they searched him, all he had was the two bus tickets and a miniature checkerboard for fun on the road—not a scrap of paper with his name or home. But Daddy knew this much, picked it up talking to various ones—late Saturday night a northbound bus stopped at the station and a man and a child went into the diner. The man bought the child some sweet milk and fried pie but nothing for himself—just sat and watched her eat it like she was magic and would turn it to money or joyful days. I say *her*. The child was a girl about three years old. Then while she was chewing, he excused himself and went to the toilet. Well, the waitress of course had waitress-curiosity and asked the child, 'Is that your Daddy, sugar?' The child kept chewing as calm as a king and said, 'No, just a man that's kidnaping me.' The waitress knew she was pushed for time so she said, 'You sure you know what kidnaping means?' The child said, 'Stealing you while your aunt's asleep.' Then the man walked out of the toilet. Time was up. The bus was loading. Nothing to

do but call the Law—which in that town was mainly
my Daddy, the sheriff being nobody you could rely on.
And Daddy went—introduced himself just as the man
bent down to the child to lift her into the bus before
him, asked to see some identification. He claimed he
didn't have any, and later at the jail when they
searched him, he didn't—had two bus tickets (I never
asked to where) and a dollar and some change. So
Daddy asked his name and he said to Daddy—smiling,
I guess, 'Is that what the world is waiting to know?'
Then he shut up, wouldn't say another word, not even
to hush the child when Daddy commenced to quizzing
her. But all she knew was that yes, she was kidnaped;
the man had told her so; he was being good to her and
she knew his name but couldn't remember. Daddy was
deputy as well as jailer, and in his judgment it all
smelled funny. He said to the man that in view of not
having any name or papers and in view of the awful
wave of crime—the Lindbergh baby was just in the
past—wouldn't they just spend the night in town and
wire back home for identification? The man shook his
head so Daddy had to say, 'I will give you one last
chance, son. What is your true name and where are
you headed?' The man thought awhile and looked
round the little knot of people that had ganged to
listen. Then he looked to the child that was still in his
arms. She was looking at him. He said to her, 'Are you
happy with me?' She didn't speak but nodded so he
said to Daddy, 'I am somebody that wouldn't harm
anything. I am trying to get home with what I love.'
Daddy said, 'Son, I for one hope you make it, that
you've got the right to, but long as this child claims she

is stole, the right ain't yours till you prove it to me.'
The man said, 'I ain't no mathematician. I can't prove
nothing.' Then he set the child down and she stood by
his leg, but he did not touch her or even look down,
not one time again. He said, 'If you are taking me,
what about her?' Daddy didn't have time to worry
about that. The waitress that had called him was
standing by, and she volunteered to keep the child till
news arrived. And the child went to her, not looking
back and the man not watching her go neither till the
instant before she passed from sight. Then he spoke
towards her back—said, 'Meet me. Promise to meet me
please'—but she never turned, never promised nothing,
just *went* like her memory had slammed against
him."

Milo's upright body shuddered suddenly, from his
high chin and neck down through his hot thighs, his
one touching hand. She stopped of course and took his
apologetic grin. "Excuse me," he said and he looked
upward from her to the dim low ceiling, then arched
farther back, searching above them. "Must have been
an angel flying past."

"Or a lonesome ghost walking on your grave." She
smiled a little too.

But Milo was serious. "Don't rush me," he said. "I
am too young to die. I have got the best part of my life
yet to live."

"What part is that?"

He was still looking backwards in search of the
angel. "Being a man, being free to live any way I want,
have a wife and children and give them things—little
things they need, things they don't need or maybe just

live right by myself alone as a rock, no good to nobody, holding back all I have for myself." He rolled his tired head back towards her.

"Too late," she said.

"Too late for what?"

"Holding back. You have give it all already."

"Who to?"

"Well, I can't speak for nobody but me."

"What have I give you that Tom never did?"

"That's what I am trying to tell you, boy."

He closed his eyes, his chin touched his chest, his hands hung loose by his hard damp flanks. "Tell on," he said.

"He stayed with us—in the jail, I mean—for two days, waiting on information. It took two days to find the child's home, but when a Missing Report came in and she fit the description, Daddy and the waitress put her on the bus back south to home, a tag around her neck with her name and destination. I never saw her, being otherwise busy—didn't want to see her. And he never saw her again neither, never asked about her, never mentioned her name no more than if she had powdered to dust when she took that waitress's hand and left him. He talked about other things though—mostly me. He took an interest in me from the start. When I went to see him the second time to take his Sunday dinner, he asked me to sit down and watch him eat—'It'll prove I am human' is what he said. I told him, 'Shoot, everything eats—germs *eat*.' He smiled and said, 'Right, but did you ever hear a germ reciting Scripture?' He handed me the Bible I had left him that morning, open to the Song of Solomon and said 'Hear me.' Then looking at me the way nobody had, way nobody has till an hour ago, he said what he had learned since morning, having used his spare time thinking of me—'Set me as a seal upon thine heart, as a seal upon thine arm: for love is strong as death; jealousy is cruel as the grave: the coals thereof are coals of fire, which hath a most vehement flame.' He stopped a minute then and stared at me, waiting for me to answer somehow, but what do you say to something like that when it comes at you sudden at age fourteen? I was going to say 'I will' that's what but he put out a hand to stop me and smiled and went on reciting, 'We have a little sister and she hath no breasts. What shall we do for our sister in the day when she shall be spoken for?' Then we could both laugh a little—I was forward in my growth as I said, but fourteen is fourteen and I was small here."

She touched her breasts that pooled back full but firm, and Milo said, "They must have got a heap of exercise since then."

She tested his face for meanness, found none. "If acting as teethers for a middle-aged man with false teeth anyhow is your idea of exercise, they have." She brushed them again lightly upwards as if in amends for what they had borne. "*He* never touched them, if you're thinking that—never tried. I have tried to recollect all these years if he ever touched me anywhere —with his hands, I mean—but as much as I wish it, I don't think he did. He wasn't shy. He could love you with his eyes hot as most men could with *two* sets of hands. And he kissed me right straight—that first Sunday evening when I come to collect his supper dishes. I had spent so much of the afternoon with him—hearing him recite and then sitting silent, that three feet between us—that Mother said to just grab his dishes and leave. I tried to do that, asked him to shove them through the little trap-door and tried not to face him as I stooped for the tray, but just as I braced to stand, he spoke—he never whispered, never thought about fear. 'Look here,' he said. I looked. Oh tears were standing again in his eyes—his eyes were blue. I knew right then, if I ever doubted, that he had not been stealing that child, not meaning her harm noway, nohow so I said—I whispered—'I know what happened at the bus last night, and I know where the waitress lives that's got the child. I'll go and see about her or take her a message—what shall I say?' He said, 'Don't move. Don't speak of her again. She was never mine. I been sitting here all afternoon forgetting her.' I could see by his eyes how true *that* was—talk about a seal set on his *heart*; his heart and eyes were coals of fire. But then he shook himself like a boy out of swimming and stood his full height—I was still stooped above his supper tray. 'Stand up,' he said. 'How come?' I said. 'Because you are no good to me down there.' I said, 'Am I any good to you anywhere?' 'You will be,' he said. 'How?' I said. 'The first step is for you to stand up,' he said. So I stood up—I have met two people you could not disobey. 'Now come forward to me.' I stepped forward to him and he kissed me then."

Milo had leaned to her through that last. Now he plugged her mouth with a kiss of his own—a sudden hard attempt to become her dream, her pitiful past. He thrust into her, past teeth toward her gorge, and she let him go but did not meet him nor welcome him so he rose and rested halfway above her, propped on his arms.

"Thank you," she said, but she looked to the wall and brushed her lips with a cleansing hand. "Of course I didn't think of nothing but that—that three or four seconds—the whole next day, sitting in school. I would keep my hand to my lips when I could to hide any sign that might be there, any permanent seal. Oh I know there was nothing—not outward nohow. The boys still joked me at recess and lunch, but what I knew, they would not know for years if ever, ever—that something can rise up in your life where nothing stood before and be a burning angel, that awful, that grand, gutting you like a dry cotton gin with the fire he makes, the fire he is. I don't mean angels in Sunday school pictures with lace on their pants, humming *Silent Night*. I know the Bible—they got flaming swords and will wrestle you all night to change your name. I don't know much but I know an angel when I see one. I have seen two"—she waited a moment but did not look up. "The first one— the one I am telling about—changed my life at least if not my name. (Rob changed that. It's all he's changed.) I went home from school that afternoon and crept past Mother upstairs to him. It was Monday, the day Daddy got word about the child and the man's name, but I didn't know that. He did—Daddy had told him already, that the child was headed home alone and that he would sit with us till a State man came to escort him down to face what he'd done, most likely tomorrow. So he knew the time was short if I didn't, and the first thing he said when I walked up to him, right up to the bars (I was still afraid, sure, but if he meant me harm, well, harm it must be)—he said, 'I told you last night you could be some good to me, and you took the first step.' I nodded to that and he said 'Well?—' and waited, not smiling. So I said, 'What is the second step?' He said, 'For you to get your Daddy's keys.' I said 'No' to that automatically, having lived in jails all my life where escape is the main terror you have. But he wasn't mad. He just explained—'I never meant *escape* for a minute. I mean that, Kate'—he pointed to the narrow cot in his corner. 'I mean you to come up here to me when they are asleep.' 'What for?' I said. I knew the first half of what he meant, but what I needed to know was why—why me, why now, why here and what lay beyond me when he was gone? Well, think over all the reasons he could give, the reasons any other hot boy would have given, the lies that he might believe were true—and I've had thirteen years to think —and you won't never come across *his* reason. 'I want to get me a child,' he said—'Soon.' I thought a whole minute, then I said 'Am I old enough?' He nodded and then said, 'Go on downstairs now and do your studying so your Mama and Daddy don't get suspicious, and when you bring my supper, don't even speak, but when they are sleep, get the key and I'll be here.' I nodded and left and was in sight of mother before I knew he had still never touched me except our lips. I had an hour to think before supper. Daddy was asleep on the big divan, but he had told Mother the news about the man and the child, and she told me though she had forgot the man's name already—I still hadn't asked, thinking I had no rights over him. So I thought that through and decided this—right then while Daddy was nodding in the front room, I'd get his extra cell key from his desk, and when I took the man his supper, I would hide that key in his folded napkin and leave like he said before he found it. Then I would not go to him in the night but would wait till sunup and go to him then. I figured it this way—if he was just lying to me to escape or just to take my first love and run, then I would give him his freedom direct, not make him use me to tell his lie. And I did it all—barely looked at him when I shoved the tray in, the key in the napkin—and when I came down I asked Mother would she please collect the dishes as I had extra studying to do. Then I went to my room—I had that much, a room to myself —and I stretched stiff on my back and waited. All night long, not shutting an eye though I cut off the lights—I can think in the dark. I seined every sound from the air like minnows—Mother and Daddy undressing for bed and the sheriff of course roaring up an hour later with a Negro drunk that I thought would ruin any future I had, but after a while the Negro's rich brother came in and bailed him out, and then there was nothing but my Mother's breathing—her lungs were half-eat-up already but we didn't know it. Mother's poor breathing and my heart that swole in my chest like a child, planted already and growing furiously to beat the daybreak. I would try to ease it and soothe time away by saying in my head over and over, 'Nobody ever asked you for nothing that they really needed, could not live without, and may never ask you again in your life. You are giving something you never knew you had, a precious gift to ease his pain.' I said it till I three-fourths believed it and day was creeping at the edge of my window. Then I stood up and went in my bare feet, my long nightgown to take his gift and begin my own. Well, he was gone—oh gone ten minutes, his bed was still warm as my hot hand and all that was left was my Bible open to the page he had learned and this message wrote with a dull pale pencil. '*I have laid here and watched for you all night and now it is day. Why have you failed me that needs you now and will need you always and carry your face on my heart like a seal to the waiting grave?—Tom.*' He had signed it. That was his name, all of it I knew." She halted, face still turned to the wall, eyes unseeing.

Her voice had held firm and clear to the end but Milo almost whispered now. "When did they bring him back?"

"Never."

"Where did they take him?"

"They never touched him no more than I did, never laid eye on him again no more than if he had *been* that angel and gone to God."

"Or a ghost to start with," Milo said. They both shuddered involuntarily, both looked up in sudden panic to the ceiling that shrank back from them as though the room were quickly flooding with unseen life. But the moment passed—threat or blessing unfulfilled. She and Milo could face each other, spared, relieved, a little abandoned and Milo could speak. "So you have waited all this time."

It was not a question but she began to answer. "Not *all* the time. Twice I give up and slashed my veins—the first time, the morning I found his note. But I lived and thought I was saved for a purpose so I waited again. Of course Daddy had to get a new jail—I had ruined him in Gaffney—and we came here and I waited here, not thinking at first that Tom would never find me if he came back to claim what I was saving. When I realized that—that my roots were cut, the one last thread that strung me to Tom: my sorry address, the Gaffney jail—well, I slashed again. And I mean *slashed*. I really tried, not like a movie star that takes a cold butter knife and strokes the bony heel of her hand where blood don't run. That was before blood plasma was invented, and I had the rarest blood type known. Nobody else in Warrenton had it but Rob Pomeroy, and he donated it arm to arm while I was fading—the only thing he ever got in me far enough to matter, but it seemed to give him rights over me so when I lived and he began hanging round me like a wet spell, I looked up and smiled—out of pity pure as mother's milk, and when his Mother died (that had stunted his life) and he come to me the night of her death and said 'Kate, I need you'—I went to him." Kate looked to Milo, studied him till he broke beneath her gaze, leaned to bury his face in the trough of her chest. Then she laid one hand into his hair, pressed him deeper. "How could I know you would come again? Who was I to earn God's notice like that?"

He accepted the force of her hand for a while, exactly as long as his breath held out. Then he surfaced for air, turned aside to speak. "And all that is true?" He could feel the affirming nod of her chin in the crown of his skull so again he whispered—"Then what must I do with what I know, with who I am?"

Kate said, "I couldn't tell you that. I may look old enough to be your Mother but I'm just twenty-seven. What can you learn in twenty-seven years?"

He said "I asked *you*" and rose from beneath her heavy hand to sit again in the natural seat of her hardly used body.

"You can learn to recognize the Lord when He comes—or any messenger He may send."

"But what if you are the messenger boy?" He grinned, downwards.

She did not accept his grin nor reflect it. "You can know what message you are bearing, can't you?—not stump in the dark when light would do, when you're *built* out of light?"

The doorbell rang above their heads (Rooster's alarm), and Milo's body showed its own alarm—face flushed, legs tensed, trunk rose from Kate to stand or run, it did not know which. But Kate lay calm, staring back and up at the bell. "It ain't nobody that can harm us worse than we've harmed each other." She looked to Milo. "Climb off please. Let me answer my door."

Milo held in place. "Wait. What does *that* mean? —we have harmed each other? You are changing tunes like a fast piccolo."

"It means whatever time makes it mean." She sat to the side of the ruined bed, then stood naked facing him a final moment, then stooped for her robe, fumbled it on, smiling as she turned toward the open door. "It mainly means I have looked my life in the eye this afternoon—my sorry life—and seen it was happy, very nearly happy. Won't it happy to you?"

Milo nodded, smiled—not to mean Yes or No nor to lie but to speak when spoken to, a lesson he had learned the day he could talk.

Before his smile faded Kate said, "That is the harm—that I never knew till now: all that time I was nearly happy." Then she was gone, leaving "Thank you" behind on the door sill, firm—but nothing else, neither "Leave" nor "Wait."

So he stood to the floor and at once felt the downward weight of his groin. He looked to the tan squab wobbling there. "Thank *you*, old son. You deserve the prize but the day isn't done. Honors come at sundown. Don't fail me yet." Then he looked round the room for signs of his clothes, knew Kate had left them to dry in the kitchen and tipped to the open door to listen—Kate's voice, faint, and an answering man. Milo slowly peeped out towards the sounds, and there on the front porch ten yards away was Kate and a strange young man with a camera, Kate pointing behind her towards the bedroom and Milo, saying, "Still there is one job you could do so as not to waste your day entirely. Private job. Take a boy's picture that's in yonder now."

Milo did not pause for fear or understanding. Bare as at birth he crossed the dark hall in one silent step to the opposite kitchen, went straight for the oven door ajar and was in his warm clothes and out the back before Kate and her new man had touched the front screen, even into high weeds beside the house and crouching there before he realized three things: that the man was from the *Warren Record* and had gone to the woods to photograph the hunt but had not found

Rooster, that Kate did not even know half his name and that his feet were bare—shoes where he dropped them by Rooster's easy chair.

Through the open windows of the living room, Kate's voice came. "Wait here please sir. I'll see if he's awake. He's my husband's cousin, fifteen years old. Boys like to sleep but he'll be glad—his mother'll be glad, Rob'll be glad—to have his picture. Rob loves him like a son, having none of his own."

The sound of that raised Milo from the weeds to stand for a moment entirely visible while his face and hands worked with the upward rush of desire—to walk to the house again (barefoot, ruined), stand for the picture, say a decent goodbye, leave his name, *say* her name (he had not said it). But what could she ever do with that? Worst of all, how could poor Rooster use it? —a picture of him and the story the photographer would strow like stink over what would be plain (his face like a mirror with a memory, his hands still rank)? Nothing. No use. This much was ended.

He ran for the car and had it rolling silent downhill when Kate walked back to the man and said, "Never mind. Excuse me. He's gone, looks like," and the man left too and Kate saw him out and stood awhile on the bright porch steps—still bright at six— not looking either way, not searching, not waiting, as straight and unshaken as if truly healed, unharmed within while fraction by fraction with perfect aim Milo's white seed (his shape, his life) flailed upward against the pull of earth toward her ready womb.

*   *   *

Milo thought of Kate—his mind a quick knot of remembered pleasure, astounded pride, shame for himself and her before Rooster and the radiance of someone who gives his gifts as clouds give rain—till he came to the road at the bottom of her hill, cranked the engine, turned right towards the hunt, shook his head at the thinning houses of town and spoke aloud to the empty car, "What in the world did I ever give anybody but trouble?" No answer came but the gnash of the engine, dry steel on steel as though oil never was. So he spoke to the start of the cool air and woods—green shade, failing sun. "Thank you, Lord—I've got a mind that drains. It's what saves my life, with all I see." And then it drained in a silent rush, in a tenth of a mile like a tank unplugged. Then it plugged again and began to fill, dim thought on thought, expectation and desire— saving his lost brother, penning the snake, redeeming his face before Rooster and Macey and filling Lois like a trunk with treasure in the oncoming night brim with his proved skill, his undreamt prowess, garlanded prow.

The old car bore him like wings through that, and then as he turned to the dirt side road that flanked the woods before the old Ryden place, while his mind was with Lois, a tire blew beneath him, the car slewed right toward a shallow gully, humped twenty yards over bone-dry trash before he could stop it, look and speak again—"Damn if it ain't night." In the pine-walled road it was nearly night—"Too soon for early October," he thought and leaned to the sky to explain the dark, saw clouds ganging for a storm, leapt out, kicked the right front tire and walked to the car trunk, praying for a spare. It was there, ready, and Milo said again,

"Lord, You are fighting on my side today," and bent to the trunk to look for tools as thunder slammed on him from the thickening sky. "*Easy*," he said—to the sky, the Lord—"I am bare as a baby. Let me fix this tire please before You start."

Among Rooster's mess he found all the tools he needed but a lug wrench. He rocked on his heels, said "Damn" again but felt no despair though he knew this road was empty for the night, not a chance in a thousand of a helping car. Still he scotched the back wheels and took the jack round and on nothing but faith, bent to the strain of jacking the right front— mind drained again, so empty of worry that he paused in mid-job and said to himself, "You ought to been a Nigger, Milo—little as you care. Well, *God* takes care, don't You, God?"

He looked up from hunching above the front bumper and stared a dark man in the dark eyes, close. "Wooo," Milo said. "I was praying for help. You're the fastest answer to prayer I've had." He did not stand but squatted fully and looked to the new man to see all he could—white, middle-sized, in baggy clothes, no luggage in sight, hands hid behind him.

The man said "Am I?" His voice was from Afton, from home anyhow.

"The Lord didn't send me a lug wrench, did He?" Milo smiled but could not see if the man's face replied.

But the man's right hand came out and extended a thin bar of iron. "This help you?" he said.

Milo took it, examined it by eager touch till he found the lug hole, the chisel end. "Well, I didn't know Daniel Boone carved lug wrenches—this ain't the latest model but yes sir, it'll do. I'm much obliged." The man did not speak, stood with empty right hand on his hip. Milo said, "Would you reach in the car please and switch on the lights? Battery's low but these clouds are swarming. I can't see nothing."

The man took a backward step as to obey, then halted, tried to speak but stammered like someone rusty for talk. What he finally said was, "Would this help you any?" and his left hand showed with a small glass lantern which he stooped and lit and held to Milo before the swelling flame could show his own face.

Milo took it, raised the wick, set it by him in the dirt, laughed and said "Whew, don't kerosene stink?"

The man said "Yes."

Milo took his jack handle—"Don't get me wrong. I'm grateful to you"—gave the wheel three more hoists, then moved his lantern round and began with the wrench. He worked with clenched intensity for a minute or two, not thinking of the man nor of courtesy. So at last he said, "You say you live around here?" No answer, no sound. Milo's head rose to see. Where the man had been was just night air. Milo stood, walked round, looked behind the truck—nothing. Then he walked to the midst of the road, looked ahead. Fifty yards ahead a man—his man surely—was walking in the gully on the Ryden side, right arm out like a rudder, a wing, gently slapping the saplings it could reach. Milo thought, "Go then if you're in such a rush." Yet the man walked slowly as if slowly knowing he was lost or abandoned. So Milo spoke in his natural voice, knowing sound would carry on the loaded air—

"Mister, I thought you were helping *me*."

The man stopped, half-turned, waited awhile, then came back to Milo a little faster than he left, stopping five feet away, partially smiling in the lantern light but mainly puzzled. "I'll help you," he said. "Any way I can. I am just heading home. No rush about that."

Milo said, "Well, good. Keep me company a minute and I'll ride you home. Anyhow you went off and left your stuff—your wrench and your light. Don't never leave a light, hard as they are to find." The man went on half-smiling and nodded.

Milo, having nothing else to say, returned to his wheel. The man followed round to hold the lantern though that was not needed, and Milo worked so hard and fast that he had only one thought, a saying of Papa's—"Everybody's crazy as they can be. Carry a knife and take pity when you can." Then the tire was on, he could lower the jack, hand the man his wrench and say, "You saved my life. Tell me where you're headed and I'll take you to the door."

The man pointed forward the way he had walked, again tried to speak, failed, took a new tack—handed Milo the wrench, said, "You'll need that again before I do."

Milo thanked him, went round to load the tools and bad tire, and when he returned the man had killed the lantern flame and stood in the same spot, staring at Milo, straining to speak. Milo spoke for him—"You look awful tired."

The man nodded rapidly. "You hit it," he said. "You hit it on the *head*," and soft laughing started, stopped in midair, cut down. "I am lost," he said.

"I figured you were. What you trying to find?"

"My home," he said.

"Who are you?"

The man began to laugh again. "That's what I've got to remember first, ain't it?"

Milo said, "It would be a big help." The man only nodded and Milo thought, "I could spend all night with this simple soul" so he said, "I tell you—my own brother's lost somewhere in these woods with a mad dog and a twenty-foot snake and a whole posse's hunting him and I'm late to meet them. Looks like to me the best thing for you is to stroll up this road—if this is your road—till you get your bearings. There's landmarks all up and down, thick as thieves." He took two steps towards the door of the car. "I thank you again and good luck to you." He reached for the handle.

The man didn't move but he struggled to speak. Milo had the door open and was on the running board when clear words came. "You ain't going to leave me now, are you, boy?"

Milo thought, "Let me turn on the lights and see this fool," and he reached for the switch, then thought of Rooster's weak battery and said aloud, "No. But listen, my main duty's to my *own* that's lost. All I can do now is take you with me and maybe you'll find what you're looking for—you know, hunt for birds and you may catch a bear."

"Thank you," the man said and moved for the passenger door, climbed in. Milo slammed his own door, cranked the engine (saying "Lord, let it start"), and they rose from the ditch and drove in darkness twenty-five yards till he lit the lights. From the moment they rolled, he could feel the man's stare on his right profile, and now he turned to meet the gaze, study the stranger. But the dashboard lights of the car were dead, and the man was darker than before.

So Milo did not speak but faced the road and watched what he could—black trees, dead weeds, a scuttling possum—thinking, "Friend, you won't find home by staring at me, won't find nothing in me but my dinner and that's fading fast." It was the first thought of food he had had, and testing his stomach he knew he was starved, thought, "How come Mrs. Pomeroy didn't offer me something?—all that work I did for her—and how am I going to do justice on Lois, weak as a wormy pauper in winter?"

The man said "Stop"—plea not order—and Milo stopped as soon as he could with the brakes he had, their rear end slinging round in the dust like a scrap yard behind. But the man didn't move, only stared on at Milo.

Milo said, "Cap'n, you're full of surprises."

"I'm not but a private," the man said and laughed.

"Well, Private, you recognize where we are?—do, you must have radar, dark as it is." Then Milo strained out through his open window to take his bearings. "Damn," he said, "if I won't lost too. This is where I'm going." He drew in and drove them to the ditch again.

"Where is it?" the man said.

"The old Ryden woods. House is in yonder somewhere. Now we got to find it and a storm coming on." Thunder had gone on griping above them. Milo opened his door, slid quickly to the ground but the man didn't move. Milo said, "Come on and bring your lantern." The man still faced him but did not move. "It was *you* yelled 'Stop.' "

The man said, "I did but I don't know why."

"Well, I can't stand here and answer riddles. Light that light and I'll lead you *somewhere*."

For his own reason the man slid across and used Milo's door, stooped to set down his lantern, fished for matches and bent to obey. As the wooden match bloomed in his hand, he looked up. He said "Who are you?"

"That's one thing I know. I'm Milo the meanest Mustian alive, and whoever you *were*, you're going to be ashes—look at your match."

The match had burned to the man's clasping fingers, lapped at them like a lover's tongue, but the man only studied the flame, then smiled, carried it on to the lantern wick and held the smile as he rose facing Milo—"Lead," he said.

"That's my name—Kindly Light." Milo took the lantern, led off toward trees dark as any grave.

But he was not the guide he promised to be, and within five minutes he thought "I am lost." The path had stopped at a low wall of vines, and now all his lantern showed was thicket—rusty briars, oiled poison oak and deep dry pine straw underfoot as a treacherous mat over holes, sharp rocks (and his feet bare). Still he did not pause, only slowed a little. The man slowed behind him, three steps back. And he went that way not scared but angry till his right foot sank to the ankle in a hole and he lurched forward and the lantern fell. His first thought was of his ankle not fire so he sat and rubbed his foot.

But the man came up, passed him, reached for the lantern, held it above him and looked ahead, his back to Milo and Milo's foot. Then he said "You are lost."

Milo said, "That makes two and one is a cripple."

But the man still showed no concern for Milo. He started ahead and had taken three steps before Milo could recover to speak. "Now who's leaving who?"

The man stopped, turned, raised the lantern enough to show he was smiling. "I am not lost now," he said. "Come on."

Milo stood, hobbled after him to stay with the light, and the man wasn't lost, not if the Ryden place was his goal. In less than three minutes he broke through a final tangle into what clearing remained and stopped on the edge. Milo came up beside him and the man held the lantern out far as he could reach, his straight arm trembling as the feeble light crept to the empty house—broken windows, open door. Not looking to Milo he said "They are sleep."

Milo said "They are dead."

"Dead?" he said. "Who were they? Who am I?" He turned on Milo, exposed his own face to the lantern now, wrenched by mystery, the fear of loss.

Milo stood his ground two feet from the face, studied it slowly. "You're a middle-sized fellow in your early thirties in war surplus clothes with red hair, blue eyes; and if this was your home, you're bound to be a

Ryden unless you're an owl or bat or snake. Nothing but Rydens ever lived here till two years ago, then Miss Jack died and the wildlife arrived."

The man turned and moved through the clearing toward the house, stopped a little way short of the steps, did not turn round but said "*Dead*, you say?"

Milo took a step forward, his ankle well now. "Dead—but you ain't alone. There's one Ryden left— Hawkins is hunting these woods tonight; you may see him yet—and *I'm* your cousin. That is if you're sure you're this bunch of Rydens. Miss Jack didn't have but one boy to my knowledge." The man went on to the steps, climbed them, still did not face round though Milo continued, "Of course there are things in the world I don't know."

The man pushed the half-open door fully open, stood on the sill, held his lantern inward. The warm shine lit the front-room windows, and Milo shuddered once against his will. The man said, "Where is her boy living now?"

"He is—" Milo halted, then walked to the foot of the steps himself. The man would not turn so he told it to his back. "I'm sorry to be the one to tell you, but I am your kin and that's better than a stranger—he is six feet under the peaceful ground in the South Pacific. Guam, I guess."

The man never flinched and his arm outstretched with the heavy lantern hung like steel on the air. At last he spoke. "Now tell me his name."

"Tom," Milo said, "—for Thomas, I guess."

The man thought awhile, then shook his head (the general sign for No) and stepped to the center of the bare front room—picked by Hawkins of all that would move or bring ten cents at a rummage sale. He set down the lantern in thick white dust, but his head shook on as he stood and faced the next dark door, to the bedrooms, kitchen.

Milo had followed to the front-door sill and spoke to answer the man's apparent No. "It was Tom all right. I know that much. Papa and Mrs. Provo were speaking of him yesterday."

"Who are they?"

"Jasper Mustian my Granddaddy and Mrs. Selma Provo that's in Warrenton at the fair with her niece and a snake show. Tom was a favorite of Papa's—Papa said—till he run away from home when he was a boy, and Mrs. Provo met him down in Florida. He got there somehow and roomed with her, left owing money though I think she said he give her the snake we are hunting tonight. It's her niece I am mainly waiting for here—she's older than me by several months (I am nearly sixteen; well, nearer than *fifteen*), but that didn't matter to her night before last. She bent to my need like a baby willow—"

The man threw himself on Milo like a train—that huge and black—and when they hit the floor, a pine board split. That was the only sound for a while. They struggled in total silence, Milo losing—the man's hands (he seemed to grow dozens in the dark) like pig-iron bands on Milo's wrists, knees, ankles, neck. Then Milo began to suck breath loudly and above his fear, he managed one thought—"This fool ain't breathing"— and for all the rolling and force of his body, the man breathed no harder than a sleeping child. But he made a large error—he rolled Milo in his grip to one side and Milo freed a hand, grabbed the man's butt—desperate —and found his last hope, the wrench still there. So with final power he clubbed the man's head behind the ear. The man said "No," rolled limp, and Milo rode him—vaulted in an instant to straddle his chest, pin arms with his knees, clamp his wrists to the floor.

Before he could think, Milo saw the man's face— prone beneath him, the lantern light stroked it—and though Milo spent no time around mirrors he knew his own face: it was there on the man, himself asleep, only red-headed, older. So he tensed his pressure on the man's pinned arms and risked one hand to shake the man's chin, saying softly as he shook, "Why must you mistreat your kin-people, sir? They are all you got and you're close kin to me. Look at me now and see yourself." That last he whispered in the man's nearest ear, then sat back and watched him swim up from sleep.

The man said, "How come you didn't kill me?"

"I tried," Milo said. "How come you won't die?" But because the man remained limp beneath him, accepting his victory, Milo smiled down at him. "You were just confused from your long trip, won't you?— thinking clearer now?"

The man waited to answer that, testing for clearness, and though he showed no trace of resistance, Milo's grip never slacked as he started. "All I know is this and I give it to you to beg your pardon. I have got no memory past an hour ago. I was just walking down that road and found you—"

"I never *passed* you," Milo said.

"I can't explain that."

Milo thought a moment, then said, "I can. You
ever listen to the radio?" The man seemed to hear but
did not answer. "If you listen you've heard of amnesia.
Everybody's got amnesia on the radio (grope around
for years not knowing their names; feeling for home,
kin, recognition; would give their leg for just a piece of
paper with their three *initials* much less their name).
That's all you've got—a little amnesia. Relax, ride it
out. It'll pass in a flash one day and you'll know."

The man's voice rushed in—"Don't confuse me.
Let me say what little I *do* know. I was walking in the
middle of that dirt road, and if I had a goal or plan, I
never knew its name, but it won't worrying me till I
found you in trouble and you started the questions.

"How come you had a wrench and a light?"

"That's the least of my worries, I tell you—maybe
I'm just some helpful somebody that patrols the roads.
No, what worries me now is *not* worrying then—but
moving down the road as natural as if I had made it
myself. I was headed *home* and if you hadn't stopped
me I'd have been there now."

"*You* brought *me* here—remember that?—and I
didn't cause Miss Jack to die nor Hawkins to sell her
stuff to Niggers."

The man said "Please" and Milo stopped. They
were silent awhile, the sky growled on beyond the
porch, storm nearer now. The man finally said, "I am
here anyhow and all I know—I don't *know*, I *feel*—is
I'm waiting for somebody."

"Who isn't?" Milo said. "*I* am."

The man said "Who?"

"I told you once. That's when you come at me."

The man said, "Excuse me. You were crowding me, throwing all them people at me that may be my own flesh and blood, maybe not."

"Well, the girl I'm expecting isn't no flesh of yours whoever you are—won't be none of *mine* after tonight. The fair she travels with is gone already. Her and her aunt are just waiting on Death—the snake's named Death—so I got to give her what I got tonight or bid her goodbye empty-handed in the morning."

"What you got to give?"

"I'll put it this way—Milo (that's me) is riding you now cause you acted so wild, but when the three posses meet here like they should and the hunt is over, Milo aims to sit a better saddle."

"That's what you call giving?"

"What else could I give but my red blood to dying men?—and the war is over."

"And the name?" the man said.

Milo said "What name?"

"Your riding saddle."

"Lois," Milo said, "—an orphan like me (my Daddy's dead), like you too, ain't she?"

The man thought, then looked backward at the lantern and went so still in every nerve that Milo felt the further peace and let his own grip ease a little. When the man turned to him again from the light, the face that had been so grieved and torn seemed smoothed from within like calming water. But he did not smile. He said to Milo, "When will she get here?"

"I was wondering that myself—worrying some.

She is hunting with Papa, and all I know is they left a note saying meet here at sundown." Milo's hands left the man's wrists, and he looked round at door and windows to check for surviving traces of day. There were none, not within that thatch of trees and a storm sky yearning like a bride for lightning. Lightning flashed. Thunder answered terrifically. Milo looked on out as the first loud raindrops thunked the tin roof and not turning back, said, "I ought to go find her and find my brother and lead them here. This is going to be hard." He had meant the storm—which crashed in now —but harder than the rain was the blow on his head from the lug wrench gripped in the man's free hands.

What came after, came in two places—in the room itself (bare of all but prone Milo and the kneeling man) and behind shut eyes in Milo's bloody head, a sleeping vision. When he had slumped to his side from the blow and his wet wound glistened even in the dark, the man knelt above him, dabbed in his blood as though blood were money—that rare at least—then rolled him to his stomach to spare his head, decently arranged his arms and legs, rocked back to study—and studied him for what to a living man would have been five minutes (time unmeasured being ghastly, mute as trees that crash in empty woods). Then the man spoke —"Dead. All my life I have meant to kill a man and have been on the lip of killing many—for money, liquor, women, my name—and was always stopped by God or the Law or just going to sleep, and now I've killed my own blood cousin." He wiped the drying

wrench on his palm, smelled at the brown blood, tasted
it at last with a slow dry tongue. "I am sorry," he said,
"but I've sent you to Heaven as pure as this rain"—the
rain was torrents—"by keeping you off of my Lois
tonight. Surely the Lord will grant me pardon for
killing my cousin to save my child that I have not seen
in countless years but is set like a seal"—he scoured his
heart—"and when I have come, been *sent* to bless her,
to ease her life with the gift I have, to give her good for
all my wrong?" He was now on his knees, but he stood
looking up, head thrust into dark near the sounding
roof—"Am I pardoned or not?" No answer came. "Am
I *sent* at last to give my gift or must I still roam?"

There was an answer, not in words nor at once, but
as the wick of the lantern dried and the white flame
struggled, giving less light—none—then a new light as
slowly swelled in the room, in Milo's vision. It seeped
at first, then flowed, then streamed from the man who
stood rock-still till the room was as clear with his light
as with day, till the light became warmth, sealed Milo's
wound—became heat, became fire—consumed the
man's feet, hands, face where he stood, till he no longer
stood, neither man nor ghost but a messenger hung in
astonished air, then sent to its work.

Yet it left through the door (not the walls as it
might), and its infinite progress over porch, down steps
calmed the rain to mist so that Milo, drawn from the
floor by light, followed stunned but awake in hot dry
air as it moved ahead seeing him no more, knowing
him no more than hawks know their young years after
birth, than light knows the air it rides to earth.

It entered—or assumed into itself—Miss Jack's

garden privy. Then the sound came out of dry wood raised on a rusty hinge, and the light began fading—so suddenly that Milo halted five yards away, still having power to consider his safety. Then the light was gone except a blue haze (more heat than light) that clung to the rotten privy boards—as guard or beacon Milo did not know, but he moved on through the black air towards it, right hand blindly extended for its gift till he stood in the privy no larger than a grave (but darker now) and said above the stink half-tamed by age, "I have got your message. Rest easy now. I will bear her whatever gift you send, not touch it myself and will guard it from others. Rest easy now. You have come too far." No answer came. No gift appeared. Even the blue haze had leeched from the wood. His head rolled back to look above.

Death fell on him from the unseen ceiling—at once sank its teeth in the meat of his shoulder, a hundred teeth so delicately used that he did not feel them. But he felt its weight like a dry landslide flinging him to the dirt, its instant first coil whipped round his trunk, both arms inside, then even as he rolled and struggled to his legs to hold his own, stave off a second coil, constriction began in the first coil, gently. And steadily with each breath he sucked, the coil embraced, gained final ground. His hands could not even rise to claw it and thrashing only consumed his scarce wind so he thought, "I will use my final breath." What he yelled was *"Tom"*—to his own surprise but not to the snake's; its aim never faltered and before the cry had left the privy, it had thrown its second coil by the first, the gradual rhythm of death unpausing. Milo could think but he could not speak—mouth gaped open on empty lungs—and his thoughts were rapidly addled by poisons (the trapped wastes of his own suffocation), but he managed this much: "I commenced this hunt with a prayer to be worthy of whatever I found, and I've *found* things—my first drink of liquor, a nice crazy lady that cooled my burning, a spirit returned and a monstrous python strangling me now. Was I worthy of so much in one short day? If not—and I don't have time to decide—I'm sorry and I beg Your pardon, Lord. Take me on now to some better place than a garden-house floor and I'll try to improve. Or considering these unusual events, if You manage one more and release me now from the jaws of Death, I promise You this—" He paused to consider (not wanting even now to commit himself to what he couldn't keep) and found this much he could safely risk—"I will never forget the stuff I have seen and learned today, and if I ever have occasion to use it, I'll use it as free as water in spring." He meant that to be his last thought if not words, but in the last conscious moment he had, a question came—"What *have* I learned and what use *could* I be if this won't the end, my day won't done?" Then through the roaring of death in his ears, he seemed to hear as if whole states away, high frantic barking from dogs, seemed to see clusters of light above him, hear a rifle fire.

The coils relaxed, air found its own way into Milo's chest, his blood gathered speed and vision swam wildly back to his eyes, hearing to his ears. The first sight—lit from flashlights above—was Lois knelt above him, hair and clothes soaked but eyes dry as sand, with one hand prising Death's teeth from his shoulder, laying the plugged head gently to earth but not looking at it, only watching him. And he watched her, not alive enough to smile, but the first sound (above the dogs) was Rooster. "What have you done to deserve this, son?" And other voices clattered near, stunned, disbelieving.

So Milo strained to read their faces—above him in the privy, packed close as wet weeds was the sheriff, Hawkins Ryden, Papa and Lois (all the rest were huddled at the door, all but Mr. Capps who was chasing his hounds scared by the snake at the end of their trail), and every face but Lois's was blank amazement, all staring at his body down from his head. He tried to lift up and see what they saw, but his strength was still out. Then he tested and found he could speak, softly. "Hadn't you seen boa constrictors before?—little old buggers, ain't poisonous." (It was still around him, still woven round the privy like Christmas garland.)

Lois smiled down. "That isn't no boa constrictor. That's a python."

Now he could smile. "I'll remember that."

Papa bent from the waist with no sign of pain—something he had not done in Milo's lifetime. "Son" —he was using his careful voice to prevent bad news— "what have you done?"

In his gratitude Milo almost told them—his lips were parted, he was drawing wind to say, "Rode Rooster's wife till she hollered 'Quit!'"

But Lois herself had looked down by then, seen what the others saw and with her strong hand she lifted his head, said "Look," pointed to his legs in Death's loose grip.

He was buried from thighs to ankles in money, new green dollar bills crisp as beech leaves in fall and drifted as thickly. He cast his eyes up where Rooster's light probed the privy ceiling, and there in the eaves where Tom had vanished (or what Tom became), where Death had waited was a cardboard box on its side, lid open, a few last dollars still waving on the edge.

Lois said, "Where are we and whose is this?" She pointed again but would not touch the money.

Milo moved his head in her hand, towards her. "We are in your rightful home and this is yours." He also tried to point to the money, but his arms were still pinned.

Lois said, "Is it yours to give?"

He said, "It was yours to start with, Lois. I am just passing it on for a friend."

Rooster—nor nobody else—understood them. All he knew to ask was "How much is it?"

Hawkins Ryden horned himself in (a swollen foot in a narrow boot), took one look and said, "I estimate it's ten thousand dollars. If it is, it's the insurance Aunt Jack got for Tommy dying—claimed she never got it, but we knew she had and was too mean to say so, knew it was hid and I've looked under every damn board in that house. Well, here it is and it's every cent mine." He squatted to snatch the first fistful.

Milo kicked up a leg and struck Hawkins in the chest. "Never," he said. "It's *hers*, I told you."

Papa said, "Beg Hawkins' pardon, son. And get

up out of that snake and go home. You are talking like a fool because you ain't eat supper."

Rooster said, "*That's* it. I knew I wasn't myself someway. Let's all go eat." Hawkins by now had torn off his shirt, squatted bare to the waist and was knotting the sleeves. Rooster said, "You going swimming before supper, Mr. Ryden?"

"I'm making a sack for my money," Hawkins said. "I am Miss Jack's nearest living kin, and like I said I paid for every crumb she ate for years, and she ate a many a crumb."

Lois had worked through that, not listened— Death's jaws free and Milo raised a little in her arm, she unwound the first coil, faded already of its grand bronze fire (its beauty was its life) and set loose Milo's upper body.

He rose with it now like a steel trap sprung, sat rigid with anger. "Didn't nobody hear what I just said?" he said.

Nobody answered till Macey unseen in the huddle outside yelled "Yes, you are heard."

"Then what must I do to make you believe me?" He was speaking to all the visible faces.

But again Macey answered—"Try telling the truth."

So he looked for Macey to tell it to him—he had asked, no one else—but his look was balked in a thicket of legs. He said "Macey, step here."

Macey's face bloomed between Papa and the sheriff—knee-level to them, eye to eye with Milo and not so much as glancing at the useless snake nor grinning at the girl who cradled his friend but interested only in smiling for Milo to greet him back from his mighty match.

Milo's mouth opened but his mind thought this, "How can I say to a face like that, simple and faithful as a white dinner plate, that the truth I bear was given like it was? It would break his heart—missing out on that." So he said, "Macey, gather this money up for Lois."

Macey's hand went out like a trained bird dog, took a handful. Hawkins closed on his wrist, shut the bloodstream down.

Milo calmly said "Sheriff, help Macey please."

Nobody moved. All stood frozen by Milo's fate— he had lost his mind in his quick ordeal. All but Macey. His fingers spidered in Hawkins' grip, securing his bills.

Milo said, "Sheriff, listen. If I'm not right how come I am *here* and how come three separate posses turned up at the final moment?—because you were *led* to hear what I know. This money is hers, the house, the land—and this stinking hole."

Rooster said, "Son, you are here because I asked you and Yancey to meet me here when you took the stuff to Kate—how was Kate, son?"

"She was fine," Milo said.

"And where is Yancey?"

"He's quit his job."

"No he ain't," Rooster said, "but getting back to you, we all met up in the woods awhile back between here and the road—having missed your brother, the dog, the snake—and when lightning commenced, them two bloodhounds that had been as much good as an old maid with asthma lit after a trail and drug us here in the drenching rain, thinking you was your brother—it was his scent they knew. Well, you won't but we saved you anyhow. You must smell like him is all I can say."

Macey said "He's wearing Rato's underwear."

Milo said "Am I?"

"Yes."

"How do you know?"

"Because when we went swimming week before last, I noticed you had on Rato's drawers. Too small for you."

Milo said "Maybe so" but he did not look.

And Papa said, "Week before *last?* No wonder you've lost what mind you had—swimming at the end of September. God help you."

Milo was ready for his final move—against his nature, they had forced it on him. He stood entirely, shedding money, one coil still round him (so he lifted fifty pounds like a fistful of feathers). He put his lips to Rooster's ear, said secretly to him, "I know you can't do your duty at home and up to now that's been your secret, but if you don't do your duty *here* and take this money into your safekeeping till I can get home and talk to Mrs. Provo and prove my truth—well, there's other boys waiting to fill your shoes, fill *all* your shoes."

Rooster stood awhile—Milo still like a kiss at his ear—and then raised a hand to Milo's neck, harshly at first, a seizing claw. Then the pressure eased, rocked the full neck gently, and when Rooster spoke he whispered too, but what he said was "Who ruined your head?"

He had only just seen the dried hole there.

Milo said, "Tom Ryden returned. This poor child's Daddy that tried to kill me, then left me alive to do his one good deed."

Rooster nodded slowly. "You going to explain everything to me later on this evening?"

"All I can," Milo said.

"About this money, I mean," Rooster said (they still whispered). "I don't want to know nothing else— you hear?—nothing I can't use in my various duties."

Milo said, "Don't worry. I'll give you your life."

And Rooster released him, used his hands like a swimmer to stroke back Milo and Papa towards the door. He picked two steps through Death's remains till he stood in the midst of the money himself, smiled at Lois, Macey, Hawkins still there on the ground. "You all step back. I'm the only Law till a better Law arrives, and I confiscate all disputed findings till the truth is clear and justice can settle." In one hand he still held the warm pistol that had finished Death.

Macey dropped his handful at once and left. Then Hawkins stood and spoke to the pistol. "You're mighty right there's a better Law, and when it hears all Hawk Ryden's been through for Tommy-damn-Ryden and his Mama he deserted, it'll bring me this money on a shining tray and beg me to take it with six per cent interest."

Rooster said, "That very well may be but the duties I *can* do, I'm doing—step aside." Hawkins went and Lois rose at the order, leaving only three in the privy now—Lois and Rooster and Milo by the door, Death at his feet. But Rooster held the only light, and as Lois stood into it, started for the door, he noticed her (something he had not really done before) and with his free hand (he had holstered his gun) touched her bare arm that was damp and cold. "Excuse me, honey. I didn't intend my first word to you to be orders to *leave*. I'm trying to do what I think is best, and killing your snake was part of the best, but I'm sorry that duty laid in my path. I know he was you all's daily bread—the *world* to you—and I'll make it up to you if I ever can."

Lois said, "No need. Thank you just the same. He was not mine even. Some boy that boarded with my Aunt Selma gave him to her when he ran off and left her unpaid, and since she was leaving her husband then, it gave her the idea of traveling with snakes so she took me when my own mother died, and her and me and Death and several dozen snakes (that came and went) traveled together these thirteen years since I was three. But don't you worry. I have had this dream of stopping moving, of sitting *still*, and Death didn't have no part in my dream." She looked down a final time to the dirt, the colorless weight still faintly seething in baffled refusal to accept its end. Then she looked to the door where Milo stood—or wavered in weakness—against banked lights from the others outside. His face was towards her but too dark to read so she did not smile (which was her desire) but looked to Rooster, gave the smile to him. "Maybe I owe you *thanks*," she said. "Maybe you have forced me to find a life."

Rooster said, "Honey, you don't owe me so much as a look—a kindly look in a rainy week. Good lives are lying round thick as seed. But I would take anything you care to give. And I mean it nicely." He still had the light and could see that she looked beyond him to Milo so he took that too and said, "Can you drive a car?"

Lois said "Yes."

"Then will you do me a favor and carry him home?" He thumbed towards Milo. "He's had his day. He needs attention—feed him good, scrub his cut, strap his chest for broken ribs. I'll get most of these boys back to hunting now, and then I'll collect this money and hold it and skin this snake for your aunt to remember Tommy by, and we'll come on to the Mustian place when we've found poor Rato and killed his dog."

Lois nodded. "Who is Tommy?" she said.

Rooster turned to dark Milo who shook his head, then said, "The boy that died a debtor to your aunt." Then he asked Milo, "Son, if you lead this girl to my truck, she'll save your life. Can you walk that far?" Milo nodded. "If you can't we'll tote you."

Milo said, "I could walk to Europe."

Rooster said "I ain't asking that." Then he handed Lois his great flashlight—"We got plenty lights" —and she went on to Milo, and though they did not speak, they walked together through the door, the slack-lipped speechless men and Macey, across the clearing past the house again abandoned and into woods.

At first Milo had walked ahead, Lois holding the light, throwing it ahead between his legs, but she had quickly seen his weakness—his unsteady knees, wandering bare feet—so she moved up beside him, not explaining why, then took a little lead. He permitted that, eased back slightly to take his own time and could see her smooth legs work against the light through briars and branches, fearless, not pausing. Warned as he had been, punished but spared, Milo strained not to think—and managed it awhile. There was only the one place to keep his eyes though—on the ground ahead, Lois's light and the lower third of Lois herself—so his straining failed and he thought one thing, "Her legs are like two tan polished tusks—curving that fine, pledging that strength." Then he looked above to halt that tack, saw only black trees and said to himself, "I have not been with her in woods before." (She had stopped him on Friday night in the open, forced him to work beneath just the stars.) He shook his head sharply to fling that aside but went on looking up (for spiritual safety), feeling his forward path with his feet—till he ran full-face into Lois who had stopped and turned to wait. He drew back as if from scalding iron, said "What's wrong?"

"I was wondering that myself," she said. She kept the light downward, a pool for their feet. "—Wrong with you, I mean."

He said, "Looks like I'm a little tired."

"Tired of what?"

"Not tired *of* nothing but *because* of some things —mainly not getting my sleep last night."

"How come?" she said.

Milo knew she knew—that he had stood a cold blind beggar half the night, chattering at her door, refused as if he were crusty with sores—but he could not say it. "I was worrying about my brother," he said.

"I'm sorry," she said. Her free hand found his wrist in the dark—no fumbling at all—and shackled him with one finger, one thumb.

"That's all right," he said. "You have to worry about your kin. What else have you got?"

She said "Yourself"—he slid from her grip but did not step back. "Milo," she said, "by *sorry* I meant what I did last night, holding you back when you needed me."

"That's all right. I won't really *needing* nohow, just wishing for company. I don't need but three things —food, water, air."

She could tell by his voice that he was not smiling, but the light stayed down—she did not look. "I know that's where you are wrong," she said. "You needed your parents to get here at all. You needed your mother when you were helpless—"

"Boys have been raised by wolves," he said. "A scientific fact."

"—Now you need Lois to take your love and make us a life." Her hand moved out to take him again.

But his wrist was gone—he had shrunk back a step on his silent feet. "Let's go home," he said, "and settle some problems and get your money."

"I don't want money. I want you," she said.

"Lois, I'm a child—ain't you noticed that? Why choose me out of all you've seen, traveling the world? By morning you'll own ten thousand dollars—got with no pains but one dead snake. You could buy you the world's *best* boy. Why me?"

Lois raised the light, not enough to flood him but enough to show her his face again, clearer than since the previous morning—an ordinary face such as crowds the world, with wet straw hair hooked across his forehead, a jaw and lips that could no more lie than tat a lace band and blue eyes that seemed unable to blink —that open, *unclosed*—which calmly bore her study now.

But more than bore—he saw her too by light cast back from his own pale skin and was strongly drawn— against all warnings from the grave, all vows—to study her darkness by his own dark shine till he felt indeed the need she had mentioned, had it rush upon him like hot dry wind. "I must cherish," he thought, "and weigh in my two naked hands each half of her"—for he suddenly saw that she came in halves—her lifting breasts, high cheeks of her tail, the double folded lips of her fork. But while he thought she receded before him—dark hair, dark eyes grew darker, then black like cold stars flinging toward colder space in infinite flight at speeds beyond thought—so he lifted his hand to touch her, halt, reclaim, use the Lois he had known, had his first joy from, who had stood here moments— was it moments?—ago and begged his touch.

She whispered "Wait" and in midair he waited, strove to read in her now lightening face the sight she saw as she studied him—the face that shone beneath his own with a light not his, the face she had loved since before her birth, that rode her dreams (un-named) each night. When her face was as warm with reflected light as the face she watched, her lips broke back on a helpless smile—greeting and gift. "I have met you," she said, "where I promised I would."

Milo nodded, his hand sank slowly—to his own

flank not hers, and the buried probing light within him
slowly died. They both stood dark. The flashlight was
out, had been out for minutes.

Then she found his hand with her own dry hand—
the cool hands of kin, demanding only company.
"Where am I?" she said. Her voice was all question but
firm, unafraid.

"You were home," he said, "and you'll go back
soon. But come on with me to *my* home awhile. One
more person's got to take my message."

She did not speak, did not move to lead. The lead
was his. Having borne his message to half his mission,
he took lead and moved, and in total dark—light dead
in her hand—he led her out (hands still joined calmly)
through harmless thorns into dripping ferns, then cold
pine straw, then the edge of the ditch, the road—
moonlight.

When his turning lights struck the windows of the
room where the women waited and climbed towards
the house, the women went quickly and stood like
members of a relay team in the chilling dark to
welcome him home—or as if they manned a frail
lifeline, flung into water at a faceless victim, fearfully
hauling him unknown ashore. Selma waited in the
doorway, leaning for support. Emma waited on the
porch between door and steps, beneath the light. And
Rosacoke was posted on the edge of light at the foot of
the steps, waiting while Milo opened his door, slowly
felt with his foot for the still-dizzy ground, then
stumped down and came towards her ahead of Lois

(not slowing for Lois, not looking back) till porch light struck him like a second blow, opened his dry wound, flamed his stains and he passed before her (Lois coming behind) still not slowing. Rosa said to halt him, "Where is Rato? What's wrong with you?" He did not pause an instant for his sister nor even for his mother—"What hurt you, son? Where is Rato, son?" —but moved to the door despite his day as smoothly as if he rode a belt or hovered till he stopped a foot from Selma's face, raised his eyes to hers, waited in silence, his face his message.

"Tom," she said—speaking in wonder but quietly enough for Lois not to hear six feet behind.

He nodded, not meaning to lie, not lying.

Emma came up behind him, examined his wound with a hard gentle finger. "Who hurt you, son? Is Rato alive?"

He nodded, not looking back to his mother.

So Emma, deprived of his new face, went on— "Then come on and let me clean this gash and tell me all you know."

He shook his head No and spoke to Selma. "I got to tell *you* what I seen."

"I know that," she said.

"Death is dead," he said.

"I know that," she said and turned in the door and limped down—but fleet and young—toward Emma's bedroom.

His hand went out to the screen-door handle to open and follow, but his mother's hand on his shoulder held back. "Son, are you sick? I'm your Mama. Look here. Tell me what's going on."

He did not look but opened the screen and took a strong step to leave her grip. "You can come if you won't interrupt," he said, "but nobody else." Then he went toward Selma and Emma went behind, accepting for the first time yet in her life a child's condition, abandoning Lois and Rosa to the dark alone together, cold to each other as the evening air.

In his mother's room Selma already sat on the white iron bed she had lain in to rest (Emma's own big bed was across the room, and Baby Sister slept in it now, deep as drowned), but rest was the least thing she thought of now. She stared to the open door till Milo entered, then her eyes clasped to him as he crossed the room (Emma shut the door, threw the thumb-bolt loudly) and took his place by the mantel that hit him shoulder-high now. Their gaze was mutual—unblinking, unsmiling, broken only by Emma passing between to her low washstand where she poured out the water to deal with wounds, wrung rags, came towards him, saying, "Sit down, son. You are taller than me."

He was, this year, though they neither had noticed, but he did not sit nor acknowledge her further than to lean his head to her side slightly. Then as Emma washed, he spoke at last to Selma. "The first thing I have to tell is a story."

"That is what I can understand," Selma said.

He nodded—or Emma moved his head once for him; in any case Emma said, "Tell the truth, not stories."

"Stories can also be true," he said, still watching

only Selma. "See if this story is." She nodded her readiness. He started, speaking low. "Thirteen years ago south of here"—he pointed south, Selma briefly looked—"a young fellow turned up late one night, a Saturday night, in a bus station diner with a child, a girl about three years old. He got her to eating fried pie and milk, then stepped to the bathroom and left her. But not alone. A waitress came up and asked the child was that her Daddy? The child said No, she was being kidnaped so the waitress called the Law and the jailer came. The child held out she was being stolen though she didn't show pain so the jailer asked the man to name himself, tell his destination—gave him every kind chance with the bus cranked to leave, people ganging round—but the man asked the child, 'Are you happy with me?' She nodded she was so the man set her down —he had held her till now—and said to the jailer, 'I am taking this thing that I love to my home.' But the jailer forbade him, said the man must stay till they found his name and the child's rightful parents. The waitress offered to keep the child, and the child went to her, not looking back, not telling the man goodbye nor nothing so he said to the child, to her vanishing back—"

"He said, 'Meet me, darling, at home, if you can.' " Selma had said it, raised by the memory—old pain—to stand and suck for air as though the room were filling with water, chin-level, cresting against her dry lips.

Milo nodded—his own nod now (Emma's washing had stopped, she listened in silence). Then when Selma had breath, seemed steady on her feet, he asked her finally "Is that story true?"

"Every word," she said.

"But how do you know those last words he said?"

"She told me then—soon as she came back—and has said them in her sleep many long nights since long past the time she knew his name or recalled his destination for her."

Milo frowned, not deeply but enough for his mother to notice and study—a frown in his eyes as though they were pained by lies like smoke—so Emma said, "*It's* true. She told me last night but who told you?"

He still spoke to Selma and the frown deepened. "I can't tell that but I know—don't I know?"

Selma nodded, took one step forward—hand out toward him—then retracted and let the hand lower itself. "But do you know the rest?"

"I am *knowing* it more than gradually. But you got to tell it."

She sat on the bed again, heavily pressed. "Why?" she said.

"Because I am bearing an overdue message that's burning me, but I can't give it till I know the right party, have perfect proof. Tell me who was that man and who was that child and where are they now and why were they there, running from who?"

"He was Thomas Ryden—called *Tom*, your cousin —and he's buried overseas—in Guam, isn't it, Emma? —and the child was Lois, *is* Lois now beyond that thin door with your own sister. The reason they were caught in Gaffney that night is another story—" Her eyes flew to Emma for refuge, relief.

But "Tell it," he said, unsmiling, merciless.

So she told it to Emma who had heard it before. "Mrs. is my stage name—Mrs. Provo. I was born Selma Provo and that's how I'll die, it looks like now. But I had one person that was closer to me than husbands ever get—my sister Edith, younger than me by nearly ten years and pretty from the start. (I was born looking like a parboiled rabbit and still do, don't I?"—she glanced from Emma to the dim mirror above the mantel—"an overworked hundred-and-sixty-pound rabbit.)" She returned to Emma and they swapped quick smiles. Milo did not smile. "Our parents had died when the flu came through in the first World War, and me and her were all each other had. Papa had farmed up in north Florida, and we were raised there—land black as oil and string beans up to your earlobes for sale—but when they died, Edith and me were all but orphans—no brothers, nobody but an old maid great-aunt down in Clearwater. So we went down. I was ten years old, Edith was barely two, but we hunched our shoulders and humped our backs and Aunt Helen laid her boarding house on us to tote till she died. Tote we did—it was tote or starve. Other people think they have seen many wonders, but did you ever see a child of two with only black ringlets to shield her from harm cook three meals a day for seventeen men? And I mean *men*—railroad gangs, circus hands, drummers of every item invented—but that's what Edith had to do sometimes when I was sick or had started to school (I quit school soon, lacking heart to burden Edith). Cook and set table and serve and wash dishes and scrub and sweep and strip dirty beds—well,

we did, that's all, and for twelve long years till our great-
aunt died at eighty-eight on her two strong feet one
Christmas eve out looking at the stars in her backyard.
Hers I say and *hers* it was, every inch till that night
when her heart burst in her and flooded her throat and
the place was ours, not because she left a will in our
favor but because we were all the people she had. She
had outlived the rest—too mean to die. I had thought
for years I would shout with joy when that day came
and I did—oh privately, just me and Edith back in the
kitchen, the boarders still hungry through death and all
—but after that slowly as we took over in name and
fact, had a few pennies to call our own, I began feeling
sad in a fresh new way. I loved Edith still, leaned on her
hard as ever—we had held each other up more than
twelve years by leaning together like sides of a roof—
but being alone with only just her, I saw for the first
time how young *I* was—not but twenty-two. I say *alone*
—what I mean is, you are not alone till you wake up
one morning and the show is *yours* to make or break,
nobody older, nobody to run to, nobody to blame, not
even one mean tight-kneed aunt, *great*-aunt at that.
Here I had worked like an ink-black *black* through my
whole childhood, burning my strength and my will to
live, my ten-cent hopes, like some kind of coal, soft
fast-burning coal. And here I had eaten up all my
girlhood, started on my womanhood—and stood stock-
alone, raving hungry—for love, I mean. I had lived
without love for twenty-two years. Oh it can be done—
to live without love. Right now there's people that do,
I guess. There's people that live at the North Pole too
—named Eskimoes." She stopped, chuffed three little

laughs like balls of smoke, then moved her eyes from Emma to Milo as slow and cautious as if moving a bowl brim-tip with water, as pained and reluctant as a self-named criminal forced toward a judge. She chuffed again. Milo did not smile. "But I was telling about Edith, wasn't I?—my baby sister. It turned out she was worse off than me—for love, I mean. I had had a few years of a mother at least. She had even missed that, recalling only our old aunt and me—and say what you will, nobody that aims to tell the truth will claim two sisters ever get closer than puppies in a litter. I know I said differently a minute ago, but women don't love each other—do they? They weren't meant to. Anyhow Edith was thirteen then—maybe fourteen, I'm poor on figures—and if you are young and are not a peg leg and are looking for love; well, a boarding house is the place to find it—or one of the many substitutes. What she found was a child named Tommy Ryden. I say *child*—he claimed nineteen but if he was seventeen I'm a poor damn judge of what times does to eyes—and I say *found*. I saw her find him. He come in one cool night that January—just after Edith and me were free—January nineteenth, General Lee's birthday; that's how I always remember the date. We still kept the same room, the same big bed, and we had turned in and rolled separate ways when the door knocker knocked. I moaned and said something like, 'Let him sleep out, coming late as this,' but Edith was already up, in her bathrobe, heading down. I said, 'Edith, it isn't Jesus asking for pity.' 'I know that,' she said. But she went anyhow, so straight and unfearing—you could usually scare her by dropping dust—that I got up and stood at

the head of the steps to watch her go and be her
protection in case of a drunk (it was Saturday night).
It wasn't a drunk. I often wished it had been. Drunks
are mainly out to hurt themselves. It was Tommy on
the porch, age about sixteen with no more baggage
than a lightning bolt. She said 'Good evening.' She
must have smiled—her back was to me—because he
smiled back as if smiling were something he had
personally invented, held a patent on. 'It's night,' he
said, 'and I beg your pardon but I'm lost and looking
for a warm board to lie on.' Edith said 'Who are you?'
'I'm a Christian gentleman from up north,' he said.
(Our aunt's porch sign was still by the door—*Room
and Board for Christian Men*—and *up north* was
North Carolina of course.) Then he said, 'How
much will you charge for a bed?' Edith said, 'How
much have you got?' 'Nothing,' he said and she stepped
back—to shut the door, I thought—but she didn't. She
said, 'Then that's what I'll charge' and led him in to
the little front room and put him in there with a man
that was advertising a show—some circus was coming
and he went ahead of it, putting up signs on any bare
barn. Well, she turned to leave him in the dark
doorway and climb back to me but he said 'Wait.' She
waited. He said, 'My name is Tom and I just want to
say, however old you get to be, there'll always be one
boy named Tom that worships your name.' 'Then my
name is Edith,' she said and waited awhile more and
turned and dragged herself up towards me as if I was
prison gates, cold iron. But I never said one hard word
to her—not to ask how much that boy had paid or
when he was leaving, least of all how come she had

welcomed him in to all we had—our home, after all—
with no word of who he was but *Tom*. There have been
Toms that cut women's throats in their sleep. This one
didn't but he might as well—Edith's, I mean. He had
cut her *heart* out by eight the next morning—just by
drinking the coffee she poured, saying 'Thank you' for
every move she made. (If you ever work in a boarding
house, you'll think the word *Thank you* is some foreign
thing you learned in a dream, that nobody else ever
learned or uses.) All I did was stand and watch. My
philosophy was—still is today: if you're anything—
man, woman, fox—that's on the run, and there's all
grades of hounds, and you see cover yawning in the
midst of your path and that cover doesn't show a *Keep
Out* sign, then take it and pray it's not a bear's cave or
a rattler's hole—though people have lived with snakes
before. And Edith was on the run. *I* knew—from me,
from our aunt that was barely cold, from her life that
was dry as a baked tin can. The worst trouble was—so
was he, so was Tom. And from the same thing—no
previous soul had loved him enough to say, 'Stand still
please. Let me *look* at you,' then look awhile and say,
'Thank you. Yes. I am coming to you. From this time
forth you will be my life.' Well, Edith said it before a
week passed, but it wasn't what Tom wanted to hear,
not then anyhow. He stood still exactly long enough—
excuse me, Emma—to sling one baby deep up her like
a hook. It hooked and grew—and Tom was long gone,
having taken up with his circus roommate—and when
I saw it growing, it was too late to act. All I could do
was wait, wait with Edith, keep her out of sight, tell
her what seemed lies—that Tom would be back like he

said he would, would be here now if she knew his
address and could get him word. 'Word?' she'd say. 'He
doesn't need *word*. He *aimed* to do this and did it and
smiled and said, "Pray it's a girl that has your hair." ' I
mentioned Edith's baby ringlets? They were long by
then, blue as black cockerel feathers swagging down her
back. Well, he aimed dead-center. It was nothing but a
girl, and you've seen her hair already, both of you—"
Selma's voice failed—not a crack nor a frog, just silence
when she moved her lips to continue so she waved again
with her hand towards the door, towards wherever
black-crowned Lois lurked. Emma looked but not
Milo. Selma's voice returned. "But his hook went on
past the baby still deeper, struck Edith in the heart,
and she died while I was bathing the child. I had been
the only one with her, you see; done all the work that
Edith didn't do—she was cheerful and awake through
the whole quick thing—but when I tied the cord and
turned with the baby and went to the washstand, Edith
said, 'Selma, don't take *her* away.' I didn't look round.
I thought she was joking. I said 'Hush up and rest' and
went to bathing, saying backwards to Edith, 'This
child hasn't cried. That's a good sign, isn't it? She just
started breathing as easy as walking—a quiet soul, let's
wish her that.' Edith didn't speak. I thought she was
asleep and finished my work and wrapped the baby and
went back to her, saying 'Name it now.' But she was far
deeper down than sleep so I named the child Lois for
our own mother, then called the doctor. Her heart, he
said, wasn't big enough to drive a cat much less a girl
through sixteen years of field-hand labor and a secret
child. That was October tenth, sixteen years ago—my

God, *today*. It's Lois's birthday and we all forgot." She looked at last to Milo. "Did you remember and give her something?"

"I think I have got her the grandest gift, but you hadn't finished your story yet. Tell to the part I have already told." His previous continuous frown was deeper, as a guard dog lying at your side will tense at threats that reach his ears and subside without your notice or care.

"That is the hardest part," Selma said, but she nodded to Milo and told it to him. "Two months later right after Thanksgiving—when I had nearly got myself back together and Lois was thriving but I was dreading the Christmas season—an envelope came addressed to Edith. The first mail she ever got and too late, postmarked *Wilmington, Delaware*. I couldn't be sure who it was from, but for three or four days, I couldn't bear to open it. I held it to the light but could not see through so I laid it in a drawer till I worked up my grit. It was a Christmas card from Tommy, saying, '*I have been running the snake show lately. They have gone on down to winter quarters where I'll join them soon and will trust to see you, but meanwhile I hope it is time for this—so here is a gift to buy something with for yourself and anybody else you have by now that I ought to love.*' The gift was ten dollars. No way to return it—still no address—and anyhow in 1932 ten dollars was something I'd have taken from Hitler. So I took it and bought my baby some clothes (a cap for ears that protruded at first and the rest I put into flowers for Edith). I say *my baby* and she seemed to be that from the first bath I gave her—still seems to be

and treats me mostly kindly though she knows her real
mother died at her birth and thinks her father died
broken hearted a few months later, leaving her to me,
to take my name. But her father came sooner than he
said he would—Christmas day about suppertime. Imagine how happy a day I had had—alone as a Catholic at
a Baptist convention, a three-months' orphan my only
company, even my worst class of boarders—tramps
—gone to *some* roost. I was back in the kitchen
warming Lois's milk when a soft knock came. My heart
lifted slightly and I took Lois with me and went to
answer, hoping it would be somebody, *something* that I
could welcome. It was Tom—who else?—looking five
years older, so thin and tired that whatever I had
meant to say or feel, I said 'Merry Christmas.' He
smiled and bowed and said 'Who is that?' and I
handed him Lois—right out the door to the porch
where he stood. The second I did it I saw my mistake—
the way he took her, held her to him, studied her with
no more questions, as natural and happy, as *relieved* as
if he had come in a dead-straight line through hails of
pain hoping to find this very thing that he had started
long months before. I knew from that second I would
have to fight to keep her mine, keep her safe from him,
make her all the amends she was already due. So I put
out my arms to accept her back—not saying 'Come in'
—but he came with Lois, not giving her up till we
stood in the kitchen and he laid her on the table (she
had not whimpered yet) and asked where was Edith.
'What do you mean to do with her?' I said. 'What?' he
said. I said, 'What if Edith was to walk in now and say
what you know—that this child is yours—and then ask

you what future you saw for her?' He thought about
that, then answered to Lois—'I'd tell her I wasn't no
gypsy,' he said, 'no fortune teller. I *wait* for the future,
let it come when it will.' I said, 'How about the past?
Can you understand that?' He didn't look at me. He
studied that child as if she was Scripture—and she let
him study, lay still, serious. Then he turned to me. 'Yes
I do,' he said. 'I have killed Edith, ain't I?' 'Yes,' I said
and he went back to Lois and stayed there with her like
she was his till her milk was ready. I took her then and
he watched me feed her, but I couldn't watch him and
we didn't speak, barely spoke for two days—not because we were either one *enemies* but maybe because
barely knowing each other, we loved and wanted and
thought we needed the same one thing—that simple
child—and were both working out our plans in silence
to win her for good. Well, if Tom had a plan at the
end of three days, it was nothing but *wait*. Some
roomers turned up towards the end of the week so Tom
told me he would head on down to the show's winter
quarters and rejoin his snakes. He gave me another ten
dollars which I took out of need—and partly pity, my
second mistake—and I took his address and promised
to write in case of bad trouble. We were on the porch
steps before he said what he really felt, what laid my
heart open clean as a blade—'Selma, I know you have
reasons for grief—so do I—but I want you to know I
am finally happy, having this child I made that will
love me, need me all of her life, all of *mine* and mourn
me beyond whatever grave I choose.' I said, 'Tom,
don't count too hard on that. You said you were not a
prophet—remember?—and nobody's bound to love
anybody else. Half the time, blood runs thinner than

water.' He nodded to that, said, 'I well know that—my past life shows how thin blood can get—but I'll be to her something she cannot fail to love.' 'Oh what will that be?' I said and laughed, no longer swallowing the bitter taste that had coated my throat since Edith went. And I laughed on louder, 'And *when* will it be?' He did not strike back but when I had calmed, he went down the steps and turned in the walk and said, 'Don't you see that is all *I* need to know, all *I'm* trying to find?' I could not laugh again but I gave him my back and threw my last bolt, 'Don't fail to send me a postcard—hear?—when you're something to love. Con tact us then and we'll both come to you through snakes or *snow*. I promise that.' Then he—"

Milo said "Wait." His face that had frowned in gathering doubt was clenched now in pain, and his calm heart lurched into double speed—for no reason he knew. But he fought to understand. "How much of all you have said is true?"

"Every word," Selma said.

And his mother said *"Milo,"* meaning to warn him against disrespect, seeing him only for what he had been, to now, to her for fifteen years—her oldest boy yet a boy, a baby. But the boy suffered. She could see that much—his face white and drawn (all the muscles drawn *up*), his careless hands that seldom touched himself now kneading his chest. Emma took him by the shoulder, said, "Son, now *rest*. You have heard enough," and he looked down at her for the first time since morning, spread his lips to speak but silence came, then tried to yield to her guiding arm, follow her toward rest.

But Selma said "W*ait*, oh wait, don't move" and

put out her own detaining hand that again hung before her, sealed in air.

He could not move—only his eyes which returned to Selma. What came after, he read in her face which mirrored slowly, a moment late, his own pain and fear, her added amazement. What he felt, more than pain, was pressure—the sense, in the final words Selma said, that the room around them, above, beneath was suddenly full, packed with a presence unseen as air but offended, potentially hurtful, growing and with each ounce of weight demanding from Milo's pressed skull and heart what they could not give—mere truth, plain justice to the unseen nameless rush around him.

Selma felt the same rush but studying Milo and its work in him, she knew its name—Milo's face being finally, fully Tom's from within, Tom's as he always looked on leaving, as though he were drawn, torn, washed away by hateful powers not his own flawed heart, as though your duty was to fling yourself into night and storm to hold his lips one moment from drowning (when you yourself had strangled long since in abandonment). And she felt the demand on her own tired chest, finally knew it was just if not right. Facing the hurt and baffled boy four yards away—and thirteen years and the rest of time—she managed to move her head a little, side to side in the sign for denial. Then at once the full room began to empty, pierced by the final approach of truth. Selma's head moved freely, her lips and voice said "No" clearly. Her hand that had been trapped out to detain now loosened, moved round once in farewell.

And Milo was free, dispossessed, also abandoned,

allowed to speak—exhausted and low. "Now tell what is true."

Selma said, "It was true if you leave out Edith. There was never an Edith."

Emma said, "Selma, you lied to me."

Selma smiled, "Emma, I have lied to worse than you."

Emma said, "Then this will have to change my opinion—"

"Hush," Milo said. "Opinions ain't worth the meanest hant in Hell. This evening I have found— been led to find—ten thousand dollars which I got to give justly to the rightful owner." He turned back to Selma. "Tell on," he said. "The pure truth now."

But Emma stepped between them. "You two couldn't tell the truth," she said, "if God walked in that oak door now and said, 'Judgment Day! Sheep here, goats there.'" She turned on Selma—"Making me hear that long story twice because I thought it was pitiful and true and you and that black-headed girl deserved help—why, I couldn't sit through *Gone With the Wind,* and you have the nerve to use my roof as a shed for lies and, pardon my French, a strumpet's den. Get yourself ready and *I'll* drive you to your trailer." Then she turned to Milo. "I hope you are crazy—I hope to God—because if you ain't, you have grown overnight to be a worse fool and scoundrel than your Daddy and that's fast moving, son. I spent twenty years of my life with a fool—a drunk one at that—who thought the world, meaning me, owed him air, food, blood just because he could smile most women's hearts out. Well, I gave mine once but never again. I'm ugly as a mud fence daubed in misery and I've sinned my share, but one thing I have done with my life—I have *learned* some things, learned you don't use your eyes to judge people by, learned you don't get nothing worth taking home till you've paid hard money of one sort or other, tears, stinking sweat. *Found* ten thousand dollars! Been *led* to find it!" She seized Milo's arm as though it were lethal, must be fought for life. "I reckon you were led by an angel of God and are licensed by Heaven to talk like a fool. But where's the money? I don't see you stooping your back with the load." Not glancing at Selma, she pushed Milo before her towards the door—leaving Baby Sister asleep to guard Selma. "This day is over for *you*, big man. You get upstairs and get in the bed but kneel down first and beg salvation. I ought to call the Law on both of you." She threw the door open on Rooster Pomeroy and light struck his badge, his smiling teeth, a loaded paper bag resting on his holster. (Rosacoke waited in the dim hall behind him—and dimmer behind her, what seemed to be Lois.)

Emma stepped back and tried to say "Speak of the devil," but the shock had her breathless, and the sheriff anyhow was studying Milo. "Son," he said, "what must I do with this money?" He unrolled the greasy mouth of the bag (it had held his lunch) and drew out more cash than his pudgy fist could hold—bills tumbled round his feet and were stirred by the draft.

Milo freed his arm from Emma, stepped back, said "Come in." Rooster entered the bedroom and Rosacoke followed at a sneaking distance. Milo slid Emma's hand off the white doorknob, pushed the door against

Rosa. "Not you," he said, "but get Lois ready."

"For what?" Rosa said through the locking door.

"For me, when I call her."

"Who are *you?*" Rosa said.

"Amen," Selma said—or whispered through tears.

But Milo said "Milo," then "Everybody sit."

Selma sat on the bed, Rooster sat in the smallest straight chair in the house (money and hat like a scales on his knees), Milo himself leaned back on the mantel. Only Emma stayed up.

She had found her voice and she turned to the sheriff. "I know I don't have many rights. I have had that ground in my face tonight, but this *is* my bedroom (or was till last night) so before anybody starts another long lie, just tell me one thing—is Rato alive?"

Rooster gestured to the chair nearest Emma (a plushbottomed rocker). "If that's all that's worrying you, sit down," he said. "Lady, *lay* down flat." Emma waited upright so he said to Milo, "You told her about the snake?" Milo nodded. "Then we *know* he's all right. What's left to harm him?—just a little mad dog that loves him like a Daddy, and if by mistake it should snag him with a tooth, they got enough serum on ice in town to cure him of whale bite. No ma'm, I left my men looking for him—his Granddaddy's with them— and they'll be here with him by bedtime sure."

Emma sat and said "Thank you."

Rooster said, "Son, I have counted this money— nine thousand eight hundred eighty nine dollars. You were talking mighty high in Miss Jack's johnny and of course I knew why—that snake choked round you—but now that you're calm and got your good nature back, tell me all you know. Whose money was this?"

Milo spoke as himself for the first time since dark. "It was what Tommy Ryden got for dying in Guam— ten thousand dollars from Uncle Sam, less eleven dollars Miss Jack spent or lost. But with her dead now, it belongs to—"

"Hold on." Rooster smiled but meant it. "We ain't there yet. Where did you find the money?"

"Where you found me."

"Why were you in there?"

Milo strained to remember.

Rooster read the strain as embarrassment, charged in with help—"Just say 'Call of nature.' "

Milo did not say it, said nothing because he could think of nothing, retained his frown.

"Why were you at the Ryden place at all?"

Milo's frown—no longer of pain but of blankness —deepened further.

"Because I had told you to meet me there—you and that sorry Yancey when you come back from Kate." Rooster waited, no confirmation came though Milo faced him square as Truth on a courthouse. "Ain't that why?"

Emma said, "Son, are you feeling bad?—dizzy maybe? You've got every right to."

Milo said "No," facing each one separately, then staring at the light bulb bare in their midst. "I just do not remember."

Emma stood and moved towards him, laid a gentler hand on his shoulder now. "Come rest," she said and Milo yielded, took a step to obey.

Rooster said—almost whispering, "Just one minute. You claimed this money didn't go to Hawkins, that your black-headed girl was the rightful owner, that you would get me proofs, had a message to give." Then he also rose, approached Milo kindly—"Remember all that?"

Milo said "No," no longer frowning.

Selma said, "Sheriff, the message was given."

"What was it?" Rooster said.

"It was private," Selma said.

Emma nudged Milo another step towards the door. Rooster set his hat on the floor and rose, then he laid on Milo a look of reproach as heavy as mild. "Son," he said, "you have misused me when I trusted you, took you for a man."

Milo faced him, unflinching but too tired to wonder what misuse he meant or defend himself by revealing secret favors he had anyhow forgot or never known of—Kate's life refreshed, her dryness watered, Rooster's name prolonged one generation more.

Rooster opened his palm on the cud of money. "Well, I hope this will make Hawkins Ryden smile. Wonder what he'll do with it?"

"Make misery," Emma said, voice hard as a spike, "or at least not ease the misery he's in—wife and children hanging barefoot and boney on a front porch that won't support a feather bed. It'll be a black sin and I'll always wonder why—but I wonder a lot." She took the doorknob to lead Milo to rest. "Sheriff, find my boy and bring him to me."

"Yes ma'm," Rooster said and restuffed his bag, bent to take his hat.

Selma said "Wait." They all turned to her—she

was white as paper—but she spoke to only Rooster. "You almost spoke of Tommy Ryden this morning. I heard you. I know. How come you stopped?"

Rooster said, "So I wouldn't harm his rest if he's resting somewhere though I doubt he is—all the pain he caused."

"Who to?" Selma said.

"Well, his poor old Mama and Daddy that he left just like they were weeds that could live on air."

Selma said, "Most people do that. That's what Jesus intended—put your hand to the plow and don't never look back."

Rooster nodded to that. "Jesus ought to been shot. But he plowed all right—right through everything he touched."

"Name one thing," Selma said.

"Well, *me*," Rooster said.

"Did you know him?" she said.

"*Know* him? I've lived with him every day of my grown life and slept with his memory at my side every night for thirteen years." (Milo slid from his mother's loose grip and her hand eased on the doorknob to listen.) "No, I never seen him to know who he was, not even a picture though we spent our childhoods three miles apart. The first I remember hearing his name was when he left home in the early Depression. I was already working in the Law—a deputy—and early one morning his Daddy come in to the office and said their boy was lost and would we find him? Boys was getting lost like buttons back then, but I said I'd try and asked Mr. Ryden to describe him please—height, weight, hair, the usual stuff. He thought awhile but he didn't know—didn't know what color his son's eyes were. I thought to myself, 'I'd have got lost too,' but I said, 'Then how will we recognize him?' and he said—no waiting, 'Find the pitifulest girl in every town you try and shake her till she rattles—he'll fall out eventually.' I asked him again how old the boy was. 'About fourteen,' he said. So I said 'Why the pitifulest girl?' 'Because,' he said, 'Tom's hot as a pistol, he's looking for love and aims to spread joy, but nothing but a fool would let him in.' Well, we never found him and I never told this to another breathing soul, but I'll tell you tonight —a little later on, one fool let him in down in Florida, a woman considerably older than him that ran a rooming house. Let him in—excuse me—in more ways than one and had herself a baby as a souvenir, a girl I believe."

"How do you know that?" Selma said, looking only at him.

"Oh the Law kept up with Tommy Ryden—well, not *kept up* but at least a step behind. He was too fast for us—too fast for everything but one Jap bullet, just a little slug of lead."

Selma swallowed that, hard, to preserve a calm face. "What did he ever do but run away from home?"

"Run away from everything else," Rooster said. "But the reason we was *really* hunting him once was, he stole that child he claimed was his—went to see that woman when the child could just walk, acted sweet as ever, give her handsome presents and walked off with that child clean as a cut when the fool wasn't looking, *run* off by bus and got to South Carolina—headed God knows where—till they caught him in Gaffney on the woman's complaint. That's how I knew. But I never told his Mama and his Daddy was dead. The woman raised a yell to the Florida police, and they notified every sheriff in the country. Well, they held him in Gaffney for a day or two till they knew who he was and could ship the child back and extradite him—and he run again, out of jail, out of *sight*. Not before he plowed up another soul though, sitting tight in jail." Rooster stopped, bent his straw hat double, wrung it like a rag.

"Who?" Milo said.

Rooster wouldn't look up, not wanting to hear.

"What soul?" Milo said.

Rooster faced him, said "Kate my wife's"—quietly, all but whispering as though in the midst of a warm room of people—two women, a boy, a sleeping child—a secret was still a matter of tone. Then he smiled and said "But you knew that."

Milo did not nod but did not deny.

"I knew you knew—soon as you said Yancey didn't stay with you. And I must have known Yancey wouldn't stay—must have sent you on purpose. Reckon I did?"

Milo did not nod.

Rooster said, "Thank you. She don't mean harm. She can't help herself and I can't help her—I told you that. Ever try being somebody else? I mean trying to do your job in the dark when the girl you were loving wasn't studying *you*, wasn't living in her body but was hid in her mind with some other face you never even saw? You don't blame me do you?—I mean for sending you in, for my whole life even?" Rooster was smiling—

not broadly but fully, clearly, in total surrender, total shame.

Milo did not nod.

"It don't make me nothing but a fool," Rooster said. "Does it, son? Think around a little—there's other fools living. Think—and I think of her every night—of that poor lonesome fool down in Florida."

Selma said, "That's me. Thank you for the thought."

Rooster wheeled on her, at first in relief (that other fools existed), smiling—"*What?*" Then sitting, dumping backwards on his squatty chair in cold astonishment.

Selma nodded. "I am her—that took Tom in every way you mentioned, some you didn't and won that baby that's out yonder now and hung my unused love around her and took his visits twice yearly like *food* till that last visit when he came with the snake—a baby python that he may have stolen—and seeing I didn't flinch from it like a woman, said, 'Selma, never say I left you empty-handed' and handed me the snake, then left in the night with Lois that loved him even harder than me though she doesn't remember."

"Can you prove it?" Rooster said.

"Prove what?" Selma said.

"That you are the foo—that the child is yours and Tom was the Daddy?"

"Look at me," Selma said. "Ain't I proof? Ain't these scars enough?" She laid both palms loud and flat on her forehead, drew them slowly downward over eyes, neck, breast, then abandoned the rest as too ruined to show.

Rooster said, "Lady, you are holding up fine. If

you had a *car* that was fifty years old, you'd think it was due to knock on you a little."

"I am forty-one years old," Selma said—and could smile at that. (Even Emma smiled.)

"Proved," Rooster said and ducked in apology. "But what I'll need is legal proof, something Hawkins Ryden can't chew up in court."

Selma said, "I've got stacks of that locked in my trailer in a little strong box—her birth certificate (I didn't lie then), Tom's letters to me and her, and his picture. But I haven't seen the picture since I last saw *him*. It's sealed in a blank envelope, no name." She paused to justify that to herself. "I owe myself *some* favors, don't I?"

Rooster said, "Yes'm. Then the money is yours." He stood and went to her, his stuffed sack extended. Selma's hand hung open, limp at her side. Rooster reached to take it, then paused, remembered—"You know I had to kill your snake?" Selma nodded. "It was *snake* or *boy*"—he pointed to Milo—"so I chose *boy* having no time to think. Maybe if I had—but I saved you the skin, already nailed it to the side of Miss Jack's to cure-out for you, make you shoes for life."

Selma shook her head. "Let Hawkins have it. After thirteen years, what is it to me?—not one scale on it Tom ever touched."

"On you neither," Rooster said and smiled. "Washed by time—like the Luray Caverns!"

Selma also smiled. "Like Kate your wife."

Rooster thought that through, continued smiling, took her limp hand firmly, closed it round the money, said again "It's yours."

Even Milo smiled.

Selma sat on the bed (backwards, not looking, the sack unnoticed in her unnoticed hand) and studied Milo—for *Milo* he was again, only himself, a tired wounded boy, harmless, powerless, abandoned by Tom as finally as she, with less of Tom now in his face and person than most cousins share, however distant. Why had she ever sweated blood over that; why crawled up and down the Eastern seaboard with a ten-cent show and the snake he gave in hopes of seeing him one more time, that one night Tom would stroll in, make amends; why lied to Lois that she was her aunt when she herself had made every *grain* of Lois? Well, all that was over, *done*, thank God. Seventeen years she had worked in that harness. "How did it ever hold me?" she said, astonished, relieved—to Milo and all he had meant tonight.

Milo barely heard and did not understand, but he shrugged and grinned with his eyes shut for rest.

"Thank you," she told him, then left him with her eyes—forever, she thought—and looked to Rooster, held the sack out to him. "Not it isn't," she said.

Rooster's face fell open in silent shock, and Emma winced deeply (meaning "Not only strumpet and fool but wasteful"), but Milo gathered new life from the words, the "No" itself—his shoulders, chest, chin filled with sudden strength, his eyes with the last glow of mission, message. "Right," Milo said. "It was never yours. It is Lois's—and has been since Tom Ryden fell and bled to death."

"Lois doesn't know that," Selma said.

"Yes she does. I told her an hour ago—with Death

wrapped around me and ten thousand dollars like a blanket of leaves."

Selma said, "But she doesn't know *why* it's hers—and never will. I have spent every minute since I got her back, soothing her Daddy out of her memory (any dreams she had), filling any gaps he left in her with all the love I could find to give, and I'm not about to gouge her up again." Again she offered Rooster the sack, thrust it towards him. He did not move so she turned back to Milo. "It's nothing but money. You take it, son. Make your family happy. I give it to you."

"Thank you," Milo said. "But it's not yours to give."

"Let us be," Selma said. "Open that door please and give me your arm and a ride back to town, and we'll leave your life and live our own. Haven't we earned that much—*me* anyhow, after all my pains?"

Milo said "No."

"Who are *you?*" Selma said. "Who gave you the right to ruin my little life I have made?"

Milo no longer knew but he had the right. He knew that at least, and in two silent steps he stood at the door, hand on the knob, half-turned to open.

Selma stood. "Emma, stop him. Emma, save my baby for me—she is *mine*."

Emma said, "Selma, you have to tell her. I don't understand no more than you—least of all understand my own boy Milo—but Milo's right. Let him tell her, Selma."

"Just give me one reason—what good will it do her? How can she use that ugly news? Emma? Sheriff?"

"As a warning," Emma said.

"Of *what?*" Selma said. She searched every face, even Baby Sister's. They all were thinking. Baby Sister seemed drowned.

Finally Milo said "Of love."

Emma nodded—"Of the ruins love has made."

Rooster nodded—"Of the ruin life is if love has to lie."

Selma settled on Milo. He bore her look but had no further answer—*was* and had been for two days his answer. She shut her eyes, nodded, "You tell her please."

Milo opened the door on the dim deep hall. Lois and Rosa seemed a county away, propped straight as slats on the opposite wall two yards apart. Milo saw only Lois and only Lois moved—when she came forward to him, Rosa kept her own place. It at least was hers.

When Lois stood well into the room and the door was shut, Milo stepped to Selma and took the full sack, then went to Lois—hand's breadth from her face—and spoke to her eyes (no one else could have met them), "This is the gift your father left you. He died to get it and meant you to have it. His name was Tom Ryden. The house where you saved my life is your home and this is your mother." He nodded towards Selma.

Lois put out her hand and took the sack as though she had spent her life taking gifts, her unquestioned due but for which she was grateful. Then she said, "I have known that all my life, but it slipped my mind till an hour ago. I will always love—"

Baby Sister said "Wait" and every eye jerked to

the corner bed where through cracked eyelids, sleep-roaring ears, she had seen, heard all. Now she rose to her knees in the nest of cover, eyes squinted, lips down. "What in the Sam Hill is love?" she said.

Milo suddenly knew, took two steps towards her, spread smiling lips to tell, warn, delight her, then dropped—silent, senseless—in a heap by her bed.

THREE

IF MILO was well he slept without dreaming (or if he dreamed it was only of rest—a walk through shade or stretched in green woods, shielded from day) so now when he woke, he knew he was healed—he had slept that calmly since they laid him here though for only nine hours. Rooster had carried him up in his arms at eight in the night. It was five o'clock now— well before dawn, still dark—but he woke because of a sound not the hour. Someone said his name and before it was finished, his eyes were open—on total dark. His first thought was, "I have not dreamed. I am all right," but the voice spoke again—or asked again, both times the name had been a question: *Milo?* clearly. The voice was near and seemed a young woman's so his second thought was, "I am *deathly* sick. I am dreaming a girl is in my room." He clamped his eyes twice to force them awake, and then he could see—but only dark shapes by the crack of hall light that slid beneath the door. The shape was a girl and the girl seemed Lois —her height, size, long hair streaming, arms and shoulders bare. She stood at the foot of the bed and waited—her question asked. Then Milo thought, "I am not alone. I am sleeping with Rosa who will wake any minute and raise a yell." And he longed to say, "Fool, this ain't a fair. It's a home. Go to bed." But his left hand slid up to test the headboard—the cold carved grapes of his own bed—and his right hand slid across warm sheets to test for Rosa. Rosa was gone if she'd ever been there. Milo said to himself, "Wherever we are and whenever it is, Lois is standing in her slip by my bed." He was fully awake.

Lois asked again—"Milo?" and waited.

Milo thought, "She is not asking after my health. She is offering me the only thanks she knows. Wherever all the others are and however crazy it will be, how can I lie still, not welcome her?" And his left hand moved from the headboard to greet her but rising, brushed his bandaged head (bandaged by his mother after he fainted), the hidden cut like a savage warning. So his hand lay still. He said to himself, "I was nearly killed for *taking* once already. I am meant to give." He did not speak, lay quiet but breathing—not faking sleep—and waited for Lois to understand that, that his service was ended. At last she did, turned, moved to the door, stood a moment half-naked in naked light, then left, shut Milo again in his dark—the deepest dark being what even after Sunday he did not know and warned by his wound (by Death itself) could not learn yet: that givers and takers need not be separate, can be two joined hands locked yet shifting, each becoming the other awhile (if the gift from one hand at least is love—the attempt to accept, forgive, pledge shielding).

He lay a moment in the various darks, satisfied, free to rest again. His eyes shut slowly. Then as if delayed between eyes and mind, that last sight struck him—Lois in the door, having failed to give thanks, turning to leave, maybe for good. And other sights followed in a hot rush within him—Buck Russell watching his black girl leave, not knowing—never knowing—if her rising belly was his first child; Selma Provo accepting Tom's gift of Death, thanking him and rising next day to find him gone forever (with Lois for a while); Lois herself at the age of three leaving Tom by the bus in South Carolina with a promise to meet which could not be kept; Kate Pomeroy feeding Tom the key to freedom and waiting too late on her single bed; Milo himself four years ago at the age of eleven on the Afton store porch one Saturday evening, staring up the road at his staggering father who came toward him smiling (it had seemed a smile), then a truck tore between and halted beyond, and the air where his father should have stood was a hole; even Rato on Saturday vanishing in trees after Death and Phillip—maybe also for good. Milo rose in the bed at the thought of his brother—lost? found? dead? or trapped in pain? His kin was his duty whatever his wounds, and he flung his bare feet to the cold floorboards, felt his body, found himself still in Rato's drawers, groped toward a chair for the rest of his clothes, then heard down the hall Rosa's door shut gently, footsteps quicker than Rosa's on the steps, heading down, away—Lois surely, dressed and leaving. He found his trousers and shirt, pulled them on, reached the door in a step, stood a last dark moment— head knocking, swimming—and said aloud the thing he had earned for his trouble and care, "What use on earth is a warning from the dead when the dead are at rest?"

No answer came. They were resting at last.

So he opened the door, lurched into the hall, the watery light and tracked Lois, trackless.

He had been so fiercely seized by the chance—the certainty—of loss that he ran without looking past the cracked kitchen door (warm light streaming) through hall, front door and stopped on the porch in what was still night—air chilled and damp—staring uselessly toward the hidden road, thinking, "Gone. Gone. Another one gone. Young as I am, they are *leaving* me."

Emma's voice said "Son."

He wheeled on his mother where she stood in the door, dark against the hall behind her. "What?"

"*Ma'm,*" she said.

"Ma'm?" he said.

"Rato is dead."

For an instant he thought she spoke of his father —Rato was also his father's name—and that they had lost his father again, must endure the cut, the long year of healing, again. *How?* Then he saw his mother's hands stiffly extended and went toward them. Her hands were full, not empty for him to fill and comfort. He leaned in the dark to see what she offered—a wad of cloth which he took, held up to the light to examine. A blue shirt torn as if by hate and mottled with emblems of blood like entrails—rust brown shapes of livers, lungs, a great dry heart. It had been his own shirt a year ago, but when he grew, it had passed to Rato— his brother Rato.

He replaced the shirt in his mother's hands, then looked to her face and shook in surprise. Her eyes were strangled with grief again, the thing he had vowed at his father's death to spare her in future. Again he had failed. He could only speak. "Where is he now?"

Her head shook side to side in mystery.

"Then who brought you this and where was it lying?"

She tried to speak, then finding no speech, stabbed with a finger toward the kitchen behind her. Then speech came or hideous noise—"Huunh," the cornered plea for relief.

Milo took his mother's elbow, lifted her the one step into the hall, led her as though she were blind to the kitchen.

The kitchen was the largest room in the house and always the warmest though its walls and floor were applegreen. There were two cook stoves—one electric, one wood—and two broad tables. The one in the center nearer the door was dark wood—the family eating table. The other was by the opposite wall, smaller, lower, covered with red oilcloth for work, and when Milo opened the kitchen door fully, nudged his mother ahead, he looked past the three men at the eating table over what seemed watery space, long time, to the smaller table where Lois sat with Rosacoke facing—Rosa's open palm in Lois's hand, Lois studying it till Milo entered, then meeting his eyes with her eyes blank, not smiling, not frowning but not unkind, only waiting for his eyes to show their need.

And he felt a need like wind upward through him

to rush somehow through all the dense space (the hot crowded room, his fool mistakes), seize Lois, take all the thanks she could give, give all she had shown she needed from him, his thanks returned for these brief days—his whole life to come his gift to her.

But before he could so much as show that need and though she stood to receive it, dropping Rosa's hand, he was called back to duty. Two of the men at the big table stood—Rooster and Mr. Favro the preacher (Papa was the third, he stayed in his chair)— and Mr. Favro came to Milo, arms hooped to force unwelcome harbor on him. He accepted duty. His eyes left Lois (she sat again slowly, turned slowly back to Rosa), and took Mr. Favro's stifling embrace, the voice like warm oil ladled on his neck—"Death is dead."

Milo nodded into the hot shoulder—"I know that."

And Rooster said softly to Milo's eyes, "Of course he's dead. Me and Milo killed him."

Mr. Favro had not heard. "It's nothing but a brief postponement now, nothing but a nuisance. You will all be lonesome for a few hard months, then the years will slide and there he'll stand in New Jerusalem— waiting, smiling, clothed in light to welcome you in and show you the ropes—"

Milo drew himself back, stood free to draw breath —not so much as thankfully glancing at Mr. Favro— then reached behind for the shirt his mother held, extended it toward Rooster. "Where did you find this and where is he lying?"

"Somewhere under them peaceful stars." Rooster pointed behind him to the still-dark window—(no one could see stars; they took them on faith, the night having cleared). "After you fell out and I got you in bed, got the ladies easy, I drove back towards the Ryden place and met your Papa coming out of the woods with that bloody shirt and the posse behind him. A bloodhound had found it, running from the snake, and the posse found the hound curled down in a ditch with the shirt in his mouth. Your Papa said he recognized the shirt, and they combed around for another good hour in the dark thick as weeds till all of the flashlights were finally failing and they gave up and struck for the road and met me there. When I seen that shirt I knew the worst so I said to your Papa, 'Come on, Mr. Mustian, I'll ride you home to rest till light. He'll wait till morning. Wherever he lies, he's peaceful now.' Your Papa agreed so I thanked the posse and sent them home. We come on here and your Mama called the preacher and here we've sat. But don't you worry. It'll be morning soon, hasn't failed in *my* lifetime."

"It is morning eternal where Rato is." Mr. Favro slammed in his wedge, first chance. "And Milo, son, if you look at him right, think about the harmless life he lived in the time he had, never bothered a soul—"

"Never spoke to one." Papa said it for himself but aloud, firmly.

"—If you study him, I say; follow his example, he'll shine for you through life's dark nights like the North Star of old to wanderers lost."

Milo said, "Are you speaking of Rato or Jesus?"

"Well, *Rato*," Mr. Favro said, "though the same goes for Jesus."

"Then say again what his example was—Rato's to me."

Mr. Favro looked to Emma for help—it had been her boy—but she stood dumb and dazed against the door. So he faced round to Papa. "Mr. Mustian, what would you say to that?"

Papa said, "I won't the one making claims for Rato. He won't an example of nothing to me. All I knew was, Rato was different. All he needed that other people needed was something to eat. And then all I could do was feed him—or have food standing by ready, don't you know? But Preacher, you're the one with education. If Rato was ever any kind of example, you are the one to know what of."

"Of never hurting things," Mr. Favro said.

Emma said "That's it."

Milo stood a moment alone with himself, not seeing even Lois. Then he said to Mr. Favro, "If morning should come and we go out and find Rato's body lying truly dead—then will be time enough for me to tell you what a lie you've told."

Mr. Favro's eyes flew to Emma for defense. She had barely heard much less understood so he stared at the blank door and yearned in silence for all kinds of rescue.

But Rooster said, "Son, tell *me* what you mean. I may not last till day." He smiled.

Milo thought again alone, then stepped past Mr. Favro, frozen, to the center of the room by the black wood-stove. He looked past Lois, past Rosacoke to the old glass pane (watery as a pool) that hung between him and the butt-end of night—what stars there were, whatever lay waiting in woods to be found—and he spoke to all that. "He was never no example of nothing to nobody—Rato, I mean. And if he's dead now it's a sorry damn sight for us to have to live with—the life he had in his fourteen years. To be born with half the mind most people get; to spend your childhood alone as a hawk (but not hunting nothing, just hanging around); to go to school and never learn to write your own name, never play a game that needed two people; and when you turned twelve and your nature took life of its own accord (grew a mind of its own), just to keep on thinking it was nothing but plumbing; to stand in your life and never look forward to being grown, giving somebody something—their food and their pleasure; to think you would sleep every night of your life like a dog in winter, curled on yourself to save your own little heat, not touching nothing but the ground beneath you or a few cold leaves; nothing to do when morning came but get up and shake and wait out another day, waiting for nothing but the last lay-down, the night you'd die—" Milo turned on Mr. Favro like an enemy. "I know I'm a child but I hadn't stood still. I have *learned* some things, and this is one thing—if Rato's dead he's in Heaven, all right. He's had all the Hell he ever could have earned in four hundred years much less fourteen."

Mr. Favro could only shake his helpless head, but Milo's new tone had called his mother partway back. She kept her place by the open door, but the look she sent him—not anger but loss—washed the preacher aside, straw in a flood. "You never learned that talk from me," Emma said.

"From *me*," Rooster said, "from me and my family and it's every word so." He looked to Milo, smiled again, but Milo had his mother's gaze to bear, could not flinch from that.

"I thought you loved your brother," Emma said.

"*Loved* him?" Milo said—his hands separated like cold steel jaws; the bloody shirt ripped into loud clean halves—"That was my heart tearing in *two*, can't you see?"

Emma shut her eyes, nodded.

So having shown his mother the old heart beneath the hard new hide, Milo turned to Mr. Favro, showed the shirt halves that still seemed to quiver, shriek, bleed.

Mr. Favro studied at a distance, nodded too, then looked to where Papa hunched at the table, cooling his coffee with a thin strip of breath through dry blue lips, not hearing what they said, no longer caring, bolted in age and exhaustion, no hope. Mr. Favro took two steps toward Milo, spoke to him softly, "Now you are the man—not just by default. You'll need all the help you can get, believe me. I'm not *all* fool. So I'll pray for you daily."

Milo said "Thank you," then said "Pray *what*, sir?"

"That the Lord will hand you day by day every gift He held back from poor Rato."

"Don't worry," Milo said. "He's handing already. I'm thankfully taking."

"But don't stop with taking," Mr. Favro said.

"I ain't," Milo said. "I been learning things—but I told you that. These past three nights, these two clear

days, I been handing out stuff like the whole Red
Cross, like loaves and fishes to people on the hills."

Mr. Favro nodded, showed he could smile, then
thought it out slowly. "Everybody isn't waiting out on
the hills, and food isn't all they're waiting for."

Milo said, "I know that too, but there's all kinds
of food."

Mr. Favro had turned and with slow hand showed
what he thought were the nearest needy, waiting now—
Papa numb in his age; Emma clubbed again by
abandonment, by her helplessness to help (even briefly
shield) the few things she loved; even Rooster smiling
and round as a clock (his full need a secret to all here
but Milo).

Yet Milo turned to Lois. She was not facing him
nor listening but was leaning deeply over Rosacoke's
palm, speaking softly to her. The inward curve of her
back and neck, her black hair spilling forward onto her
breasts, the calm of her profile (cleared now of sleep)
seemed signs to Milo that she had truly gone beyond
needing him, had at last accepted his gift from her
father as full final payment of all Milo owed and was
already launched on her own free life. But he was not
free. He said to himself, "It takes two to say goodbye"
and reaching blindly behind, laid the torn shirt halves
on the larger table, took a step toward Lois.

Mr. Favro touched him with a hindering hand,
said, "Son, there are others here that need you more."

Milo paused but did not face him. "They may,
yes sir. They very well may but I never said I was all
man yet. *I'm* part-fool too. Anyhow they'll wait. They
know I'll come. We all got time. Morning still isn't

here." He crossed the remaining way towards Lois, stopped only when his hip nudged her shoulder. She still whispered rapidly to Rosacoke. "Morning," he said.

Lois looked at last, saw his face clear of grief but not being sure of which duty he had chosen (her or his sister), she only half-smiled—"I wish it was"—and looked at the dark still gripped to the pane.

Rosacoke also faced the window, her hand still in Lois's. "Maybe we have had the last day of all. The sun has maybe failed. It'll happen one day—why not today?" When she looked for answer, she looked first to Papa (and all eyes followed), but he was asleep upright in his chair, his wind grating quietly. So Rosa looked to Rooster—"Maybe this is the end?"

But Rooster looked to Milo, answered to him. "Could be I guess. What could *keep* it from being? You've had *your* day. Maybe I've had mine—maybe never will." Milo watched him but did not offer hope so Rooster faced the worst. "*Nothing* to keep this from being the end except I am five miles from my lonesome wife."

"That's no reason at all—" Every eye but Papa's crouched at that, searched wildly for the speaker. It had burst from Mr. Favro like shrapnel from a shell, and once said, it left him as scattered, ruined.

Each sought the face that seemed to him suddenly to offer denial or at worst, protection. Emma looked to Milo's back, was balked; Rooster to his left profile clung there; Rosa to his face that would not face hers. Milo looked to Lois, offering her freely what the others craved.

But again she was back over Rosacoke's palm, studying as though another girl's skin, a child's skin (though already polished, thickened by work) would yield what hope and safety there were—a promised future for someone at least.

But a cry split the house, swift and clean as an axe —one threat realized. Then they all looked to Emma. "Baby Sister is having a dream," she said. "I'll have to go calm her. And Selma just got her poor eyes closed." She looked to Mr. Favro. "Excuse me please. I'll be right back."

"Surely," he said. "But I'd better go too. I've done what I can, what the Lord indicated—fed what little I had to His sheep. Send for me soon as you know any more." He bowed to Rooster, bowed to Milo, said "Rosacoke—" She looked up and nodded and he vanished past Emma.

"Just a minute," Emma said—to the air he had stirred—"I'll see you out." But he was past hearing or answering so she said to Rooster, "Sheriff, would you excuse me once if I leave you here with these children awhile and try to lie down and wrestle myself somehow before day?"

Rooster stood, said, "Yes'm. I just wish I could help. You have had more than your share to bear, Mrs. Mustian."

"That's all right," she said. "Just find my boy."

Rooster laid his hand in pledge on his heart. "I will find your boy wherever the Lord has left him," he said.

Emma nodded, shut her eyes. "If you don't that's the thing I could not bear." She wavered a moment—

blind—put out a hand, found the cold door jamb. Her eyes split open. "Yes I could," she said—to only Milo. He knew that, nodded and she left too, silently closing the door behind her.

There were two sounds left in the kitchen then— Papa's hoarse sleep and Lois's voice into Rosacoke's palm, not so much to Rosa as to herself, discovering lives for others as she spoke. "I am just a beginner at this," Lois said, "but one thing here is plain enough for any child to read." She traced the deep J of Rosa's life-line—"Looks *carved* in, don't it?"

Rooster took a step to look and Milo leaned forward. Rosa said "Who carved it?"

Lois said, "You. You've been planning your life since the minute you were made."

Milo stood back above them, said "What is her plan?" And Rooster nodded, stood to wait also.

So Lois began to tell it to Milo—looking up from the hand to him not Rosa as though this separate person's life were as urgent to them both as breath, rest, morning. "She has two years of freedom left."

Milo said, "How old is she now? Can you see?"

Lois looked. "Eleven."

Rosa said "He knew that."

Lois said, "Sure he did. He's testing me." She continued to Milo—"Two more years. Then one fall day out walking in the woods, she will see a boy and hand him her life."

Milo said, "What will be his name?"

Lois strained to discover. "It's there, all right. She has chose him already—or had him chose for her—but I can't name him. As I said before, I'm new at the future."

Rosacoke said, "Can I ask something?—why will I lose my freedom to him?"

Lois said—still to Milo not Rosa—"Because you'll love him."

"Why will I love him?"

Lois did not need to study further. "Because you have had the life you've had, are who you are."

Rosacoke said, "Oh I knew that much." She studied Milo—"I ain't been free, wouldn't want to be" —turned again to Lois. "I thought you could find me a better reason." Lois did not look for another reason, only shook her head. "Then tell the rest of my plan," Rosa said.

Lois knew without looking, continued to Milo, "Then she will live in misery for years."

"Why?" Milo said.

"I never promised to explain," Lois said. "—Because it's her plan."

Milo said, "But it isn't her *right*."

"Oh," Lois said, "it'll end, it'll end—the misery, for a while."

"How?" Milo said.

"She will take a baby from the boy, then marry him."

Rosacoke thrust in—it was her life—"You mean, marry and then take a baby from him."

Lois looked back for that, reworked the hand with a firm finger, plowing as if it were a field, then shook her head. "It is planned the way I said it. The child is a boy, will come in July, but you will only be married at Christmas."

Rosacoke counted the months on her fingers. "All right," she said.

But Milo said "Stop," stepped powerfully in, pressed his own flat hand over Rosacoke's, scoured against her like a polishing wheel.

Rooster said "Wait," stepped forward too, stacked his hand palm-up on the others, looked to Lois. "You ain't lying, are you?" Lois shook her head. "Because if you are, I'll lock you up *now*, won't wait for day."

"I know too little to lie," Lois said.

"Then look," Rooster said, "Oh *see* please ma'm, if there's any baby here." With his free hand he stabbed at his open palm.

Milo and Rosa were first to look—the hand seemed a baby itself, smooth, chubby. Then Lois bent. It took her eight seconds—(Rosacoke counted silently). "Yes," Lois said.

Milo said "When?"

Rooster left his hand with Lois but looked to Milo. "When?" he said.

Milo thought, then his head shook slightly. He did not know.

But Lois said "June."

Rooster's palm flipped over and became a sudden fist locked on Lois's wrist. "You *know* that?" he said.

"*You* know it," Lois said. "It's been in your hand since you had a hand."

Rooster's hand released her and he studied it hard. As he looked—as they all looked—it slowly cupped of its own accord, preparing for the gift. He smiled down to Lois. "Say it's going to be a boy."

"It is," she said.

"Thank you," Rooster said. "And coming in June! I'll beat you by a month, Rosacoke. Think of that."

"A month and nine years," Lois said. "This coming June."

Rooster's mouth fell open, eyes gathered in pain. Then he also counted—backwards from June, not in public like Rosa on his visible fingers but with taps of his tongue on the roof of his mouth. He looked to the window, calculated the remainder of night, then said to Rosacoke, "We've got another hour and I've got to go home and see my wife. She's been by herself all Sunday, all tonight."

"You'll be back," Rosa said and stood in her place.

"Yes I will," Rooster said and he backed from the close group, shoulders hunched inward not to touch anyone, then turned his back on them, moved quickly to the door, opened it, halted, spread heavy silence like fog through the room.

Milo said "What is it?"

Rooster waited, then turned. When he spoke his face was too grave for the question, his voice too hard. He spoke to Milo. "What must I name him?"

Milo took it as gravely as Rooster intended, thought carefully through every chance and duty. "If it was my boy I'd name him Rob."

The news—amends, forgiveness, plea for pardon—took awhile to work through the space to Rooster, but once there, he smiled. "Thank you," he said. "That'll be his name—the new Apple King!—and I'll tell him you chose it." He left more quickly than large men generally manage to leave, but unrushed, unridden, already at peace with the various seeds broadcast in his life and waiting to grow.

But Milo shuddered—once (still for fear) as Rooster vanished, once (in understanding and helplessness) as the front door shut behind him (only its distant click reached the kitchen). Lois did not notice. She had already looked back to Rosacoke's hand, found a new shape there which she struggled to read, but Rosacoke saw him both times and thought he shivered from cold—the room had chilled since Emma left—so she took her hand from Lois, saying, "Thank you but I'll take the rest in surprise" and brushed past Milo who was burning not cold to the squat wood-stove. She took the lid-lifter, raised a lid—fire dying—then went to the woodbox, bent and loaded herself with the little wood left, fed it in, turned to Milo—he had been watching her—and said, "That is all the wood in the house. I'll fix you some breakfast if you get me some wood. You ain't had a meal in—what? two days? Food's all you need."

"It's one thing," he said and moved three steps toward the door to obey—go out to the woodshed coatless in darkness. It was dark that stopped him before he reached the hall—the thought not the fact— and he stopped ashamed, having never feared darkness even as a child (had spent half his life, it seemed to him now, hurling round by night in various games). He did not face round onto Lois or Rosa, and this time Rosa did not see nor understand, only went on finding the pans she would need.

Lois did or at least said to Milo's back, half-laughing, "I'll come and hold the lantern if you'll chop the wood."

At that Milo turned and went swiftly towards Lois, but silently not to break Papa's sleep. Two steps short he extended his right hand flat as a plate and delivered it to her, not forced in her face nor on her own hand but laid on the table beneath her baffled eyes.

She looked at once from his hand to him. "What is that?" she said.

"Hell," he said—he whispered—"it's my right hand. It's what you been finding people's lives in, remember?"

"Oh that—" Lois said as if whole days had passed.

"Yes that," he said and he probed with a finger at the palm's few lines. "It don't look like much of a plan to me, but whatever it is, you are in it—ain't you?" He did force it now, threw it up before her eyes.

Lois would not look, clamped her eyes as if Milo offered fire.

"*Lois,*" he said—he whispered still but with power enough now to etch cold glass—"I am making you a gift so remember your manners. You either got to take it or say why not."

She opened her eyes, on his eyes not his hand. "What gift?" she said.

"My life," he said.

"Why?" she said.

"Because you asked me for it twice in three days. Because I have learned my lesson by now."

"What lesson?" she said.

"That the worst thing of all is not paying your debts—and paying in time; that you got to give people what they need *in time,* not years too late when they've famished and fell."

Lois said, "Milo, who taught you that?"

He rose back to think and the large high kitchen seemed swarmed with his teachers, pressing on him like water in the depths of a pond, on his eyes, eardrums, sunk temples, soft throat—everyone he had seen these two days, three nights—and he forced his lips open to answer at last, say "Everybody did—"

But Papa said loudly, "I'm *one* that didn't, I can tell you that much. I been owing some debts since Hoover come in—Hell, since Woodrow Wilson crept home from Paris and turned to stone." Like stone himself, only half-returned from sleep, he sat up in his chair. "Debts ain't nothing but money—remember—and owing ain't a reason to pay, I've found, unless your debtor's in worse need than you."

"She's in need," Milo said.

"All right," Papa said, "I won't ask why (though if somebody handed me ten thousand dollars, I wouldn't need nothing but a better bed; then I'd sleep six months), and I won't ask why you are buried in debt to a stranger you saw for the first time Friday. I won't say nothing if you'll let me say this—for God's sake pay her back with something she can use, don't stand around offering her your bare-faced hand like hands was rare."

Milo thrust his hand at Papa. "This stands for my life."

"Your *life?*" Papa said. "What use is a life?"

Rosacoke said, "I could use a load of wood."

When they had crossed the pitch-black yard—Milo leading darkly first from his hot need to give, then

Lois passing ahead with the lantern from what was her own impatience to receive, then Milo up again by unthinking memory through threatening litter (spiked scraps of iron, split jars, bare roots)—when both had stooped and entered the woodshed and silently hurried, but not touching yet, out of every thread of clothes and stood a moment separate, still and in study in the flame light that rose from the lantern on the ground, what Milo gave and Lois received was this much at least: a hand as tough as a Gladstone bag on her cold left shoulder; then that hand tightening and drawing her forward till she brushed against, then was held full length (though still upright) along a stretch of skin like fine broadcloth (that seamless, warm, dry); then was kissed once on her smiling mouth, hard but dry and quickly, stopping on the surface as a child would kiss an aunt at the start of a visit while looking beyond her at deep woods, a lake or sand for play; then was steered by that hand on the height of her butt toward a dim far corner, half-laid, half-pushed to a cushion of pine bark powdered with age—that much at least Lois thought of as taking (no thought of using). But Milo paused above her on arms as straight as what stood ready beneath to serve, looked at her eyes—only them, nothing lower—and said unsmiling, "I have heard that the saddest thing on earth is to love somebody and they not love back."

"So have I," she said and by smiling fully, forced him to smile, then rocked the heel of her own tough hand in the pit of his neck (where nerves pierce the skull) and drew him forward, welcomed him down, and the rest was giving—pure gift for both, no thought

of receipt though receipts poured in so long as they
worked, as if fresh joy could flood your thighs, stream
down through your legs, drown your heart, gorge throat
and brain, offer (even threaten) a new clear life (so
long as you moved) and yet roll on, roll past, leave you
spared.

It could and did—rolled on, spared them both, left
them mildly grateful. Then though they still touched,
lay as joy had left them, they quickly grew separate—at
first with the distance of brother and sister close but
ignorant of one another; then like strangers in a
crowded room, burdened by nearness; then farther still
till at last when Milo's body fell back he fell like a
fledgling from a narrow nest, a pear from an over-
weighted tree, still faintly aware of gratitude but
forgetful already of to whom or why and mainly free,
mainly grateful for that.

Yet relieved as he was to have paid in full, he
could still not accept his joy to be free, not face this
final assault by the hound that had sought him since his
father's death but closely, fiercely all weekend—that
people depart (undetained by love, unprepared for
their journey) and we watch them go and they do not
return.

So he half-rose and looked for Lois's face. It was
turned away. He gently hauled it round till her eyes
met his and their lips mirrored smiles. Then again he
showed her his open hand. "Look and see if you ain't
there," he said.

This time she looked, no longer afraid of her
certain absence, wishing in fact that there might at
least be a shallow trace of her life in his, some sign of

her passing, and she turned the hand all angles to the
light—nothing, no sign, his whole life so plainly
illegible that she could not have guessed so much as his
name, not to speak of their mutual fate to meet, touch
twice, exchange sweet gifts, discover blood kin. "I am
not," she said and she shut his hand like a quiet door,
returned it to his thigh stretched separate beyond
her.

Milo said "Why not?" quite seriously.

"You didn't plan for me, that's all."

"Who have I planned for?" He spoke gravely now
in need again but of foresight, vision, *news*, not a
simple girl—"And where will I go?"

"Nobody else knows that but you."

He did not answer—agree or deny. He was turned
away, his face to the light.

"Do *you?*" she said.

"Yes," he said. He spoke to the light. "I have got
two plans—one old as my hand, one I just now made.
The old plan was for me to live on here and work like a
mill from day to dark every day but Christmas doing
what my Daddy did (my sorry Daddy, the days he
could walk), what Papa does now tired as he is—raise
eight acres of neck-high tobacco, plant the seed in
March under muslin beds (seed that make mustard
seed look like cannon balls), lose half my plants to
frost and blue mold, then transplant the rest in early
May and nurse it all summer like a millionaire's baby—
losing half again to wet weather, dry weather, worms,
blight, maybe all to a five-minute hail storm one
evening; pulling leaves in late July, tacking them in
barns hot as biscuit ovens till they kill out gold; then

hauling them to town to a tin-top building and watching bone-tired some fast-talking stranger frown at it—not feel it—give you fifty cents a pound like he's Jesus healing wounds. Hell, I don't even *smoke*. But in my old plan, I die doing that year after year." He halted but did not turn his head.

"Nothing else?" Lois said.

"What else?" Milo said.

She said, "Well—fun, a little enjoyment. Don't you plan to laugh any, take any vacations, rest up between years? Won't there be somebody to lighten your load?"

"Mama will cook what meals I eat. Rosa will wash and iron my clothes till she starts that life you promised her."

Lois waited for him to continue, to hope, but he lay on silent and that silence mixed with the chill of the dark clasped her—the heat of their moving gone—so that when she spoke she also shuddered. "I was speaking of a wife." She touched him, unintending—her hand at the small of his cooling back.

He turned to face her. "Oh sure," he said, "maybe two years from now, maybe three if I'm lazy, I'll pick out one of those girls I've known since I first went to school—Nancy Gunter or Sarah King or Sissie Abbott if she'll shut up—and we'll drive to town every Saturday night and chew earlobes in the dark theater and after a year or so of that, get married, live up in the room I sleep in now." He stopped, having reached another blank end.

"You mean that to sound like fun?"

"Well," he said, then waited to think—"I never

claimed to be a comedian. But I'll get home for a while most nights or for dinner at least, and then I can saw me off a slice of fun—if that's what you mean, what you and me was slicing a minute ago but better than that, on warm bed sheets."

"That wasn't all I meant."

"Me neither. I'm flogging myself too hard. Children are bound to come rolling in, and I guess giving them their Santa Claus will be some pleasure—and raising them up till they take their own growth." He paused still facing Lois and smiled to break her stare. "Doesn't that sound like fun to you?" She did not answer nor reflect his smile. "Well, it's what nine-tenths of the humans born since God said 'Adam!' have thought was a life, planned out for themselves— all my people, my Mama, my Daddy (it was what strangled him), Rosacoke if you foretold truly. It was *my* old plan."

"What's the new one?" she said.

"It depends."

"On what?" she said, hope again in her voice (though against her will).

"On Rato really being dead," he said.

"If he is?—" she said.

"I'm leaving at daybreak."

"*Leaving?*" she said. "Leaving Rato's body for a posse to find? Leaving your mother and sister to scratch like me and my—mother. You are all that's left."

"Papa's left."

"For exactly three years."

"You seen his hand?"

"I seen his eyes."

Milo thought awhile. "I'm leaving still and I'll tell you why—any world where Rato Mustian dies bloody for saving a dog that wouldn't bring a dime in a cat-food factory, any world where—" He stopped. All his kin ganged before his eyes, living, dead (and he knew more dead than the average boy)—all his friends, enemies, speaking acquaintances—and all seemed ruined in various degrees: hobbled or addled or stove-in deeply. He spoke again to clear his sight. "Any world like that is in serious need of somebody's help. I volunteer."

"Why?"

"To change some things."

"How?" Lois said.

"By telling what I know, the things I have learned these past three days. My learning's just started but I've learned some things."

Lois said, "Start with me. Tell me please now."

He turned again from her to the lantern—flame as steady as hammered iron—and waited tensely for his knowledge to gather, the wounds and visions of three clear days to narrow in the gap between his eyes behind his skull, transform into words. And he clamped his eyes to force the conversion, but only colors came—the reds and purples of his own thick blood as it thinned in his eyelids, received the light—no word, not one. His heart clenched hotly and to spare it danger, he faced round violently onto Lois, forced his throat to speak (eyes still shut). "Everybody has got to—" Again he was refused, not permitted to say what all the others— his mother, Rosa, Mr. Favro, Selma, even Rooster, even Macey—would have rushed to offer, and his throat was locked silent as if by a hand or a coarse wool throttle. So he hung there darkly above dark Lois— only his back receiving light now, and what the light showed was only his back, curved like a vine that flails for grip, the next foothold on food and life.

Lois touched him gently on his tight ringed throat. His eyes split open but his head shook fiercely and her hand fell back. "No," he said, "I have not learned nothing. I have just seen things that passed and are gone." He waited for strength to drive to the next— "But I'm going too. This isn't my place. I have got to find rest."

"You are just fifteen."

He nodded. "Fifteen, but I've lived more lives than most men at fifty. Time isn't what wears people out. There's Niggers round here—in sound of my voice —that can bend their back and pick cotton faster than you can dance (and sing while they do) but are well past a hundred and can picture slavery clear as I can Rato. Look at your Daddy—"

She looked, half-hoping, to the lantern—simple light.

"He was younger than me by a year when he left, fourteen years old and already finished, finished here, ground down. He had had his share of the local day, and he either had to go or die in his tracks in Ryden dirt—ground *fine* as dirt—had to find some life, a few more days, a little rest."

"What did he ever find?"

Milo studied Lois beside and below him, at his mercy entirely. "You," he said.

Her eyes shut, head shook No three times. Then

she waited, then asked, "What good on earth was so much running for that little rest?"

Milo turned her question like a weapon on himself. "I never said I was running from a fight. I'm running toward my life and I'm game to wrestle every step of the way. What I won't do, *can't* do is stand in my tracks—my ancestors' tracks—and be whipped dry, dead but can't lie down for sixty more years."

"You *could*," Lois said. "You could die in a ditch. But at least you've *got* tracks. How many people have? And where was my father taking me that time? Where did he beg me to promise to meet him?—not in cold midair."

Milo looked to his feet as if testing their power, then answered her first question not her last—"I could but I won't"—and stood in a perfect thrust, went to his clothes and dressed in the light, his back to Lois.

So she watched his back.

Then he went to the dark rear end of the shed, quietly gathered an armload of wood—the fresh pine quarters he had split on Friday just before supper, before the fair, with Rato watching.

In the short time it took him, Lois stood and dressed too, thinking he meant to return to the house (and her to her mother), hand Rosa the wood, eat the food she fried and begin his life—the old first life in his old home here.

But when his arms were full, he walked unseeing past her—she was stroking her hair into place with her hand—and stopped at the open door of the shed, set the wood down there, stood, clapped his hands to shake off bark and looked to the sky.

The sky had faded though only a little—to the sharpest eye—from black to deep gray so that when Milo faced round on Lois, she saw him clearly by two lights now (gray sky behind, lantern on his face) as she had only seen him in deep dark before (Friday night in the field by the fair and this passing night in the Ryden woods), the image of her oldest memory—her father, her final promise to him, to meet, keep faith—the message given, gift delivered.

Milo said "I am going." His hand flapped mildly against his side. He turned, took a step.

Lois said, "The wood. You forgot Rosa's wood."

Milo stopped beyond the door, half-faced her again. "No I didn't. She'll come looking soon and it'll be here. It ain't going nowhere."

Lois said "Are you?"

"Yes."

"Where?"

He pointed away from the still-dim house towards his own dim left as though a clear destination lay there, enduring his journey. Then he seemed to smile fully (though she only guessed that) and said, "You still never said your plan."

"That one," she said. She pointed his way.

"All right," he said, "but you got to come now, leave all—clothes, money, your new belongings. We are hunting not hauling."

"I know that," she said and went toward him, past lantern and wood into still-paler air—the sky at least; the ground was black so they both looked downward to choose their way, and though Lois kept her hand near his, he did not take it till he suddenly stopped on the edge of the yard ten yards from the field, the woods beyond. Then he found her fingers, took hold to stop her, but she had seen only just after him the dark shapes ahead that broke from the pines and entered the field and moved their way—a high hunched form that came on slowly and, slightly ahead as if clearing a path, a low form that hugged the darkest furrows.

Lois said "Who?"

Milo said "God knows" and the cold wrapped wound behind his ear fried out like a brand. He dropped Lois's hand—or freed it, not so much abandoning as leaving her ready for what this was should it come to claim her, renouncing his claim. Then he started again, also entered the field—Lois one step behind—to face what shape, what claim bore down.

Nothing but Phillip and Rato behind—bare to the waist, maybe five pounds nearer the bone than before —but safe, spared and there so sudden, unquestionably as to silence Milo, fling him back on his heels, Phillip prancing around him, wetly panting.

So Lois spoke, pointing first to Phillip. "Is Phillip safe?"

Rato said, "Always was. Nothing but worms and he's cured of that, found the grass he needed hunting you all's snake."

"That's dead," Lois said.

Rato said "I'm sorry."

"Thank you," Lois said. "Where'd you lose your shirt?"

"In a fight with a fox."

"But you're live," she said. "That's all that counts."

Rato said "We're live," thinking she included Phillip, and as Phillip had already streaked toward the house, Rato nodded to Lois and followed his dog, past Milo as though Milo were air, a piece of the day.

But Milo turned and watched him go. He could see him now, even Phillip far ahead—light had swelled that much in that brief meeting—the back of the house, Phillip skipping the steps, waiting Rato on the porch, Rato moving on slowly, knowing the house and its contents would wait, the house seeming washed by the new light, home. So Milo followed with a longer stride —Lois fell in behind—and in eight long steps, he was near enough to Rato to touch, shield, cover his bare cold back (a black rake of claws had dug the lean meat, had abruptly halted at the spine, postponed).

But Rato turned, faced Milo, grinned. "Morning," he said.

"Morning," Milo said. Then they both looked up to the lifting sky—Lois followed their eyes—and found they were right. It was morning (clear, cloudless, the oldest gift), would be morning oh six hours yet.

REYNOLDS PRICE

Born in Macon, North Carolina in 1933, Reynolds Price attended small North Carolina schools and received his Bachelor of Arts degree from Duke University. As a Rhodes Scholar he studied for three years at Merton College, Oxford, receiving the Bachelor of Letters. In 1958 he returned to Duke where he teaches in the Department of English. There he began and completed A Long and Happy Life *which was published in 1962 and received the award of the William Faulkner Foundation for a notable first novel. In the summer of 1961 he again traveled to England where he worked for a year at the stories which were published in 1963 as* The Names and Faces of Heroes. *He now lives and works in Orange County, North Carolina on a hill covered with beech trees above a pond.*